Christopher Coleman

Chapter 1

HEAVEN DIDN'T FEEL as she had always expected it would, but it was still comfortable and warm, enveloping, pressing on her like a heavy blanket.

Accompanying the comfort, however, was only darkness, with thin strands of light appearing sporadically to her right, waving at her and then disappearing into the dark. This darkness was also unexpected, opposite how she had always envisioned the afterlife. Where was the glow of illuminated clouds, behind which, presumably, was the source of the glow and the promise of everlasting life?

Everlasting life. It was the beginning and ending of everything she now remembered. There was almost nothing she could recall about her life before Marlene.

It was to be there though, she thought, *on Earth. Not in the realm of death. Everyone was promised this type of afterlife.*

A stronger beam of light forced its way through the clouds of darkness, edging through her slitted eyes and striking her retinas like lightning. The pain in the back of her head was debilitating. She opened her mouth to scream and a flood of water poured in, rushing down her throat, thirsting to invade her lungs.

She flailed her torso wildly and tried to breathe through her nose, but there was only water again. She was in Hell, she now realized. And why wouldn't she be?

She opened her eyes wide, lifting her head from the soft, pillowy pocket that had been its resting place since she had first awoken.

And then the memory came.

It was of Hansel, his eyes both soft and deranged as he swung the oar with a viciousness she'd not thought possible in her son. She remembered the flash of light and then instant blindness in her left eye, and finally the blurred look of sadness on the face of her teenage boy.

She was suffocating now, drowning, and though her mind knew she was being tortured in the depths of Hell—and that this was to be her fate from here until eternity—her body floundered, reacting to its instinct for survival.

She pushed herself from the soft sediment beneath her, feeling now that the weight enveloping her was not some embrace of God or the Devil, but the pressure of water. She swam toward the light above her, her body heavy and slow. The weight came not just from her clothes and shoes, but from the inside, like she had eaten a pile of stones.

The effort of her swim to the light was enormous, but when she felt the tips of her fingers break the surface of the water, and experienced the cool air upon her skin, she was inspired, and thrust her head toward the light.

She believed instantly, by both the color of the water and the smell of the air, that she had just emerged from the lake behind her Back Country cottage. And one lift of her chin confirmed it. There stood her humble home, only a few dozen yards away, staring blandly back at her, uncaring about its owner and occupant who was currently struggling for survival below.

Anika grabbed for the water in front of her, furiously alternating strokes, splashing like a neophyte swimmer as she tried desperately to make it to the shore. It was a distance any child could swim, but she felt as if she were being pulled under by some invisible hand. She steadied her strokes now, accepting that each one was only going to move her fractionally, until finally she felt the resistance of the sediment against her toes below. She continued inching forward and was now in water shallow enough to stand.

She tiptoed forward, lifting her head above the water line, and eventually made it into waist-deep water where she tried walking to the shoreline, again feeling the magnitude of gravity upon her.

As she reached the bank of the lake, she turned from her house and stared across to the Klahr Orchard, and for the first time considered that she may in fact be alive.

But how?

Perhaps she had survived the blow from Hansel—that was possible—but not the water. Certainly she'd been underwater for hours. Days even.

Suddenly she felt a sharp cramp in her stomach, a pain indicator that straddled the area between nausea and diarrhea. She grabbed her belly and lurched forward, opening her mouth to vomit and unleashing what must have been a half-gallon of lake water. Another lurch and more water flooded out. She coughed spastically, trying to catch her breath, and then felt the first wave coming from her anus, first as a slow leak, and quickly escalating to a full liquid bowel movement.

She stripped naked now, pulling off every piece of clothing, trying to rid herself of every ounce of weight, and then stood on the lake bank, simultaneously crouched and hunched, vomiting and defecating lake water by the gallons.

ANIKA CROUCHED ON THE porch, gripping the beam that jutted out from the wall in between the two center windows. The support beam ran from floor to ceiling and formed a vertical barrier behind which Anika could hide and wait, only the right half of her face exposed in the window as she peeked down through the trees at the still water from which she'd just emerged, anticipating some investigative scene to unfold. They would be coming shortly, no doubt, The System men, to dredge the lake or send in divers with cameras and the brightest of lights. They would search diligently for her corpse, summoned by Mrs. Klahr, Anika's docile neighbor who had been captured in the crossfire of Anika's madness and taken hostage. The woman had seen the whole episode from only a few feet away, including Hansel's death blow, which had landed flush on Anika's temple and had sent Anika toppling to her death under twelve feet of murky water.

But when they didn't find her? When the bottom sediment of the small, regional lake rendered nothing? What then?

Only a few years ago, The System wouldn't have spent ten seconds debating whether to send an officer all the way out to the Back Country on the report of a missing corpse, and certainly not when it involved an obscure family like the Morgans. But things had changed significantly since then. The Morgan family had become infamous in the Southlands and beyond, thrust there unwittingly by the life, death and rebirth of Marlene. And the Back Country was now a steady beacon on the radar of The System.

But The System's interest went beyond just Anika and her family's notoriety; they had lost officers in the unfolding of the terrifying story, men who had been corrupted and murdered by the Witch of the North. Any news of a death at the lake behind the Morgan property would not be taken lightly by System authorities.

Anika waited in her position on the deck for what must have been an hour, and then, seeing no signs of a dive team or System men, stood and began to pace the deck, constantly extending her left arm in front of her as she did to avoid bumping into the room's furniture. Her left-eye blindness would take some getting used to.

She walked to the porch screen now and looked out across the lake to the Klahr house. She thought of Hansel, and as the vision of her son rose in her mind, she collapsed to the floor and began to weep. The feelings of love and longing and protectiveness suddenly felt brand new, as if she'd never experienced them for anyone before. It was as if the continuous months of addiction had destroyed her ability to feel anything resembling caring or devotion. The potion had consumed her to the point of total immersion.

Anika closed her eye now and let her thoughts go fully to the potion, exploring down to the depths of her cells whether the addiction still existed in her. She visualized in-

gesting one of the thin vials of liquid, the fluid which she had
so delicately measured out and then handed over to Hansel
to dispense. The decision to cede this power to her son had
made him an accomplice to her addiction, and she'd always
known it was a monstrous thing to do, but there was no
doubt it had kept her alive. Had she controlled the potion
for the duration of her addiction, she'd have been dead early
on.

Perhaps that would have been a good thing, she considered now, but there it was.

Anika brought forth a vision of the potion sliding down
her throat, opening her mind to the feelings it had rendered
in the past, and then gagged, a small amount of lake water
spilling up her esophagus into her mouth.

She turned and ran from the porch and into the bathroom, falling to her knees over the bowl of the toilet and
vomiting more lake water into the empty ceramic basin.

Her craving was gone, and, even more, it had been transformed into repulsion. She leaned forward over the toilet
again and dry heaved, and then sat back against the wall behind her, lifting her chin to the ceiling, wiping the spittle
from her face in the process. She stared at the light above her,
hoping the answers to the questions she was pondering existed somewhere in its luminescence.

Where would she go now?

Her life with Hansel was over. He'd struck her down like
the dragon she was and had presumably watched her sink beneath the surface of the lake and drown. She couldn't simply show up at the Klahr house now, a day or two after her
apparent death, hat in hand, asking for a chance to explain

herself, requesting to start life over again. There was simply no place of trust from which they could begin. She was an abomination now. By all scientific explanations, she should be dead. People couldn't survive underwater for longer than a few minutes, at most, except, perhaps, in icy waters and extremely cold temperatures. But the Back Country was warm at this time of the year, and never reached the levels that would have made any difference. Besides, even if she hadn't drowned, the blow from Hansel's oar should have killed her.

That Anika was alive was nothing short of impossible.

But the potion made it possible. The potion was the reason she still lived. Or had been reborn. She wasn't sure what had happened exactly, only that she was conscious and breathing. It didn't matter though; whichever it was, Hansel could never accept her again.

Nor could she seek out Gretel. Her daughter had abandoned their property and family long ago, and, as Anika now sat on the linoleum floor of her cottage bathroom, she was thankful for her daughter's decision. It had been unfair of her, perhaps, to strand Hansel in this land alone, but it had likely saved her life.

Tanja.

The word fluttered across her mind like a stray moth, hovering for a moment and then fading.

The name was familiar to Anika, but she couldn't immediately place it. It was one to do with Marlene though, about that she was certain.

Anika stood now and walked back to the porch, and instantly saw the woman standing on the bank. It was Amanda Klahr, and next to her was Hansel. Had they been looking up toward the cottage on the opposite side of their lake bank, they would have seen Anika's figure in the window.

She instinctively stepped behind the support beam, but the attentions of her son and neighbor were fixed on the lake. Mrs. Klahr had her arm across Hansel's shoulders, and Hansel held in his hands a cluster of flowers. And as she watched them standing there, Anika soon realized they had no intention of calling The System. They were handling this business on their own, as Back Country folk had done for centuries before Marlene had poisoned their land.

Hansel leaned forward and tossed the flowers forward, and Anika could see his intentions for the wind and drift of the water to take them out to the center of the lake. But the breeze was blowing downstream, and the flowers flowed to the left along the shoreline, never making it anywhere close to his mother's watery gravesite.

"It's okay, my darling," Anika whispered. "I see them. I love them." She paused. "And I love you too."

At that moment, Hansel raised his head and looked toward the porch. Anika turned away from the window and stood with her back to the beam, completely out of sight. She didn't think he saw her, not with the glare of the sun as it was, but she considered he may have sensed her. Hansel wasn't Gretel, but he was her brother, and he was capable of a lot more than he knew.

Anika waited a few minutes longer, listening for signs that Hansel and Mrs. Klahr had left the lake, and once she thought it safe, walked to the kitchen, where the smell struck her instantly. It was the smell of meat.

Suddenly Anika could think of nothing but food. She pulled open the refrigerator door with a heave and her eyes landed on a lone chicken thigh resting on a stark white plate. It was raw, puddled in blood and almost certainly spoiled.

But she didn't hesitate. She grabbed for the hunk of bird flesh with both hands and brought it up to her mouth, tearing into it with her large teeth.

Chapter 2

PETR RAISED THE AXE high above his head and brought it down even and pure in the center of the log, barely feeling any sensation as the cylinder of wood separated in perfect symmetry and fell to either side of the chopping block. As always, with every swing, he thought of Marlene.

The creaking sound of the screened porch door erased the hag's face from his mind for a moment, but Petr stayed focused on the axe blade lodged into the wood in front of him.

"Petr, phone."

Petr gave no visible indicator that he'd heard Gil's voice, and instead uprooted the blade from the block and loaded another log on the stump. He gripped the axe handle again and swung the blade out low and wide, extending his arms fully, accelerating the head down perfectly on top of the flat, blonde surface of the log, splitting it identically to the last.

"Petr, you hear me? Phone."

Petr loaded another piece of wood upright on the block and stared at it, studying its vulnerability, noting how helpless it looked as it awaited its clean and hasty demise.

"Petr!"

Gil was Petr's only housemate for the semester, though Petr had been scheduled to house with two others during his freshman year. One had transferred to a different school a few days before classes were to start, and the other had simply decided college wasn't going to be his path, so it was just Petr and Gil for the time being.

Gil was portly and sociable, and he seemed to have a knack for making friends, though Petr wouldn't have yet counted himself amongst that group.

Petr squinted and nodded at Gil and then tossed the axe to the ground. "Who is it?"

"Sounds like your grandmother. Or...whatever she is to you."

Mrs. Klahr.

"But remember, it's Saturday, Pete? I didn't think you were allowed to talk to anyone other than Gretel today?"

Petr smirked and looked sideways at Gil, his eyes slits as he walked past his fellow schoolmate.

"This might be the first time I've seen you awake on a Saturday without that girl either standing next to you or on the other end of the line."

Petr hopped the step from the yard to the house, and grabbed the phone, suddenly feeling the pang of concern rising in his gut. A call from Mrs. Klahr this early on a Saturday was unusual. He and his elderly guardian had settled into the routine of speaking every *Sunday* morning, a schedule that fit Petr perfectly, and one which Mrs. Klahr had thus far respected. Petr's workload for his first semester was grueling, particularly for a freshman, his classes and study sessions occupying his days and nights during the week. That left Saturday as his day to unwind from it all, and to this point in his college endeavor, that meant spending all of his Saturdays with Gretel.

"Mrs. Klahr? What's wrong?"

Petr could hear the deep inhalation on the other end of the line, and he could almost see the look of unease on the old woman's face. He felt his heartbeat accelerate at once, and a glaze of water flooded his eyes.

"Mrs. Klahr?"

"Have you spoken to Gretel today?"

It was 10:30 a.m. and Gretel hadn't yet called or come over. Petr had left two messages at her house, which was a little less than two miles across campus, and when she hadn't returned them, he had assumed she'd just decided to sleep late. That was fine; he had some weight to pull in the house. The first nip of fall had arrived, likely to be followed in a few weeks by something that resembled winter, and that meant there was wood that needed chopping. "No. Is she okay?"

"Yes, Petr, Gretel is fine. She's on her way here."

"There? Why?"

"It's about her mother."

Petr knew instantly that Anika Morgan was dead.

"She's dead, Petr. She...well, you should come home too."

"Okay," Petr whispered, and then closed his eyes, squeezing in the tears that had begun to fall. He hung up the receiver without another word and then slid slowly to the floor, settling into a sitting position on the stone tiling, his back flat and tall against the kitchen wall beneath the mounted phone.

Anika.

The woman had become a mythical figure to Petr over the years, her bravery and resolve unlike anything he'd ever heard of before or since. She was a legend now, not just in the

Southlands, but throughout most of the New Country and, likely by now, beyond.

But Petr was so close to the story of Anika and Gretel that he sometimes forgot how remarkable the two women really were, though he was reminded almost daily in the dining hall at dinner, or regularly on Saturdays, when Petr was with Gretel, noting how the stares and pointed fingers still followed her. Even after being at the university for over a month, her notoriety lingered.

She was Gretel Morgan. Witch slayer and daughter of Anika Morgan, the amazing co-heroine of a story that included kidnapping and imprisonment, magic and murder, and the betrayal of her own family.

And Petr's family as well.

Petr also realized the pointing fingers on campus were sometimes aimed at him. He had played a part in the infamous story, and though he'd been instrumental in Marlene's downfall, his father had conversely been instrumental in her rise. And aficionados of the Anika and Gretel story knew it. When the Morgan tale was spun by New Country folk, Anika and Gretel always came out as the heroes. Petr's final label, however, was a bit more ambiguous, and he was sure he often fell on the wrong side of the ledger.

But now Anika was dead, and Petr could hear in Mrs. Klahr's voice that the circumstances surrounding the death were troublesome. He knew intimately of Anika's struggle with the potion, of her addiction to the concoction that had brought her back from the brink of death. He had seen the change in her over the years, and the madness into which she had descended. It was the main reason he had insisted Gretel come with him to school. He loved Gretel, of course, and he wanted to marry her and spend the rest of his life with her, but more than that, he needed her to be safe and away from the toxicity that had developed at home. He knew what he was doing to Hansel by taking her away, but it was a sacrifice Petr had been willing to accept.

He stood and grabbed the keys and walked to Mr. Klahr's old truck. The old hunk of metal roared right to life, and Petr thought of Mr. Klahr, his mentor and adoptive grandfather, for most of the ride home to the Back Country.

PETR HAD NEVER INTENDED to come home so soon, and considering the circumstances, he felt the strain build in his stomach the moment he reached the Back Country limits. But as he pulled into the driveway of the Klahr property—his property now—he could smell the aroma of the apples drifting from the orchard beyond the house, and he closed his eyes and smiled.

He thought of the days before the collapse of his childhood, when he and Gretel worked side by side until the sun went down, loading buckets of fruit and laughing until Mrs. Klahr called them in for dinner. It was the happiest few months of his life—there was no period that was a close second—the culmination being that day at Rifle Field and the first kiss from the girl he loved.

Petr opened his eyes and saw Mrs. Klahr standing on the porch, her hand over her mouth in a frozen gasp. As the truck slowed to a stop, she descended the steps slowly, her free hand desperately gripping the railing, her eyes focused on each delicate step. She looked so frail now, Petr thought, and he knew instantly that whatever event had unfolded here, whatever tragic incident had led to Anika Morgan's death, it had somehow involved Amanda Klahr.

He opened the truck door slowly and walked to her, this woman whom he loved as much as any person in the world, greeting her at the bottom of the porch stairs and placing his arms around her. He embraced her without a word. The story would come later; right now Mrs. Klahr just needed to feel solace.

After several moments, Petr pulled away and asked, "What happened?"

Amanda reached up and cupped her hands on her adopted grandson's cheeks, her eyes sad, exhausted. "She's down by the lake," she said. "She knows what happened to her mother, I've told her everything, and what she doesn't, I will fill you in with the details later. Just go to her now. Be with her."

Petr hugged Mrs. Klahr again and kissed her forehead, and then walked to the back of the property and down past the fruit trees to the lake. Gretel was standing at the edge of the water, her hands atop her head as she stared across the lake at the only real home she had ever known.

"Gretel?"

Gretel neither turned nor spoke; she simply gave a slight dismissive shake of her head, a motion which Petr interpreted as aftershock.

"What happened?" Petr closed his eyes and shook of the question. "I mean, I know that Anika is...dead."

At this last word, Gretel dropped her hands from her head and looked to her right down the shoreline.

"But what happened?"

Gretel said nothing at first, continuing to shake her head slowly, ruefully. And then, just as Petr was about to speak again, she asked, "Do you remember the day when all of this really began?"

She looked back toward the center of the lake, her eyes focused again on her former home.

"It began right over there. It was the day Marlene killed my father, the day she revealed herself to us for the first time, at the top of the porch. It all started for my mother months earlier, I know that, but for us, for you and me and Hansel, that was the day it really began. Do you remember?"

Petr scoffed. "Of course I remember." His voice was nearly a whisper, nearly choking on the last syllable. The day Gretel had just excavated contained a tapestry of revelations, one of which was about his own father's betrayal and death.

"I remember about your father too," Gretel replied, seeming to acknowledge Petr's silent thoughts, once again reinforcing her supernatural abilities. "But before any of that, before Marlene and my father came outside, Odalinde, Hansel and I had just returned from my grandfather's house. And you were sitting there on the porch, waiting for us. And before the truck had stopped moving, I exploded out and ran at you, crazed, screaming at you about how you had lied to me about what you knew regarding my father and Odalinde's engagement. Which, it turns out, was true, you had lied."

"Gretel, I..."

"At that moment, and only for a moment, I hated you. I had grown to become very fond of you up until then, but when I knew you had learned of my father and Odalinde's plans to marry, and that you had kept it to yourself, and acted like you didn't know..." Gretel broke off the final thought, not finding the words to properly express it. "Anyway, when I saw you sitting there that day, I wanted to kill you. And I mean that almost literally. It's how I feel about you right now, Petr. I don't want to look at you because I don't want to feel that way about you again."

Petr felt a surge of defensiveness rise in him. "I'm sorry about your mother, Gretel, but I didn't do anything. What did I do?"

In spite of her prior words, Gretel turned to Petr, the pain on her face causing Petr to grimace himself.

"Nothing, Petr. Of course you've done nothing. And of course it's not fair for me to feel this way about any of you, or to blame you or your father or The System for all that's happened over the past couple of years. It's no more your fault than it is Mrs. Klahr's or Hansel's. You were all just caught up in this, just as I was at first." Gretel paused. "But at a certain point, I could no longer say that. I became very much to blame for how the story began to unfold. And now she's dead. And I am responsible."

"That isn't true, Gretel."

Gretel frowned and nodded. "But it is. At the very least I'm responsible for the *way* she died."

"But if you hadn't..."

"I know, Petr!" Gretel snapped, and then lowered her voice immediately. "I know if I hadn't given her the potion that she would have died anyway. But it doesn't change what happened. Mrs. Klahr gave me the potion, and I gave it to my mother to save her. And in the process, I killed her and created...whatever it was she became."

Petr couldn't argue the facts as Gretel had just laid them out, and perhaps Gretel needed to go through this stage as part of the grieving process. So instead, he steered the conversation back to the present. "How did she die?"

Tears began to fall from Gretel's cheeks in a steady flow. "Hansel."

Petr wanted to follow up on the particulars, but at speaking her brother's name, Gretel covered her face and leaned forward, her head out over the water as she sobbed. Petr placed a hand on her back but she shivered him away.

Slowly, Gretel composed herself and stood upright again, wiping the last of the tears away and taking a deep breath. "I left him here alone with her. I told him to leave, but I knew he wouldn't. He still loved her so much, and he still believed it was possible for her to get better. But I knew it was hopeless."

"And you told him that. You did what you could do."

Gretel shook her head. "I shouldn't have gone away. It wasn't fair of me. Not the least bit. I told myself it was for my future, but it was a lie. And I knew it at the time."

"It *was* for your future. It still is." Petr now felt a hint of blame being cast his way, for being the impetus behind Gretel leaving. That was true, of course, and he had given a pretty tough sell on the idea of her entering school early.

Gretel shook her head slowly. "I was a coward. And I was tired."

Petr said nothing for a few beats, allowing the confession its proper marination. Finally, he asked, "How is Hansel?"

Gretel ignored the question. "I'm going to be leaving, Petr."

"Yeah, of course, Gretel. Take the rest of the semester off. This was all just to get a head start anyway. You'll come back in a couple months and start up again, and be right there with everyone else. The departments will understand. I'll even talk to the heads if you like."

"No, Petr, I'm leaving. For more than a semester."

Petr felt a knot rise in his gut. "Where? For how long?" He paused. "Why?"

"This land, it...it doesn't feel like my home anymore. It feels...wicked now, like it's been polluted to a point where it can never be clean again."

"That's why you need to come back to school. Away from here. Away from this destruction."

Gretel was shaking her head before Petr had finished speaking. "I'm not just talking about the Back Country. This whole place is contaminated. The Back Country and South-lands is where it all unfolded, but Marlene came from the Northlands. And it was the Urbanlands that sent The System. Dodd and...and your father."

Petr closed his eyes and turned his head as if slapped.

"I'm leaving for the Old World."

Petr opened his eyes again, his expression flat and re-signed, his vision now blurred from the moisture of nascent tears. "I'll come with you," he said, but his attempt at persuasion sounded perfunctory.

Gretel gave a flat smile. "I won't be gone forever, I can promise that. But...I also can't tell you when I'll be back."

"What about Hansel?"

Gretel turned away from Petr again, and this time took a deep breath. "He's the other reason I'm going. I know I'm to blame for this, for Anika, for her death, but every time I look at him, I'll blame him. At least for a while. And I don't want to do that. Which is why I need to get away from him too."

"If leaving him before wasn't fair, how can it be fair to leave him now?"

"Because it is!" Gretel said immediately, simultaneously blasting a look of scorn toward Petr, who received it without a flinch. "It isn't the same now," she continued, "Anika is gone."

Gretel was speaking quickly now, her pitch high, as if trying to convince herself of her own words.

"And Hansel has the orchard to run now. And Mrs. Klahr is still here. They'll look after each other for the next few years. After that..."

"After that, what? Your plan is to be gone for that long? For the 'next few years?'"

"I don't have a plan, Petr. I don't know. I just, I feel like the Old World is where I belong. I knew it the minute we first landed there and began our search for the answers to *Orphism*. The whole time we were there I begged Anika to take us home, back here, because of how much I missed Mr. and Mrs. Klahr. And you, of course."

In spite of himself, Petr drew a trace of a smile.

"But I also knew I *belonged* there. I won't be able to explain it exactly, except to say that I feel a connection to that world that I don't feel here anymore. I used to feel it quite strongly, but now..."

"What?"

"As perverse as it sounds, I haven't felt it since Marlene. She was a monster, and she needed to die, of course. But she also tethered me to my heritage." Gretel frowned and took a deep breath, and Petr could see that she was unsatisfied with how she was expressing her feelings. "I just have to go."

Petr closed his eyes, still not quite able to accept what he had just heard. It was a crushing rupture in a life which, over the last few months, had been nearly perfect. Not only had he been accepted to the University of the Urbanlands, where he had thus far been excelling both academically and socially, but he had also convinced the girl whom he intended to one day marry to join him there. And though Petr expected things for her to move a bit more slowly at the college, she, too, seemed to be taking to her new life without serious difficulty. She was still prone to the occasional mood lapse, and seemed to disappear from the conversation when she found herself in large groups of people, often sitting silently while her friends' stories and laughter erupted all around her.

But otherwise Gretel had seemed to move on from Marlene. Slowly she began to leave behind the topics of her family's ordeal. Even *Orphism*, the book by which she'd been nothing short of consumed, gradually disappeared from her bedside table, eventually earning a permanent place high atop her dorm room bookshelf.

And it was during these months Petr and Gretel had become lovers.

Sex was a topic that he and Gretel rarely discussed previously, except as it pertained to other people, and usually as they were portrayed in books and movies. They had become physical a few months before Petr left for school, but it was still of the adolescent variety, the kind of intimacy that occurred only with lights and clothes on.

But then Gretel had joined Petr at school, accepted to attend pre-semester classes, and by that first weekend, before Petr's housemate had arrived for the semester, and just after Gretel had finally freed herself from the stress and tragedy of her deteriorating mother, they were sleeping together.

That first time, Gretel had come to Petr well after midnight; her arrival was without notice, after having walked from her house to the other side of campus, two miles on a chilly fall night. Petr answered his door to an overcoated Gretel, her face and hair made up subtly and beautifully. Her head was cocked slightly to one side and she wore the smile of a buccaneer.

Within minutes, the two were naked in Petr's bed, and Petr could only laugh along with Gretel when it was all over in seconds. But he would rally nicely, and that night they made love four times, with each time Petr experiencing a new level of pleasure.

"I will miss you," Gretel said, again seeming to sense Petr's thoughts. "And me leaving doesn't have anything to do with you."

Petr shook his head and pursed his lips. "No, of course not," he said.

Gretel picked up one of the oars lying at her feet, and walked to the rowboat which sat beached on the bank, just to her right.

"You're going to row to the Old World?" Petr joked, the humor not at all diminishing the emptiness eating away at his intestines.

Gretel smiled. "You know I would if I could. But for now I'm just going to take a scull."

Gretel locked the oar into the oarlock, matching it to the one already fitted on the opposite side, and then launched the boat as she had done a thousand times. She sculled two giant strokes, her body facing Petr as she did, drifting quickly away from him, her eyes focused on something not present, something much further away than him or the lake or the Back Country.

At about the halfway point, she deftly turned the canoe left and headed down toward the s-bend, in the direction of Rifle Field. With each stroke, Gretel grew smaller in Petr's vision, and just as she was at a distance beyond recognition, Petr saw her smile and wave. She was always happiest on the lake, he thought, free of the enormous burdens that had weighed her for as long as he knew the girl.

Petr lifted a hand and held it out in a motionless wave. "I love you," he said. It was the first time he'd said the words aloud, though he had felt that way about her for most of the time he knew her.

He watched her disappear behind the thicket of trees at the bend, and then turned his attention to the house across the lake and the porch where he first saw Gretel through the kitchen window on the night they first met. It seemed like twenty years ago.

He looked to his right now and something on the screened porch caught his eye. There was movement. Petr wiped his eyes and stretched his cheeks, clearing away any lingering tears, considering that perhaps the prism of glisten had created a reflection.

He moved a step closer now, dipping the toes of his shoes into the water and craning his neck up. His eyes were clear, and since the porch windows had no glass and were covered only in mesh, there was no glare to trick him.

There was someone there.

He could see the silhouette of a body—female at first look—rising up from the floor of the porch. It was a few steps away from the window, but the shape was unmistakable.

Petr squinted and took two steps into the water, cupping his hands over his eyes to narrow his focus. Were his eyes tricking him? Was the shape simply a floor lamp? Or a shadow? No, it was definitely a human shape, and Petr quickly considered the possibility of a ghost. Why not? If any house was likely to have a spirit haunting it, it was Gretel's, and since Marlene had died there on the property, hers was not an unlikely choice.

The outline stood motionless for a few more moments—Petr was waded up to his thighs now—and then, like a wisp of smoke, it vanished into the background.

Petr gasped, his eyes now wide and shocked, his mind moving quickly to process further possibilities of what he'd just witnessed. He pivoted now in the water, turning in every direction, hoping in vain that there was someone who could validate that what he'd seen was real.

He ran back up the lake path toward the house, organizing his thoughts into words as he went, saying them out loud to himself so he could be economical and precise when telling Mrs. Klahr, and later Gretel, what he saw.

But as Petr passed the line of fruit trees and came even with the house, he saw Hansel seated on a large tree that had recently fallen near the garden shed. Another few feet and it would have destroyed the structure, along with a bevy of harvesting equipment.

Hansel was staring out toward the lake; clearly he would have seen Petr as he made his way down to see Gretel, just as he would see him now, returning. But Hansel was entranced, and made no movements to indicate his awareness.

"Hansel. Are you okay?"

Hansel sat unmoved.

Petr walked over to the boy and sat beside him on the log, allowing him several feet of space as buffer. He was clearly still in shock from his mother's death, which apparently he had directly caused, though Petr realized he still hadn't heard the details.

The two sat silently for more than two minutes, and just as Petr was about to speak, Hansel said, "She wants to blame me. And she probably will for a long time."

"What happened, Hansel?"

Hansel turned to Petr, his eyes now alive and focused. "But one day she'll know it wasn't my fault."

Petr nodded, not having enough information either to argue or confirm Hansel's words.

Hansel stood now and turned toward the house, the shock still evident in his body language.

"Hansel," Petr said.

Hansel stopped but didn't turn toward Petr, and Petr could sense the resentment in the boy. Perhaps the blame Gretel was foisting on Hansel, he was now transferring to Petr. "What?"

"This might sound like a strange question, but was there anyone else living in your house? With you and Anika?"

Petr turned toward Petr now, his eyes scrunched in a look of confusion and disgust. "No. What?"

Petr gave a half smile and shook off the question. "It's nothing. I...I'm not sure why I thought to ask that."

Hansel frowned and walked through the back door of the Klahr house, and before Gretel returned from her rowing session, Petr sprinted for his truck and drove directly to the Morgan property.

WITHIN MINUTES, PETR had parked the truck and was standing at the bottom of the porch steps, staring up and reminiscing about the night his father had sent him from the cruiser, ostensibly to retrieve his police binder, which he had purposely left behind in the Morgan house. Petr had thought a lot over these couple of years about how much his father had used him during the Marlene incident, about how willing he had been to sacrifice his only son—and Petr's childhood—for the perverse promise of immortality. And as each month passed, and Petr got further away from that dark time in his life, he hated Oliver Stenson even more.

Petr walked deliberately to the top of the steps and then stood staring at the front door for a beat before gripping the handle. He was suddenly frightened at the thought of entering, remembering that Marlene had once taken up residence here, bivouacking in the basement like some subterranean predator, emerging at night under the mask of darkness to kill, including on the night she had murdered Mr. Klahr.

Was she here now?

Petr knew that was impossible—Marlene was dead, there was no question about that—but perhaps someone had come to avenge her. *Somebody* was standing in that window, he was almost certain of it now, and this new possibility that it was someone sympathetic to Marlene suddenly flooded Petr with terror. It was a notion that now seemed like a very real possibility. She was a witch, after all, ancient and legendary, which meant she probably had family and followers in the darkest of the world's corners, ready to retaliate against the family that had killed her.

"Just go in," he said, and then pushed open the heavy, oak door.

The front door of Gretel's house opened directly into a small kitchen, and once Petr was inside, he could see half of the porch through the sliding glass door to his right. But the other half of the porch was blocked by the house's central support beam, so he walked gingerly toward the door, placing each step as carefully as a cat burglar. He was now close enough that he could touch his nose against the glass door, and he slowly scanned the full length of the porch.

There was no one out there.

He turned back to the kitchen and focused on that room, noticing several things immediately. There were footprints on the linoleum. Fingerprints on the handle of the refrigerator door. This was by no means smoking gun evidence that someone had just been there—it hadn't been twenty-four hours since Anika's death, so presumably she and Hansel would have been there and could have made these marks—but at first glance, the prints looked fresh.

He turned back toward the porch and slid open the glass door, walking out and feeling the fresh breeze sifting in through the screens. Petr walked to the window and stared down at the spot on the other side of the lake where he'd been standing less than ten minutes ago. Across from that spot, on the Morgan side of the lake where he was currently, was Gretel's canoe. She was apparently done with rowing and had come to visit her property.

He quickly walked back to the front door to see where she'd gone, and screamed at the sight of her standing in the front doorway.

"What are you doing, Petr?" she asked. "Why are you in here?"

"I...Why are you here?" He regretted the words the instant they left his mouth.

"This is *my* house."

"I know, I'm sorry, I don't know why I asked that. Listen to me: I think I saw something...someone...in here."

"What? When?"

"Just a few minutes ago. Just after you left for Rifle Field. I was looking across the lake and I saw...I don't know. Someone out on the porch." Petr nodded toward the screened porch from where he'd just come.

"I don't...understand." Gretel's face was a ball of confusion, as if her misunderstanding was more to do with Petr and his violation of her trust. "Why would you tell me something like that?"

Petr's mouth opened in disbelief, his eyes now wide and apologetic. "Gretel, I saw someone." He paused. "I think it was a woman."

"A woman? What did she look like?" Gretel's disbelief had morphed into indignation.

"I couldn't see her exactly, there was just a shape. I thought I was seeing things at first, but then...she moved. She backed out of sight like she knew I had seen her. That's why I came over here."

"There was only Hansel and my mother. No one else lived here. You know that."

Petr thought again of when Marlene had camped in the basement, and the smell she brought with her, a smell he was sure he could still detect remnants of now. So, in truth, someone else had lived there, but Petr decided it best not to remind Gretel of that now. "I do know that. I'm just—"

"Get out, Petr. I need some time here by myself. There are a few things I have to find before I go."

"Gretel..."

"Get out." Gretel didn't yell the words, but the effect on Petr was the same as if she had.

Petr stepped past Gretel and onto the front porch. Gretel stood at the threshold with the door open halfway.

"When is the funeral?" he asked, having given up on trying to convince Gretel of what he'd seen. Perhaps it was a ghost, he thought, in which case she would discover it on her own soon enough.

"Tomorrow morning at dawn. It will just be the four of us. We'll have a ceremony at the lake edge of the orchard."

"Just us?"

Gretel's eyes softened now and she shrugged. "There's no one left, Petr. Who would we tell?" Her look turned serious. "And we agreed—that is, Mrs. Klahr, Hansel, and I agreed—not to involve any more police."

Petr was stunned at this and scoffed. "She was killed, Gretel. No one has called the police?"

"I'm sure you can understand about that." Gretel's eyes flamed with warning, her teeth clenched. It was a look that said anything other than total acceptance of their decision would render Petr dead to her forever.

"Where is she? Where is the body?"

Gretel dropped Petr's eyes and looked to the floor. "It's at the bottom of the lake."

Petr still hadn't heard any of the details of Anika's death, and he quickly formed his own version of the story; he would find out later he wasn't far off from the truth of the actual events.

He nodded. "Tomorrow at dawn."

Gretel nodded back and closed the door.

Chapter 3

STOOPED LOW BETWEEN a pair of twin guest beds, Anika watched Petr Stenson through the gap between the wall and open stairway that led to their basement. Her nose and mouth were pressed against the side of the mattress, her eyes—one of which was now covered with a patch that she'd found in an old first aid kit—peeked just over the top, like a crocodile treading the surface of a river.

Anika had showered and dressed, cleansing her body of lake gunk and feces, reuniting with clothes she hadn't worn in a year, so accustomed had she become to living life in her filthy robe. Her wounds were still severe, however, untreated and gruesome, her face a portrait of damage.

The twin beds between which Anika hid had been a staple in the Morgan house for years, and though they had been used only rarely, mostly by Anika after her husband Georg's injury had left him nearly crippled with pain for several weeks, the smell of them now seemed to contain every memory of her previous life. She recalled how difficult life had seemed then, when her father and husband had been simultaneously incapacitated, one spiraling toward dementia, the other laid up in bed by the kick of a spirited horse. She hadn't known anything about the conspiracy against her then, the plan concocted by her father to bargain his own daughter's body for the poison of his own long life. She never thought then the ties of family could be broken so easily.

And Georg had been complicit too, unwilling to overcome the temptations of Marlene, the woman who had taken everything from her.

Everything but her children.

Hansel and Gretel had survived the story, somehow, and had even become heroes in it, they with Petr, fighting the power and evil of Marlene with all the bravery of wartime soldiers.

And Anika, of course, had played her role too, ultimately slaying the witch after returning from the Old World, the place where she had overcome desperate sickness and treachery.

But everything felt different now. Anika felt different. New. As if she had been reborn into someone else, a being with new senses and perspectives, yet still in possession of all of the memories and feelings of her former self.

And she was hungry now. She was so hungry.

Petr moved further into the kitchen, and Anika could now see only his legs below the knee, his bare calves triggering a release of saliva at the back of her mouth. She wanted to spit the craving to the floor, disgusted at herself for both the craving and for drawing the boy from the lake to the house. She had been careless on the porch, lingering too long there, allowing Petr to see her, or at least detect the shape of her through the window.

But she had been watching Gretel, had been entranced by her hair and skin and movements, and Anika had wanted to drink up every last moment of her daughter.

She thought of the potion now, and of the addiction that had blossomed from it. Beyond her own demise, it had brought destruction to her children's lives. It had forced Hansel to become a killer.

But the feeling of the potion was no longer inside of her. Anika could still feel the remnants of the addiction, and the effects it had rendered on her body, but the craving for the liquid was gone.

It had been replaced though, and even at this early stage of her new incarnation, she could feel the replacement was a thing far more sinister.

The spoiled chicken had had the opposite effect of sating her hunger, and Anika had spent several minutes washing off the bird fat and skin from her fingers and nails, nearly vomiting again as the tiny chunks of flesh circled the sink drain.

And her need to feed was growing, with only Petr nearby.

Petr walked back into the kitchen, and his body was again in full view. Anika licked her lips and swallowed, and then crouched lower behind the bed.

And then she heard Gretel.

The tenor and tempo of her daughter's voice drifting in from the front threshold was ecstasy in Anika's ears, and the knowledge that Gretel was only steps from her was torture.

Anika estimated it had been only a few weeks since she had seen her daughter, but as she searched her memory, she couldn't remember the last time she'd seen her in a state of sobriety. Whatever happened at the bottom of the lake had altered Anika, about that she was certain, but it was very different from the fog of the poisonous potion. She was aware now. As fully aware as she'd ever been in her life.

She saw the first shoe of Gretel enter the house, followed by the full stature of her body, and Anika waited in distress for the hunger to emerge.

But there was nothing.

Anika closed her eyes for a moment and smiled, and then took a deep breath before opening her eyes wide, taking in the fullness of her daughter, who looked beautiful and sad.

Anika heard the door close, and then watched as her daughter disappeared from view, walking in the direction of the back bedrooms. She moved from her crouching position and sat flat on the floor, resting her back against the bed frame. She put her hands in her head, pressing her palms to her closed eyes to keep from weeping.

What was she to do now? How was she to exist in this world after today?

As far as the world knew, or soon would, Anika Morgan was dead. Certainly her family would believe nothing else. Hansel had struck her down, and he and Mrs. Klahr had no doubt watched her head sink below the surface of the water, bloody and struggling as she went. And they had later tossed flowers into the water, an obvious sign of her memoriam.

She was dead now, a corpse at the bottom of the lake, and any surprise resurrection, any miraculous appearance to her son would only invoke the terror of Marlene and the abomination of Orphism. She would be seen as a witch from then on, undead, and a constant underlying threat to her son forever, no matter the reparations she made.

But perhaps Gretel could understand. If Anika had indeed died and been resurrected, if she was a product of the potion's powers and the practice of Orphism, Gretel could fathom it. She probably knew more about the subject than anyone in the New Country.

Anika would allow Gretel to leave today, and then watch from the perch of the porch her own funeral at dawn tomorrow. And by nightfall, she would wait for a time when Gretel was alone, and together they would find answers.

But between now and tomorrow night, she would hunt.

THAT NIGHT ANIKA DREAMED of the Old World, of the Koudeheuval Mountains and the Village of the Elders, and of an even more distant place in that world, one described to her by her father during Anika's captivity in the warehouse behind the cannery, just after she'd escaped from Marlene's cottage and been "rescued" by Officer Stenson. The place her father had spoken of was the land of Orphism's birth, where the magic of immortality was first discovered by her ancestors, where it was nurtured and revered before leaking out to the rest of the world and hijacked by villains. In her dream, it was in this land where she saw the woman, ancient and malevolent, unfamiliar to Anika. But Anika knew her identity instinctively. It was she. It was Tanja.

The daughter of Tanja.

The daughter.

It was the daughter of Tanja, as told by the village elder through Anika's interpreter Oskar, who was in possession of the only copy of *Orphism* that contained the remedy to her illness. She would learn later, of course, that it was Marlene who the elder was referencing, and Gretel had indeed found the cure in her book and brought Anika back from the edge of death.

The 'Tanja' part of the elder's description, however, was still a mystery, but ever since Anika's emergence from the lake, her name had become prominent in her thoughts.

Anika also dreamed of Noah, the gentle guide who had navigated them up and through the mountains to the amazing society of her ancestors, from which they were then guided to the Village of the Elders. There was almost no way Anika could quantify Noah's value to her voyage—she would never have made it without him—and as she thought about the man now, she remembered their farewell words on the pier and her wish at the time for him to come with her. How she wished now, more than ever, that he had come. Her life since then may have gone much differently. But Anika knew in her heart that Noah would play a critical role again before the story of the Morgans was finally written, and she gave a sigh of contentment at this assurance.

As if Noah had suddenly spoken her name aloud, Anika's eyes flashed open, ending the dream in an instant. She was in one of the basement's twin beds, staring at a pair of wooden support beams that ran beneath the ceiling. She recalled having taken to one of the twin beds to rest, waiting for Gretel to leave, and had obviously fallen asleep there.

Was it the next day? The day after her resurrection? If it was, why was she not experiencing throbbing pain in her head at the site of her wound? She could feel the damage, the oozing blood and infection where the wound still raged unhealed and gnarled, but she felt no physical discomfort at all coming from the surface of her body. There was only warmth and serenity.

Her hunger, on the other hand, was almost unbearable now, and the thought of Petr's smooth, thick calves strolling across the kitchen floor collapsed into Anika's mind like a cinder block. But Petr was gone now too, he was in no danger from Anika, and she decided not to fight the thought this time. Instead she explored the hunger, noting how it didn't seem to quite resonate from her belly, but rather it was a piercing pang that she experienced throughout the whole of her body.

And there was no sense denying anymore that her craving was for human flesh.

But Anika also felt the emotions that were still lingering from her dream, and, unlike her hunger, she welcomed these sensations. It was a sign that she was alive, at least on some level, and that she still had the capacity to love.

Anika sucked in a giant breath to clear the memories of the dream, and then, as she focused on the daylight shining through the basement door, panic set in.

She had slept through the remainder of the previous day and night, and now seemed to be well into the next day. Judging by the glow of light, it was several hours past dawn, and that meant she had missed her own funeral.

What did it matter though? It was a charade, and she had really only wanted to witness the ceremony so that she could see her children again.

And to keep track of Gretel.

Anika figured she still had time before Gretel would return to school, and during her stay in the Back Country, she had hoped her daughter would choose to come stay in her own house. It only made sense; why would she stay with the Klahrs if her home was perfectly suitable?

There were other factors, of course, not the least of which was that Hansel had just killed his own mother and may want the support and company of his sister. But Anika knew Gretel, and she suspected that, despite Hansel being justified in his actions, she would feel a certain level of animosity toward her brother. It wasn't fair for her to feel that way, but that was Gretel—grudges had always been a part of her make up.

Anika rose from the bed and walked quickly to the basement door, sliding the glass wide and stepping out onto the patio where she absorbed the gratifying warmth of the late morning sun. It was an hour before noon, she judged, well past what was certain to have been a short memorial service, but she listened anyway for any voices that might be echoing across the lake.

Hearing none, Anika turned to re-enter the house, but just as she was about step through the doorway, she caught a distant scent emanating from the woods to the east. The smell was barely perceptible, and yet it was distinct and familiar. And the source of it was substantial.

Something large and delicious.

As if the scent itself had flicked a switch inside of her, Anika's demeanor of sleep instantly evaporated and developed into one of primal urgency. She lifted her head sharply, darting her jaw to the left, then to the right, and then left again, making incremental recalibrations, automatically positioning her nose to keep the scent alive.

She licked her lips and swallowed slowly as she narrowed her eyes, blurring the vision of her surroundings while focusing her mind on the smell. Like a snake sloughing off its aged scales, Anika shed her slippers and blouse, then her pants, letting each item fall limply at her feet onto the brick-paved patio.

Now barefoot and naked but for her bra and a thin pair of underpants, Anika moved quietly onto the gravel surrounding the overgrown garden, striding with purpose past the woodpile, silently breaching the tree line, moving with stealth until she reached the interior of the heavy woods.

Once behind the shroud of the deep forest's leaves and branches, Anika's movements became those of a panther, with her new lack of physical sensation rendering her impervious to weather and pain. This made what would have otherwise been unpleasant steps through the leaf litter as simple as walking over a field of ginned cotton.

Anika sidled low and sideways as she advanced between the trunks, almost touching her knees to the ground, maintaining cover by rising tall behind each tree she approached, poking her head out in a scan for danger before continuing.

She was no more than a hundred yards into the woodland when she saw a six-point buck; it was facing away from Anika, its rump high and alert, and it made no gesture indicating it had detected the human intruder behind it. Anika stood covertly beside the animal's hind quarters, which was nearly Anika's height, and then slapped it with her open hand, sending the deer fleeting through the woods without ever turning to see the thing that had assaulted him.

But it wasn't the deer Anika had smelled back at the house; it was the men hunting it.

"I heard it, Mattheo! I heard it grunt and scramble."

"Spooked?"

"I don't know, but I think it's coming toward me."

The voices were frantic with excitement, and Anika, using an involuntary triangulation formula of the deer's position, the volume of the men's voices, and the sweet smell of flesh, calculated they came from no more than fifty yards away.

"Toward us?"

"I think so." There was a pause and then, "It's there."

The gunshot was enormous, and Anika dropped to the ground and covered her ears in pain. Her sense of smell had been amplified, but so too had her hearing.

I wonder if the taste of them will be amplified too, she thought, and before she could shame herself for the idea, Anika sprinted in the direction of the fallen deer and the men surrounding its carcass.

"You got him Mattheo," the first hunter said proudly, out of breath. "It was a wonderful shot."

Anika stood tall behind a thick, white birch trunk, ten yards from the two hunters, watching the scene unfold as she measured her options.

"I did," the other hunter—Mattheo—replied, his expression glowing and self-satisfied.

"I've taught you well, my boy."

Father and son. Not what Anika would have hoped for. Her hunger was primary now, and not to be denied, but the thought of tearing this family apart, in whatever way the scenario played out, piled a helping of weight upon her.

But the outcast lion didn't consider the parents of the wounded zebra colt; it simply hunted that prey which was most immediate, focusing solely on its own survival in the world.

Anika stepped from behind the tree and stood in the open now, the mud and sap of the woodland streaking her bare body from her face and neck to the dorsals of her feet. She scanned herself, the wildness of her appearance for the first time registering. And she hadn't yet seen her face. The concavity of the wound and the crusts of blood and healing must be abominable. She thought of that night in the Northlands, when she'd become lost in the woods off the Interways, almost freezing to death before finally being attacked and abducted by Marlene.

But the parallels she felt now didn't run along her own experience from that night. She felt much more connected now to Marlene. Sympathetic even to the craving she must have been feeling.

The two hunters who stood before her—one of whom, Anika now saw, wasn't a man at all, and was perhaps fifteen at the oldest—didn't notice her for several moments, fixated as they were on their trophy. She took a step closer to them now, then another, her eyes narrowed once again, focusing neither on the father nor the son, instead maintaining a peripheral line of sight between them.

It was Mattheo who noticed her first. "Oh my God," he whispered. "Dad."

The smile lingered on Mattheo's father's face for a few seconds, as if anticipating some profound acknowledgement of bonding from his son. "Yes, boy?"

"Dad look."

Mattheo's dad lifted his chin and gun almost simultaneously, and the barrel of the rifle, which had been low and impotent a second before, was now pointed directly at Anika.

"Dad, she's naked." It was a plea from Mattheo, a direction to his dad that this woman was no threat.

The father lowered the gun and blinked several times, as if clearing his mind for both he and his son, perhaps considering that the woman in front of him may be some type of mirage. "Who are you?" he asked. "Are you in some kind of trouble?"

Anika closed her eyes and breathed deeply, and then, without intent or preconception, she stuck her tongue out slightly, trying to taste the sweat and musk coming from the bodies in front of her.

"I asked who you are," Mattheo's father repeated, this time with less compassion or bewilderment.

Anika could smell the increased output of his glands as he lifted the rifle again, this time, she calculated, based on the sound of the barrel cutting the air, to about thigh level.

"Dad, what are you doing? Look at her. She's hurt. Why are you pointing the gun at her?"

"I'm not pointing it at her. I'm positioning it so that I can point it at her quickly if necessary."

"Why would that be necessary?"

Anika opened her eyes now and saw the man look towards his son, as if his own reasoning was solid, though perhaps not rational if he spoke of it aloud.

"Dad, why? Who is that?"

"You know the stories, Mattheo. You know of all that happened around here. Of that witch from the North and her kin."

"I know of the witch. Marlene."

Anika felt a bolt of pain shoot through her shoulders at the sound of the hag's name, but she kept her eyes locked on the discussion, inputting each word of the conversation into the calculation that would decide their fate.

"What does she have to do with Marlene? Marlene is dead. Really dead. You know that. We all know that. And that part about those folks being her kin is just story. Stories for reprobate children."

The older hunter looked back at Anika, the discussion with his son seemingly having no impact on his opinions of the woman standing naked in front of him.

"Is that true? You got nothing at all to do with that woman and her tale?"

Anika squared the man's eyes to her and smiled, and then shook her head slowly.

"You see that," Mattheo said, "She's got nothing to do with it."

"That's not what I meant," Anika said finally, the two hunters now riveted by her voice. "I was telling you that what you said isn't true. I, in fact, have quite a bit to do with that story."

"I told you," the father said quietly, his eyes never leaving Anika. "It's the Morgan woman."

"Anika?" Mattheo whispered. "Anika Morgan?"

"That cursed family's property isn't but a few hundred yards from here."

"They live there still?"

"I guess they do. The stories about that whole thing never really goes beyond Marlene. But it seems they do."

Anika felt a stabbing pain in her heart as it began to beat faster, preparing her body with the oxygen it would need for the upcoming slaughter. But there was a deeper pain there as well, a driving sadness that reverberated to her soul.

She took one step forward and the world around her slowed a bit, as if she were able to operate normally while everything in her surroundings was awash in honey. Even the brightness was there, illuminating the scene to her benefit, highlighting details that would otherwise have been obfuscated in the drama, but which she could use to her advantage.

The hunter's trigger finger fumbled for a quarter second, and Anika squatted and dodged to her right, taking another two steps toward the man. He pointed the rifle low now and shot, but Anika had already collapsed to her belly and done a full roll back to her right. She was now lying face down in front of the shooter, less than four feet away.

He took a step back as he reloaded, Anika could hear it all play out as if she'd seen this play a thousand times, and she pushed her arms straight, planking her body stiff and then rising instantly to her feet.

Mattheo's father pivoted the rifle toward Anika, his intentions now nothing other than deadly. But with the ease of a bear in a stream of spawning salmon, Anika intercepted the middle of the barrel in mid-swing, snatching the gun from the hunter's hands before flinging it behind her.

As if she'd been pushed from behind by a hurricane-force wind, Anika lunged towards the man, her heels high, the balls of her feet barely touching the ground. And before she could contemplate what she'd done, Anika sank her large teeth into the side of the man's neck, chewing a large chunk off before moving to the center of his neck and throat. There was instant silence.

Anika thought of Gretel and Hansel as she kept her pose of death on the hunter, feeling the last of his blood being pumped toward the wound. And then she thought of Marlene, the person ultimately responsible for the death of poor Mattheo's father.

Mattheo.

Anika allowed the limp body to fall to her feet, the man's head smacking the butt of the rifle that now lay useless beside the hunter. She chewed the chunk of flesh she'd bitten off from him and swallowed it, and then looked to the teenage boy to her right, pieces of camel-brown skin still hanging from her chin, the stubble of day-old beard lightly brushing against her cheek.

Mattheo's face was white with fear, his eyes glistening and unblinking. He still held his own rifle low at his hip, gripped tightly in his fist, but Anika could tell he was unaware at the moment its purpose.

"What to do with you, Mattheo," Anika said, her uncontrollable hunger for the moment sated, her mind now clear enough to consider the boy's life.

But the satiation wouldn't last long; the smell of the dead man's blood below her had already begun wafting up into her nostrils.

"I...I don't..."

Anika prayed Mattheo would run. She didn't need him. The food she had so craved was now at her feet in the form of his father's corpse; if Mattheo simply turned and sprinted away from Anika, she would be feeding on it momentarily. If he stayed, she would murder the boy, and only for the purposes of concealing his father's slaughter.

"Go."

Mattheo stood in place, frozen in shock, his fear of moving having overcome the potential punishment that might result from disobeying the killer's command.

"Mattheo!"

At the sound of his name, the boy's eyes came alive and he looked at Anika, the fear on his face turning slightly to a mixture of sadness and confusion.

"Mattheo listen to me. You have to run. Now!" Anika barked the last word, her voice scratchy and low, guttural, bits of sinew and blood flying from her mouth.

"Is Gretel dead?"

The question caught Anika off guard, and she choked on a breath as she took a shaky step backwards. She then brought her hands to her mouth in a move that resembled shyness, embarrassment perhaps, and Anika began wiping her hands in long, slow strokes down her chin and cheeks, attempting to erase the mess of evidence around her mouth.

She looked away shamefully and said, "No. Now run away from me. Tell whoever you want, tell everyone, but please run. I don't want to kill you."

Mattheo finally took a single step back from the spot where he had, to this point, been standing as still as a lake of ice.

Anika pleaded in her mind for the boy to run, almost panicky in her thoughts now, so desperate was she not to take his life. Her hunger would be fulfilled in moments, and the thought of Mattheo's murder was now almost unbearably distressing.

But she could only contain her instincts for so long. As thorough as her hunger was, her need to satisfy this new desire of human flesh, so too was the drive toward self-defense and preservation.

"Did you know her?" The words seemed to leave Anika's mouth before they formed in her mind, and she closed her eyes again, this time in regret. On some level, she hoped the boy would recognize the stall tactic and just take off sprinting through the woods in the opposite direction of where she stood. Whether she would have chased him down or not, Anika couldn't have said. It was possible that Mattheo dashing away like a scared animal would have triggered that same thing inside her that made it impossible for most dogs to watch in stillness a stick that's just been thrown to the far side of the yard.

"I didn't. I heard a lot of stories about her though. And about you."

Anika could hear the disappointment in the boy's voice. She was certainly not embodying the legend he'd heard of in the schoolyard.

"And I knew someone whose friend was killed by the Witch of the North."

That was interesting, Anika thought. She'd never really considered the victims outside of her own circle.

"My friend's friend, he was named Claude. He and his sister—I think her name was Sofia—were killed at her cabin."

The names sounded familiar to Anika, particularly the sister's, and she thought perhaps Gretel—or maybe it was Petr—had been friendly with her at one time.

"Are you like her now?"

Anika sighed and covered her face with her hands, pressing them tightly against her forehead, as if a heavy migraine had suddenly emerged.

"You have to run now, Mattheo." Anika's words were hurried now, her breathing heavy and rasping, and the resistance she was providing against herself was becoming almost impossible to maintain.

Anika noted the change in the boy's expression instantly. It was slight, likely imperceptible to virtually every other person on the planet. But not to Anika.

Mattheo's eyes shifted once to his right, and two of the fingers of his right hand, the hand that was wrapped around the rifle stock, gave a slight twitch. Anika frowned and instinctively turned her body so that her left shoulder was now facing Mattheo, knowing this would provide a narrower target for the boy while also shortening the distance her arm would have to cover to reach his neck.

It was over before Mattheo could bring the gun as high as his hip. He did manage to squeeze the trigger, and the subsequent explosion from the round put a small crater in forest floor that was only inches from Anika's right foot. But before he could make another move, she was behind the boy, gripping his neck in a gruesome twist of her arms, applying a pressure at the base that was instantly fatal, so severe that it shattered his windpipe and six of the seven cervical vertebrae that formed the top of his spine.

Anika released Mattheo's body and watched in horror as it fell in a heap of dead flesh next to his father's crumpled corpse. She felt a sudden loss of instinct, drive, as if a demon had just released her from its possession. She hugged her arms to her chest, squeezing her own body as if trying to awaken herself from a nightmare. But the smell of the flesh was real, and no alternate level of consciousness could eliminate it from her senses.

Anika squinted back the tears that had already begun dripping on top of her victims, neither of whom deserved to die, neither of whom had a chance to live once she smelled them.

Anika now accepted that she was like her now. Marlene. Driven by an inexorable need to kill her fellow man and feed on their flesh.

But Anika knew she was worse. Marlene had at least shown a great level of restraint with Anika during all those weeks and months of her captivity, and never allowed herself to give in to the hunger before the potion was complete. Anika, on the other hand, needed no potion, and thus restraint was a luxury. She had died already—at least, that was her assumption based on the evidence to this point—and her resurrected desire for raw, human meat could be had with regularity. There was an abundance of it everywhere she went.

She looked down at the bodies below her, and decided she would take only the flesh of the older hunter. Mattheo's body she would drag to the lake and sink to the bottom, where, it was not lost on Anika, she, herself, was assumed by her family to be decomposing. There was no honor in this decision; in fact, it would only help to demonstrate that Mattheo's killing was an even greater waste of life. But the decision was a type of line in the sand for Anika, and she was hoping it would instill in her some modicum of self-discipline. The boy was dead now, a victim of her reflexes and instinct, but she could still hold on to what humanity remained in her—when not in the throes of hunger—by making as many rational decisions as possible.

Anika knelt at the torso of Mattheo's father and ravaged his body with the veracity of a starving wolf pack, using her newfound strength to tear him open at the belly. She removed the organs—liver, heart, and kidneys—and devoured each in several large, predatory bites. Her hair hung over her face as she fed, interfering with the purity of the meal, and soon became heavy and unruly from the weight of blood. Anika could feel the warmth of the innards across her face, and could only imagine how she would have appeared to an onlooker.

With the insides of the hunter eaten, Anika felt no hunger for the rest of him. She wasn't repulsed by the skin and flesh, and could have eaten it if that was all there was, but she felt satisfied by the rich organ meat, and thus immediately dug out a shallow grave with her fingers and buried the hollowed out body, leaving it to be consumed by the lower-life forms that dwelled in the dirt.

Anika then grabbed the collar of Mattheo's shirt and dragged his body down the slope of the forest to the lake bank. Once there, she dressed in the spare clothes that Mattheo had packed—a decent fit—and then filled the two backpacks—his father's and his own—with as many large stones as would fit inside of them. Then, using a rope she found amongst Mattheo's father's supplies, Anika tied the packs tightly around Mattheo's waist and neck, and then pulled his body toward her off the bank and into the water.

Anika looked in both directions and could see only see the empty bank of the Klahr property in the distance off to her right. In the other direction, there was only the lake bend around which was Rifle Field. The scene was clear of witnesses, and Anika slowly pushed down on Mattheo's chest, feeling the sickening ease with which the corpse sank beneath the surface.

With each second she held the corpse below, waiting for the lungs to fill, a new level of panic rose within Anika.

She couldn't sustain this type of life for long. And probably not at all. Even if she could stomach the thought of a lifetime of feeding on the insides of human beings, it wasn't reasonable to think she could rely on her food supply coming in the form of stray hunters wandering near her property. She would be caught eventually, the murders uncovered and solved, and once convicted of the treachery—of which she would indeed be guilty—she would hang from the gallows like a common traitor, or be shot in the head as she stood blindfolded against a stone wall.

The truth was, though, even if her villainy was never discovered, Anika couldn't live like this. There was simply no way at all. She wasn't supposed to be alive anymore, and perhaps the whole truth of it was that she should have never returned from the Old Country. Maybe Anika's story should have ended once she took Gretel to the Old Country to regain her heritage. Maybe she was simply the vehicle for allowing Gretel to find the answers to the secrets of *Orphism*. Once she had left her home in the Back Country, maybe she was meant never to come home again.

But she had come home, triumphant and sick, and whatever accidental combination of poison and cure she'd received from the witch and the village elders and Gretel had now made her own death a defiant obstacle. Once a simple Back Country woman, farm wife and mother, Anika had gradually turned into a resemblance of Marlene, and was now even worse than the witch herself.

From where she now stood, about ten feet off the bank in thigh-high water, Anika could see the outline of the Weinhiemmer cannery through the trees at the lake bend. The structure seemed destined to remain the eyesore it had always been, blemishing the beauty of Rifle Field with its pocked exterior and surrounding barbed fence.

Anika, of course, held mixed emotions about the cannery. It was to that place that she and Gretel had escaped, sheltering themselves from Marlene as the witch pursued them like a starving bear. It was the night of Anika and Gretel's reunion, a night that culminated with Gretel sinking the heavy iron claw of an industrial hammer into the middle of the witch's forehead.

And now Anika had taken the lives of two people, almost blithely, a father and son, two men that certainly formed a part of some larger family, individuals who were just as innocent as she and Gretel were during their fight against Marlene.

Anika was the villain now, there was no question as to that, a monster as hideous and loathsome as the one she had helped kill not so long ago. And despite her angst and regret at the crimes she had just committed, neither of those emotions meant a thing. They weren't going to bring back the innocent man who seemed ready to help Anika; or his son, who indirectly knew friends of Gretel and whose body she could now touch with her foot beneath the water. Neither of them would ever get a proper burial, and their family—mother and wife, brothers and sisters, sons and daughters—would forever live in doubt about their disappearance and death, questioning whether it was abandonment or abduction.

And they would suffer.

Anika took a deep breath and ducked beneath the water, and then swam in the direction of Rifle Field. Out of curiosity, she challenged her lungs and their need for oxygen, and though she easily made it around the bend and to the shores of the open field, she could also feel the pressure to breathe emerging. She took this as a positive sign, since it indicated there was still life in her.

And if there was still life in her, it meant she could still die.

Anika stepped from the water and onto the grassy bank, and then headed directly to the tall, chain-linked fence that separated Rifle Field and the cannery from one another. The barbed wire that looped in wide circles at the top was as menacing as ever, the patina of rust coating the tips of the barbs adding to its deadly appearance.

It was a perfect test, she thought. If she could feel the pain on her hands and body as she climbed through the piercing barrier of the fence, it would be a signal that death could still be achieved.

Anika thought of Marlene, and the witch's own reluctance to die.

Gretel's hammer blow and the witch's fall to the cannery floor would have killed any human. But it hadn't killed Marlene. It was as if her body had acquired a resistance to death in the way any normal body immunizes itself from a litany of diseases.

But she wasn't completely resistant.

A couple of shotgun blasts was more than enough to finally finish her life. The gun shots were traumatic, gauging huge holes in her head and chest, leaving no place for the blood to flow to keep her body functioning. No amount of potion or witchcraft could heal such extreme injuries.

And Marlene herself had killed Odalinde, also an Orphist who had been emboldened by the potion for centuries.

So if they could die, so too could Anika.

She felt the sting of the barbs in her hands and face as she climbed, and then her groin and thighs as she straddled through the spiraling wire, feeling the stretch of her skin each time it caught a tip of the metal spikes, tearing at the soft flesh until it opened into long, thin cavities of red. The pain was dull, like walking barefoot through a pile of smooth but uneven stones.

But it was pain nevertheless.

Anika pulled the last of her tattered shirt through the barbed barrier, and then jumped the seven feet from the top of the fence to the ground on the cannery side. Memories of the night of her escape tried to creep back to Anika's mind, but she shunned them for the moment. And hopefully, if things went as planned, she would never have the chance to think of anything again.

She walked around to the front of the cannery and swung open the large metal door, allowing the afternoon light to fill the open space inside. Anika took a tepid step into the building, the smell of it bringing her back to the day of her escape, when she'd fled in terror from the storage building that sat on the hill above.

The dust and dilapidation still raged in the interior of the cannery, but the main room was barer than she remembered. The tubing that ran throughout remained, and the floor-bolted canning tables, but the floor itself was absent of the tools that were so prevalent that night she and Gretel had come, and was now littered with trash and bottles, some of which looked fairly fresh.

This newly strewn garbage wasn't surprising to Anika; the tale of Gretel and Anika had now become infamous, wide-spread, and as a result, various locations along the timeline of the story had become popular tourist attractions, the cannery being one of several. The System, who theoretically had jurisdiction over the abandoned building, had, of course, done nothing to prevent the gawkers from trespassing, as they were still trying to rid themselves of the tarnish the Morgan story had left on their institution. And due to this lack of interest, the loose items of value—mainly tools—had been stolen.

This was a problem for Anika, since her plan to carry out her suicide depended on her finding at least one of the sharp, mortal objects that were present during her previous visit. At first glance, however, it appeared she would need to devise a new strategy.

The hammer, of course, the one Gretel had used to send the witch plummeting to the cannery's ground floor, was also gone, no doubt stolen within days of Marlene's inhuman resurrection. Its gruesome heritage would have certainly been the prized possession in any aficionado's collection. Or perhaps Marlene had simply walked out with the hammer in her head, oblivious to the destruction it should have caused.

But what did remain was the stain of the witch's injury; the dried puddle of blood and fluid still mapped the floor just below the open ladder way leading up to the loft.

Anika took a deep breath and stared up through the opening in the loft floor, and then climbed the ladder, stopping for a moment on the top rung before pushing herself up to the wood-based tier. She walked to the open window that looked out over the lake, and immediately wished it were ten stories higher. Twenty perhaps, and with only concrete awaiting her below. That should be high enough to do the job, she thought.

But there were no buildings in the Back Country—and possibly even in the Urbanlands—high enough to facilitate a fatal fall, especially considering her freshly won resilience to pain and injury.

She turned away from the window and scanned the remainder of the loft, and then, finding nothing useful, descended the ladder and walked out of the cannery. She stood in the open air now as she considered her next move, taking in the scent of grass and trees, of animal scat and dead fish, odors previously masked in insignificance from her senses, but which now overwhelmed her.

She closed her eyes and focused, concentrating on the puzzle at hand, letting the sensory experience of her surroundings fade to the background. Her goal was death now, but death was proving tricky. Most people understood the emotional dilemmas associated with suicide, not the least of which was the effect it would have on those left behind. And the mental challenge was formidable too, of course, since most people had a mind oriented towards survival, and overcoming that orientation required a great deal of commitment and resolve.

But the physical aspect of suicide was not to be overlooked either. Millions of years of evolution had created a human body that was in some ways so fragile—its susceptibility to disease, for example—yet quite resilient when it came to the ultimate seizure of life. Anika assumed a handgun would be the most efficient, since it was the one weapon she knew of that was specifically designed for killing people. A close-range shot to the skull was as certain to kill as any other she could imagine.

But, for the moment, that option didn't exist, since the only gun the Morgans now owned was sunken beneath the lake, an incidental casualty of her own killing.

And even if she had an arsenal of guns at the house, she had no plans to ever step foot in her home again. Anika was beyond cleansing now, a pariah, and the last thing she wanted to do was to carry the filth of her soul into the home where her children were born.

The warehouse.

The structure was just out of site from where Anika now stood at the bottom of the hill, but as she walked towards it and began her ascension, the sloping metal roof of the building began to crest into view. As the shape grew larger, a wave of nausea set in, and Anika couldn't fight off her recollection of the moment when she had watched her father emerge from the back room of the warehouse, presenting himself for the first time as the crooked miscreant he'd become. He had told her the story of her heritage that night, of her mother's incredible family and their ancient and revolutionary discovery. And he had revealed every detail behind the motivation that led to his daughter's kidnapping and torture, and of his ghastly plans to kill her for his own immortality.

But he'd not counted on her strength and desire to see her family again, and when the gap of opportunity opened, Anika had killed her father, thrusting a shard of broken glass into the side of his neck.

And then she'd escaped to Rifle Field, fleeing down the very hill she was now climbing, before jumping to the lake side of the fence through the cannery window. From there she took to the water, and eventually reunited with Gretel in the middle of the lake, just between the Klahr orchard and their own property.

The irony of Anika's current trek was not lost on her. She was essentially in a journey of complete reversal, and now instead of desperately seeking escape and survival, she was looking for a way to take the life she had so preciously defended.

Anika walked through the back of the warehouse and through the interior door that led to the main storage room. She scanned the room, which, despite its abandonment, was still lit by fluorescent emergency lighting. Not much had changed from that night a little over two years ago, Anika thought. The sofa and table and chairs remained, set up just as they were then, bizarrely arranged in the center of the room, appearing almost as toys against the backdrop of towering shelving and thousands of square feet of open space.

She stood silently in the room for a few moments, focusing again on the details of her capture, hoping to recall something from that night that could guide her towards her next move.

And then it came to her.

Officer Stenson had been with her and her father for a brief time that night, just after he had found Anika on the Interways. And during his time there, he had brought out a tray of food from somewhere in the back of the building. That meant that somewhere in the back of the warehouse there was a kitchen.

Anika returned to the back room and turned left, and then walked down a hallway that seemed to dead end at a utility closet. But as she approached the door to the service room, she spotted a narrow, doorless opening in the wall to her left. The room was dark, but a dull orange crisis light revealed what appeared to be a kitchenette. In less than a minute, Anika was in the room and holding a small paring knife to her throat, saying her final prayers, asking her children to forgive her.

She stood tall beneath the glowing orange bulb, stretching her neck toward the ceiling, and then touched the blade of the knife to her throat, pressing the tip against her skin to get a feel for the pain she should expect. She would have to get the knife in deeply to ensure the vein was fully sliced, thus maximizing the bleeding. If she bumbled the cut, she would likely still die from the wound—eventually—especially in the isolation of the warehouse where she wasn't likely to be found for weeks.

But there could be suffering. And Anika just wanted to die in peace.

Anika closed her eyes and swallowed, and then pierced the blade into the side of her neck. That was the starting point from which she would begin to slice her own throat. The knife wasn't razor sharp—she could barely feel the press and puncture of the metal—but now that she was in, it seemed perfectly suitable for accomplishing the task at hand.

She scraped the knife across her neck toward the center beneath her chin, and was now only inches away from the vein that would explode beneath the trauma of the metal.

And then she heard the voice.

Tanja will kill them. Gretel and Hansel. Tanja will kill them.

Anika's eyes shot open, and she held the knife in place for a beat, terrified to remove it for fear that the fatal cut had already been made, and that removal of the blade would unleash the fountain of red death. She removed her knife hand slowly, and seeing no gusher, lowered it down by her side. She looked around the room for the person who had spoken, knowing in her heart there was no one there.

The words hadn't been spoken aloud, of course, Anika knew that much, but it also hadn't been the same voice she'd heard while sitting on the bathroom floor back at the cottage. The voice then was more of a memory, while this one, though not quite auditory, sounded real. Of course, the voice in the bathroom had also mentioned Tanja, and Anika considered that the memory had perhaps surfaced as a precursor to now, a primer for the warning she was currently receiving.

"What do I do?" Anika asked the empty room, ignoring the warm streams of blood that flowed quickly down the length of her neck.

Find her. Kill her. You were brought back for a reason, Anika. And it was not to die alone, at your own hands, in the back of an abandoned warehouse.

There was nothing tonal in the voice, no pitch or inflection to decipher; it was as if the words were bypassing Anika's ears and being implanted directly into her brain.

"Who are you?"

I am no one now. And who I was once makes little difference.

"But I don't know Tanja. I don't know where to look." Anika was now fully committed to the conversation, and willing to accept the idea that she was losing her mind. But, as the voice had just replied with regards to its identity, Anika's sanity made little difference now. She had reached the cusp of suicide, so if there was a purpose to which she could cling, a reason for living that might save her children, she was willing to consider it.

The Eastern Lands, the voice continued. *It has been her place of dwelling for many quarters of centuries now. That is where you must go.*

Anika shook her head in disbelief, beginning now to doubt her mental state even further, considering the voice may in fact be a delusion, a protective barrier her mind had constructed to ward off her self-destruction. How else could she conceive of such an impossible command? The Eastern Lands? They were a thousand miles away. She may as well have been told to look for Tanja on the moon.

"It's Gretel who possesses the abilities," Anika pled, instantly feeling shame at the cowardice in her voice. "I would never find her."

Gretel's destiny will lead her elsewhere. And her path will lead her brother to that same place one day as well. But you must do your part in bringing an end to this story. The scourge that was Marlene is but one chapter in a book of many. The kin of Marlene have dwindled, the Aulwurms of the Old World are nearly extinct. But there are siblings that remain. And her mother.

"Tanja."

There was only acknowledging silence from the voice, and the name 'Tanja' seemed to hang in the air.

Anika shook her head and folded her hands across her face. "I killed them without cause. I can't continue taking lives."

What was it you were about to do with the knife?

Anika shook her head again, this time dismissing the implied comparison. "No. This *is* for a cause. I am prepared to take my own life to prevent the deaths of others."

Martyrdom is no more a cause than is the kill of a hunt.

"They were innocent!" Anika's scream filled the small space of the kitchenette, and she flung the knife toward the porcelain sink; the blade hit the iron faucet and ricocheted to the floor with a clang. She turned her face up to the ceiling and then leaned back against the narrow counter, suddenly feeling weak and hopeless. "What am I to do?" she asked. Her voice was barely a whisper as she shook her head in desperate confusion.

Your actions are yours, Anika. You have the same will you have always had. You must never forget that. I know your hunger is strong. Perhaps it even feels irresistible. But the strength of that feeling won't reside in you for long. Soon the craving will be controllable, measurable in a way that you will be able to both satisfy and command. You have returned from the base life stronger. Less prone to injury. Formidable. And your frenzied passion to eat is a way to ensure you remain that way.

"Base life?"

The potion, in the manner in which you consumed it, built in you a type of shell beneath the surface of your original being. Think of it as if you have molted from your previous life. Whereas most people die and their souls are released from their

*bodies to continue their existence in a realm beyond, your expo-
sure to the potion—and its remedy—has created another layer of corporeality that has kept your soul in place. It's why you
remember yourself, why you have the same emotions and opinions as the Anika Morgan of last week.*

"But my body is poisoned now."

*There are a great number of people, men and women alike,
who would destroy civilizations to be for one day what you've
become for as long as you can sustain it. You have moved beyond the labels of Orphism and the potion it begat. It simply
is now. You've reached the junction of decision, where you must
choose to use the underlife for purpose, or die under the weight
of the responsibility it requires.*

"And what does this 'underlife' mean exactly? I can't be
killed by the blade? Or, if I will it to be so, can I bring an end
to this by slitting my own throat?"

*There are a great many things that can end your underlife.
And as your hunger is controlled and your feedings grow less
frequent, you will become even more susceptible to death. There
is a balance to be found. You will need help to find this balance
of desire and gratification. Someone whom you can trust with
your secrets. With your life. It is vital that you survive. It is vital
that you keep your children alive.*

Anika slid to the floor of the kitchen and laid her palms
flat in a posture of defeat. "I don't understand what is happening. I don't know what you're telling me to do. Where do
I go? Who can I trust to help me?"

She will know of Marlene's death. The voice continued
without regard to Anika's laments. The tone was cold now,
unsettling. *She will learn of the death of her daughter. Feel it.*

And her other child will feel it as well. And she will hunt all of you until you are her trophies. You. Gretel. And eventually Hansel. Find Tanja. Kill her.

Anika now felt exhausted, the adrenaline of her near death suddenly plummeting, leaving her groggy on the floor and asking drowsy questions to the voice that had now departed. She reached absently to the side of her neck and, just before she drifted to sleep, realized the deep slice she had made from her ear to the point just below her chin had already begun to heal.

Chapter 4

"WILL YOU WAIT FOR ME?"

Petr stopped to pluck a pear from a stem that protruded just at the edge of his reach, stretching his body up through the middle branches to grab a particular beauty, intensely focused on the task while he asked his question, hoping to appear preoccupied with important fruit-picking duties as he engaged Gretel in small talk. But he heard the doubt in his voice, and he assumed Gretel could hear it too.

He put the pear to his nose and took a sniff, luxuriating in the freshness of the smell before taking a wide, moist bite.

"I'll just be a few days. You know I'd do anything to stay, but it's a project I just can't miss. If it was only me, I would accept the grade and move on. But there are other people involved, people depending on my part and—."

"It's fine, Hansel," Gretel interrupted. She looked at Petr and smiled, opening her eyes playfully wide. "I already know all of this."

Petr and Gretel resumed their stroll, striding slowly as they walked, almost pausing between each step to maximize the seconds before they reached Petr's truck.

"Okay, I just—"

"And I also know that worrying about a pair of strangers from your first-semester biology class is what makes you the person you are. You're very special, Petr. Most of the people

I know—have ever known—would cling to any reason to be derelict in their responsibilities. But not you; even when your excuses are valid, you keep to your commitments."

Petr ignored the compliment. "Why don't you come with me, Gretel?"

He stopped walking and placed his hand on top of Gretel's forearm. She broke her stride a step ahead of him and turned, her playfulness slipping away as she looked to the ground with a sigh.

"Why not? Anika is...we've had her funeral. I know Hansel is still shaken by all that's happened, of course, and I'm sure he will be for a while. Forever, maybe. But honestly, generally, he seems okay." Petr paused and then added, "Almost relieved."

Gretel looked up at Petr, her eyes wild at first but then quickly diffusing, as if recognizing the truth the statement.

"There's nothing left for you to do here. Let's just go back together. Mrs. Klahr is here to look after your brother. We'll only be gone for a few days. I'll finish my project and then we'll come back. And once we're back, you can start making your plans to leave." He paused. "Or maybe you can just stay."

"I can't, Petr." Gretel's words came swiftly and with a dusting of irritation. She looked past Petr now, staring off to some empty space in the distance.

Petr dipped his head, trying to catch Gretel's look, but she kept her eyes averted. "Why not?"

Gretel let the question sink in, allowing it the appropriate consideration, and then finally directed her large, brown eyes back at Petr. "It doesn't feel right here anymore, Petr.

There's still something...treacherous here. And now that I'm back, I feel it more powerfully than ever."

"Then we'll stay at school. We don't have to come back."

Gretel frowned. "And what about when summer arrives? Or at holidays?"

"We'll stay on campus. Easy as that. Or we'll rent another house somewhere even farther from here. There are plenty of other places we can live. I don't care, Gretel, I just don't want you to go."

"You can't stay away forever, Petr. Are you just going to abandon the orchard? And Mrs. Klahr?"

"Well what is it that you're doing?" The volume of Petr's question edged just to the border of yelling, and he immediately followed it with a soft, "I'm sorry."

Gretel let the silence linger for a beat and then said, "I'm not you, Petr."

"That's a cop out."

Gretel gave a sympathetic frown. "You know I'm not, Petr. And not just in the ways you think I mean. To do with my abilities or whatever. I don't have the compassion you have. I'm not as kind or charitable. Do you think for a minute that if our situations were reversed I would go back to school for my awaiting classmates and some class project?"

It was Petr's turn to look away now. He felt embarrassed, childish.

"I will miss Hansel. And Mrs. Klahr. And especially you. And I'll worry sick about all of you every day. But I *am* leaving. And I will try my best to wait for you, Petr, but I won't promise that I can."

Another silence filled the space now, and the two lovers looked off in separate directions. Finally, Gretel gave a sad smile and started walking again up the gravel driveway toward Mr. Klahr's truck. Petr remained in his place, watching Gretel as she took the steps alone, and then he closed his eyes at the pain that filled his chest. He loved her. He forever would. That she didn't feel the same about him was obvious, though he took selfish consolation in his belief that she would probably never feel that way about anyone.

Petr bathed in the pain for another moment and then followed Gretel up the driveway, meeting her at the truck. She had already opened the door for him and now stood to the side like a chauffeur.

He stepped into the driver's seat and started the engine, and then stared through the windshield at the dirt road ahead. "Where will you go?" he asked, the resignation in his voice palpable. He then smiled and said, "You know, in case I wanted to send you a letter."

Gretel didn't return his smile. "I don't know exactly. My plan is to stay in Hecklin for a while. That's the town we lived in when we were there before. I'll look into renting a room somewhere. After that, though, I can't really say for sure. I'll just see where the land takes me. I've got my mother's letter at least, so maybe that can guide me in the beginning."

"All of that sounds incredibly safe."

Gretel didn't bite at the sarcasm. "So since I'm likely to be a bit transient for a while, it will probably work better in the other direction: I'll send you the letter."

Petr nodded at this, but his thoughts had digressed. He gave a quiet snicker and a slight jiggle of his head.

"What is it?" Gretel asked.

Petr looked over at the girl he loved. "You know, I always thought that after Marlene was gone, when she was truly dead, gone forever, and you and Hansel and your mother were back from the Old World, things would start over for us. That we would all become...closer. And I don't just mean you and me, but Hansel and Anika too. And the Klahrs. I thought the whole experience we went through would create some type of unbreakable bond between the four of us. But that never happened, did it? In fact, in most ways, the opposite has happened."

Gretel raised her eyebrows and gave a coquettish smile. "Don't you think you and I have gotten closer since then?"

"Yes," Petr answered, seeming to miss the sexual reference. "But also no. The truth is, I felt closer to you that day in Rifle Field than I do right now. I don't really know why exactly. Maybe it's because we've grown a lot since then, or have become more reserved with our emotions. But I don't think that's the whole of it. I think we were poisoned by her. Not literally, like Anika was, but in our souls."

"Petr, it's not you, it's—"

Petr laughed, cutting Gretel off in mid-sentence. "Were you about to say 'it's not you, it's me?'"

Gretel frowned.

Petr looked serious now, steely. "But that's just it, Gretel, it *is* me. I know you think you're the only one left that feels it, but I have the poison inside me too. I may not act as cold as you. And maybe I appear to value my relationships a bit more. But I've been poisoned too. She didn't just kill my father, Gretel, she killed Mr. Klahr. Do you know what Mr. Klahr was to me?"

"Yes, Petr. He was...I know." Gretel swallowed and closed her eyes.

"And she killed Sophie. And her brother. That was my fault. Those lives are my responsibility."

"That's not true."

Petr closed his eyes, blocking the developing tears, and then shook his head to reset the conversation. "I'm hoping you'll be here when I get back. But I won't count on it. And if you're not...I'll understand. I really will. And I'll assume I'll never see you again."

"You will. I can't put it to a measure of time, but you will see me again. I promise that."

"No you can't, Gretel. You can't know that for sure."

Gretel dipped her head and looked up suspiciously at Petr. "Have you not heard about me? I'm magic, you know? I know lots of things that other people don't."

Petr laughed, and before that second or two of happiness escaped him, Gretel leaned into his body and kissed him deeply, grabbing his face in her hands, letting her tongue linger in his mouth.

She pulled away slowly, the stick of their lips stretching the kiss for another moment before she backed away and shut the door slowly. "And one more thing, Petr."

Petr looked at Gretel, still slightly enchanted by the kiss.

"Please don't come looking for me."

Petr blinked back to the moment, mildly startled. "What?"

"It might not always be safe where I'm going, and I don't want you to follow me. It's not one of those situations where if you truly loved me you would come and tell me how you feel and insist that I come home and marry you. That's not what this is, so please don't come."

"Why would you say that?"

"Because I can feel it in you. Even if you can't. I know once things at school are finished you'll want to come for me. But you can't. I've promised we'll see each other again, and I want you to hold that belief close to you."

Gretel's words struck Petr like a slap, and he now felt embarrassed and emasculated.

"Promise me, Petr."

Petr looked back out through the windshield, his face now void of emotion. "I promise."

He pulled the door to the truck closed and, without another word, drove away from his home. Just before he turned toward the Interways, he checked the rear view mirror, but Gretel was already gone.

Chapter 5

ANIKA EXITED THE WAREHOUSE and began walking down the dirt road that led away from the structure, not wavering from the path until she reached the shoulder of the Interways. Her clothes were in tatters, her face a mess of bruises and scabs, and despite her unusual strength, she was tired. The hunger was showing the first signs of returning, but for now it was manageable, a budding seed somewhere deep within her cells.

The Eastern Lands. That was to be her aim now. It was a laughable quest, of course. She couldn't imagine how she would make it to the docks, let alone across the widest of the oceans to the other side of the world. And once she was there, what then? How would she find this woman? Tanja. She knew nothing about her other than her sinister genetics and ancient existence, not exactly the traits upon which to find a person in a sea of a hundred million others.

Tanja. A lingering monstrosity of Marlene's heritage that still somehow remained. How could it be? How could it be that this distant kin of Anika's was, according to the invisible voice in the warehouse, on a mission to kill her and Hansel and Gretel?

If this was the truth, Anika thought, then let her come.

Why did she have to go all the way to the Eastern Lands to kill this woman? She could just go to her children now—they were only a half a mile away at this very moment—and reveal to them, in some way, the story of how she'd been resurrected, how the universe had spared her for a purpose. And the plot of their prehistoric ancestor to murder them.

Gretel, of all people, would believe her, considering her expertise with Orphism and the potion. And then she could protect them both. Right here in the familiarity of their home. Yes, let Tanja come. Let her come with whomever she wished. She would kill them all. Kill them the same way she killed Marlene.

But Anika's feet were leading her away from home, her instincts were taking her away from the cannery and Rifle Field and the lake that led back to the Morgan property. And she immediately felt the reason why.

The hunger.

It was building again, and putting her children and Mrs. Klahr in the path of her rapacity was not something she was willing to risk. Not anymore.

Anika walked at a steady pace along the gravel shoulder of the Interways, passing the second of two mile markers before hearing the sound of the first car, approaching from behind. She quickly veered diagonally from the shoulder to the tree line that ran parallel with the road, and then stood eagerly between two trees, licking her lips as she watched the late model sedan whiz by her without slowing.

Anika continued her path down the Interways, now hugging the edge of the forest as she walked. Hours passed and the sun rose high, sticking at its apex before beginning its descent.

The subtle pangs that had bubbled in Anika's stomach at the start of her journey were now a raging fire, and when she saw mile marker 193 rising from the grass at the border of the road—the twenty-fourth marker she'd reached that day—she sat under the overgrown branches of a giant maple tree. Three or four more cars revved by, and with each one that passed, Anika felt desire and regret.

She lay back now, her head resting on a pile of dead twigs, and re-imagined the scene in the warehouse only a half day earlier. How she wished she were back there now, knife in hand, and could make the choice she'd set out to make initially, to press the blade to her neck and pull it quickly and tightly along the length of her throat.

Another car approached and Anika sat up weakly, resting on her elbows as she listened, gauging the vehicle's distance, calculating the effort it would take for her to reach the road and flag it down. Her strength was all but diminished now, and the thought of sleep was rapidly overpowering her need to eat.

At least for the night. Tomorrow when she woke, she would be famished.

Anika decided she needed a more secure location to camp for the night, preferably one that provided some semblance of shelter, so she forced herself to her feet and then walked several paces into the darkness of the woods. The setting sun was still tossing a few strands of light through the leaves, but they would soon be disappearing. That was fine, she thought; for tonight, she would sleep under the stars in a thick part of the forest and then re-assess her plan come morning.

Anika continued walking further into the interior of the woods until she was far enough away that she could no longer hear the passing tire noise from the Interways. She saw a thick maple tree to her right and headed towards it, but as she took her first step in the tree's direction, she nearly toppled to the ground, tripped up by a thick piece of wood that had been buried deep into the earth.

Curious, Anika knelt down and studied the object, realizing instantly it was a property stake. She stood again and looked straight ahead, and then scanned her surroundings, swivelling her head slowly from left to right. She narrowed her eyes now, channeling the last of the light, and just caught the wink of a reflection in her periphery. She craned her neck forward toward the flicker, adjusting the height of her eye line slightly, and through a narrow gap that ran the length of the branches in front of her, she could just make out the corner L shape of wood and glass. It was a window, and Anika knew instantly that even in the full light of day, in her previous life, she would have never detected it.

Anika moved to her left now and then took a few more steps forward, pushing away a branch here and there, ducking through the foliage until she reached the perimeter of a yard where a small wooden cabin stood alone in a carved out area of the forest. A single box truck with the words *Pavel's Seafood* sat parked in the driveway.

Anika almost doubted her eyes at first, as if the home before her was some sort of mirage, a trick of her mind like those seen by men dying of thirst in the desert. But as she inched closer to the cabin, she could smell the aroma coming from the wood-burning stove, and feel at her feet the manicured yard of gravel and wooden planter rails that ran the length of the flower gardens surrounding the property. It was a beautiful property, really, quaint and secluded but meticulous in design and maintenance.

Anika stood at the rear of the house, now about twenty paces away, and looked upon a small staircase that led to a back door. Based on what Anika could see through a window just above and to the right of the door—and what she could see was quite a bit more than the previous Anika would have seen—the door opened into the home's kitchen. The smell of herring was strong in Anika's nostrils, and some type of shellfish—mussels, perhaps—had just been put to a boil.

It wasn't the powerful aromas of the fish that struck Anika, however; she delicately waded through those odors until she found the aroma inside she desired most. He was middle-aged, fifty perhaps, and lived in the home alone.

Anika stood inhaling the air, her mouth open and eyes closed as she teetered in place, barely conscious now. Her trance was in part to do with the thought of sating her hunger, but it was mostly to do with exhaustion. Despite her remarkable discovery of the cabin, and the momentary shot of adrenaline provided by the possibilities inside, sleep was becoming unavoidable.

She walked around the side of the house, allowing a generous berth, keeping her head tilted as she passed trying to maintain the smell in her orbit. She arrived at the front of the property where a wide porch ran along the length of the facade, and she stood directly in front of the structure, staring at the face of the home like the predator she'd become.

The craving was growing stronger by the moment, and she thought of her near-death moment in the warehouse once again.

"Let sleep win," she pleaded aloud.

Anika closed her eyes and then opened them slowly before striding purposefully toward the porch. She reached the bottom of the first step, prepared to climb them and enter the home, when she noticed a substantial hole in the lattice-work next to her leg on the right. She knelt down and looked through the cavity into a dark crawlspace that looked to be rather vast, and appeared to have been filled up over the years with yard and garden supplies. The hole was the perfect size for a person to fit through.

This was a sign, she thought. Sleep is my choice for tonight.

Anika climbed through the opening and pushed her way to the back until she reached the foundation of the home, eventually wedging herself between a wheelbarrow and some type of primitive electrical blower. They certainly weren't the accommodations of a luxury inn, but the arrangement did give her shelter and a modest layer of warmth. And, perhaps more importantly, she would be perfectly stationed for the hunt when morning arrived.

But for the night, the hunger subsided and was replaced by the warmth of sleep, and before Anika drifted into unconsciousness, she had one last thought of reassurance: she had made the right choice. Even if only for another night, the man inside was still alive.

ANIKA SLEPT WELL AMONGST the mass of equipment and tools, and only began to stir when the property owner opened his front door to begin his daily routine. Anika's eyes opened with a flash but were met with only darkness, indicating the sun was still a few hours from rising. As was the case for most workers in the Back Country, the days of men who delivered seafood apparently started very early.

Anika listened intensely as the man walked across the portion of the porch directly above her head before descending the steps to his truck. The vehicle came to life with a modest bit of effort, and the man returned to his home to finish up his other morning duties while the motor warmed.

At the sound of the closing door, Anika squeezed from between the wheelbarrow and blower, disturbing a pair of mice that had been using her body for warmth during the night. She moved forward, low and stalking, and then situated herself in a kneeling position at the opening, her face pressed against a splintered section of lattice. When he returned, Anika thought, the second he reached the bottom step and took his first stride toward the truck, she would attack.

The creak of the front door loaded the muscles in Anika's knees and shoulders. She felt like a rubber band being stretched to capacity, and she had to concentrate to keep her breathing quiet and under control. Next came the dull click of the man's soles above Anika's head, and she slipped her right foot out from beneath the deck as quietly as a cat. She was in a sprinter's position now, fingertips to the ground. Her eyes were wide and, despite the dull ache of shame and self-loathing in the pit of her stomach, a smile had found its way upon her face.

She took one last deep breath when she saw the hem of the man's pants, his shoe hitting the pathway at the base of the porch. She shifted her weight forward, the last crucial motion of preparation before she would erupt towards his throat.

And then she heard the siren of a passing System vehicle in the distance.

A siren. The System.

Anika was rendered motionless by the sound, stunned in place, as if she'd been blasted with a magic spell that had frozen her in a particular moment of time and action. Her paralysis lasted for only a moment though, and she quickly ducked back beneath the porch and out of sight of the man whose life, she knew, had been spared by only a fraction of a second.

From her bunkered position of the crawlspace, Anika watched the seafood truck and the man—whose name was Pavel, presumably—drive off into the dark morning.

For several minutes after the truck was out of sight, Anika remained still, staring at the empty place where the truck sat only moments earlier. It was nothing short of a miracle, she considered, and she knew that on some level it was Orphism that was responsible for the intervention of the siren. And Orphism that had intervened, in the form of an internal voice, just moments before she took her own life.

She began to laugh, and seconds later the laughter was accompanied by tears of glee, glee that she had shown restraint and let the man live.

The voice at the warehouse had told Anika the hunger would diminish over time, but barely any had passed, and the truth was, the reason she had let the delivery man escape was not due to a lack of want—the instinct to devour him was just as overpowering as it had been with the hunters—it was the siren that brought her back from the brink.

But why? Why had she been so distracted by the noise?

The System didn't often make its way to the interior of the Back Country, but they were in charge of the entirety of the Interways, and thus a System siren wasn't all that unusual in this part of the Southlands. But something about the noise had struck Anika as relevant, and it had become part of the decision matrix which allowed an innocent man to live.

And then it came to her, as if the answer had fallen like a feather from above, drifting gradually downward until it lodged itself into Anika's brain.

Her need to feed on human organs would continue, at least for a while longer until either the cravings subsided or she followed through with her suicide. But the victims didn't have to be innocent. And they didn't have to be random. To a certain extent, she could control whom she fed on, whom she targeted. That was what the siren had meant to her.

Anika stepped out to the walkway and quickly ascended the porch stairs. She walked to the door and, not surprisingly, it was unlocked. In the shroud of the forest without a neighbor in sight, burglary was probably as unlikely at Pavel's home as a plague of locusts.

Inside, the home was small but clean, austere, making what could easily have been a home of clutter feel open and pleasant. Anika surveyed the exposed floor plan and saw what she was looking for on a small table in the dining area at the back of the house.

A telephone.

She walked with purpose towards the phone and rested her hand on the receiver, running through the script in her head before she placed the call.

She dialed 0-0-1 and a voice came on the line immediately, sans a ring on Anika's end.

"System Dispatch," the voice said. "Please state your name and emergency location."

Anika had never called the System before and wasn't quite sure what questions to prepare for. For a number of years, there wasn't even a phone at the Morgan home, and in those times, before her father had become ill and Heinrich had been injured, the thought of interacting with any type of law enforcement, let alone The System, was almost ludicrous.

How so much had changed.

"Name?" Anika stalled, as if mishearing the question, which was actually a difficult one when a name had to be invented.

"Please state your name and emergency location." There was no impatience in the voice, just a businesslike tone attempting to elicit the necessary information.

"Tanja. Tanja Aulwurm." The name came out instinctively. "And I doubt, really, that it qualifies as an emergency, but I was driving home and I saw a stray dog on the shoulder. Right at mile marker 193. It was quite large, the dog, and it was just sitting there. I don't know for certain, but it seemed to be in pain. I slowed...to see if I could help it perhaps, but then I considered it may be dangerous. In any case, I wasn't sure what to do so I called it in."

Anika knew the story had to be benign enough so as not to bring out more than one patrol car, but serious enough that The System would involve itself at all. A stray dog on the Interways: no. A stray dog that was large and injured, perhaps dangerous: maybe.

"Thank you, Ms. Aulwurm. I'm sending a car to mile marker 193 now."

Anika shivered at being referred to as Ms. Aulwurm, knowing that it was indeed who she actually was, no matter that the name had been diluted and nearly lost over the centuries.

The dispatcher hung up the phone with nary a pleasantry, and Anika knew she had little time to waste. If a car was in the immediate area of mile marker 193, it would pass by and see there was no dog and just keep driving.

Anika placed the phone back in the cradle, perused the floor for any dirt she may have tracked in, and then, deciding the scene was clean, rushed out the door and back through the woods to the Interways.

It wasn't perfect, her plan. And it wasn't humane. But Anika thought she had found a temporary solution to her problem of food.

Chapter 6

DESPITE HER HAGGARD face and crooked back, the old woman shuffled through the busy street quickly, dodging oncoming pedestrians with the acumen of a cockroach. She kept her eyes forward, focused, and tried to take the shallowest of breaths to keep the aromas from penetrating too deeply. So many aromas.

These shopping excursions were a stressful necessity of the woman's existence, and with each step outside of her sphere of comfort, she silently cursed the men and women around her.

But every purchase was purposeful, every ingredient critical, so she needed to focus on each errand with the same care she put into the potion, the potion which now sat incomplete on the table in her kitchen.

She reached the downtown market and pushed through the center of a dense crowd that stretched from one end of the street to the other, the attention of the shoppers divided equally amongst a bevy of vendors. There were hundreds of people on the street today, and though it was true this part of the Eastern Lands seemed always to be busy, the woman wondered if there was something unique happening, a festival that was getting underway, or a notable wedding for which preparations were being made.

But none of that was really unique, she thought; these people were always celebrating something. Why, she could never quite understand—in her eyes, there was nothing but misery in every direction of this place.

But it was that very abundance and destitution that had kept her here for so many decades. It was quite easy to thrive in a place with such a combination. There were always so many candidates from which to choose. So many who had lost all connections to hope and society. And when she selected them for her own sustenance, they were almost never missed. And if they were, they were quickly forgotten. For all the bodies that dwelled in this ancient place of color and music, of history and food and literature and art, there were few resources appropriated for practical things. The difficulties that accompanied such muddy subjects like murder and kidnapping were simply beyond the management of any authority.

She exited the mobs of the central market and reached the layer of outer vendors. Here the sea of people ended abruptly and transformed neatly into a nearly deserted street. These outer vendors croaked sheepish pitch phrases at the few passersby, their voices barely audible, seeming almost embarrassed by their products. The woman thought of these sellers as the "market dregs;" an almost underground group made up of those who were unable to secure a permit for the market square, either because they couldn't afford one or because their merchandise was too fringe for the big stage. Technically, these sellers weren't to be peddling their wares on the streets at all—anywhere in or outside the market square—but enforcement of these rules were, again, beyond the abilities of the local governments.

The woman stopped at the perimeter of the dregs and scanned the caravan of wagons slowly, starting with the one just beside her to the left and working her vision clockwise until she spotted the appropriate flag, paying particular note to the symbol upon it. The wagon was parked middle right of the circle, just past center, and the flag rising from the front of it was threadbare, the pole upon which it sat seemingly overwhelmed by the meager cloth it held. It had been almost a year since she'd been back to this particular seller, but the woman was certain he was the one she sought.

She walked toward the man stationed behind the wagon, his body thin and frail, his age, the woman suspected, much older than most would have guessed. As she approached him, she could see the fear build on his face, and his deadened eyes suddenly sprang to life, his breathing intensifying. He looked behind him and off to his left, as if considering whether to flee, and then turned back and stood tall, studying the woman as she neared.

"Hello ma'am," he said, his voice cracking in the middle of the second word.

"Are you not pleased by a customer? I would think you would do anything for a sale." The woman looked around her in every direction, rotating her feet as she did until she had made a full revolution, a kind of derisive dance.

The man swallowed and stared at the woman unblinking. "I am pleased," he stammered. "Of course. What...what would you like to see?"

The woman smiled, making sure to show the magnitude of her wide mouth and the range of teeth within it. "Do you not remember me?"

"It has been a long while. Over one year I think."

"Which means you do remember me."

The man nodded.

The woman let her smile deteriorate, falling quickly into a look of tension and impatience. "I will assume that since your symbol has not changed," the woman pointed up toward the frayed green flag and the two large, forward-facing red fangs painted upon them. "That your products have not either. Am I to be correct in this assumption?"

The vendor took a cautious peek to his right, assessing the interest of his neighboring vendor whose station looked as if it hadn't been visited in weeks. The neighbor was fast asleep on his stool, his head sideways, snoring softly on his hands that were folded neatly atop the wagon.

"It is not something I can bring with me here daily. You see how little business I draw. And this...item is rare."

"The symbol on your flag would suggest this is just the thing you would maintain regularly."

The man looked up at his flag, as if confirming the fangs were, indeed, still present there. "Yes, but the venom you seek is..." The vendor looked around again, this time doing a full-circle perusal of the area. "Not quite licit."

The old woman chuckled at this notion, and then paused, assessing the earnestness of the vendor's words. "Licit? Is that what worries you? That is a comedy. In the time it took me to walk here from my home, not a mile away, mind you, I witnessed no less than a dozen illegal acts, all of which,

I assure you, were far more nefarious than selling the venom of a snake."

"Yes, well..." the vendor seemed to be conceding the point, but still not willing to proceed with the transaction.

The woman stood confused for a moment, and then, as if she'd been slipped a note upon which the answer had been written, closed her eyes and smiled, this time with her lips tightly sealed. "So it is about money?" she asked. "Is that it? You need more than the last time?"

The vendor cocked an eyebrow up and twitched his neck. "Cobra venom is easy to find. The snakes are common and the price is negotiable. I have it with me every day. But the bungaru is quite a different creature altogether. It is a secretive snake, more difficult to find and more deadly to wrangle. And there is quite a delicate science to extracting its venom."

"I detest negotiation," the woman replied quickly, almost before the vendor had finished speaking. "Almost as much as I detest weakness and excuses. Tell me your new price, tell me when you will have the ingredient, and on that day I will return to complete the transaction."

"It will be more than a week. I cannot say surely."

"We will agree to two then. Two weeks. I would suggest you have it for me at this very moment two weeks from to-day."

The vendor nodded, suspicion and regret heavy in his eyes.

"And for your efforts, I will double the amount paid to you last time."

The vendor took a deep breath and his lips parted slightly, instinctually poised to counter the woman's price. But he said nothing, knowing her offer was well beyond that to which he'd expected to agree.

"As I said, I detest negotiation."

The vendor nodded again, tacitly agreeing to the finality of the transaction.

The woman loathed these outings generally, but she enjoyed the power she wielded during these dealings, and how easily she could render these fools speechless, controlling the scene entirely.

She stared for a beat longer into the man's face and then turned, and as she began to walk away she heard him speak.

"It is not an ingredient," he said.

The woman kept her back to the vendor for several seconds, and then turned slowly towards him. She lifted her head and pushed her face forward, displaying her mouth in an extreme gape, wide and wild so as to showcase her jagged teeth. She could feel them protruding from all angles, large and lethal (not unlike the fangs on the flag above her, she imagined), glistening in the midday sun.

The vendor turned away coughing, placing his hand in a canopy above his eyebrows, shielding his view of her. "It is poison," he managed in a whisper. "It is just that you are my customer, so I have the responsibility to tell you that."

"Poison is in the body of the beholder," the woman said, turning away again, and as she began her walk from the outer vendors back toward the interior of the market place, she called out the reminder, "Two weeks."

Chapter 7

ANIKA STOOD NERVOUSLY at the edge of the Interways, keeping her hand within touching distance of the black and white mile marker 193 sign. It was an unnecessary precaution, she knew, since she would hear the System cruiser coming from at least a hundred yards away. Besides, with her standing like a distressed vagabond on the shoulder, the officer would stop for certain. And if he decided to ignore her, to proceed by without stopping, perhaps in search of a stray dog that had been called in from a concerned motorist, she was prepared to wave him down like a lunatic, or even step into the middle of the road, if necessary.

She hadn't had time to fully develop all of the tactics for what was to come, but she felt confident and justified in the overall strategy. She would need to sustain herself for the sake of her children, at least for as long as she could live with her monstrous acts, and to do so she would have to find victims upon which to feed.

Unfortunately for Anika, the people of the Back Country were, for the most part, a peaceful, law-abiding people who kept to themselves and their business. There was too much innocence here, she thought, too many lives that deserved the same dignity as she and her children.

But The System held no such honor.

For all of the corruption surrounding Officers Stenson and Dodd, and the cover ups of Marlene's disappearance from the cannery on the days following Gretel's presumed killing of the witch, there was never any retribution paid by the organization. Stenson and Dodd had been killed, that was true, but there were others in The System who knew of the poor procedures that had taken place and the lack of evidence at the crime scene. There was never an autopsy done on Marlene obviously, because her body had never been found. Yet that small detail had never appeared in any police report. At least none that she had ever heard about. There were prosecutions that should have been made at the highest levels of the institution, and yet, as far as she knew, not a single person had even been disciplined.

Anika's thoughts of The System bounced wildly in her brain, and she realized she was jumping to some conclusions. Perhaps steps had been taken toward punishing certain administrators and she was unaware of them. But she didn't think it so. Petr had followed the investigation closely for over a year, and he had done quite a bit of work on his own to find answers, mainly to do with the many questions that surrounded his father's involvement in the systemic corruption. He had been stonewalled most of the way, but he learned enough to know that justice had not been done.

Besides, even if Anika was rationalizing her upcoming actions, an officer in The System would be a far less innocent kill than virtually any citizen of the Back Country.

Anika checked the numbers on the sign again, making sure she had relayed the proper information to the dispatcher, and, as if her check had triggered the scene, she heard the unmistakable grumble of a System vehicle churning down the Interways towards her.

She froze for a moment, suddenly re-considering her plan, overcome now with fear at the future action to which she had committed.

She will hunt them until they are her trophies.

The words of the voice sobered Anika only slightly. She truly believed that what she had been told was true, that her children were in some type of future peril, and that she was to play a part in keeping them safe. And for that reason, she had to stay alive.

But was this the only way?

As the cruiser rumbled into view, Anika's chest seized with hunger, and she closed her eyes at the enormity of the pressure. Her throat tightened at the thought of the food source so close, and of how she'd so deftly drawn it towards her like a master killer, as quick and strong as a cat yet with a mind that was percipient and nimble.

Anika gave a half wave toward the car as it slowed and then stopped only a foot away. She took a quick step backwards as the officer opened the cruiser door and hastily stepped to the gravelly shoulder, rising barely to the top of the cruiser's roof as she stood.

A woman.

"Ma'am, are you hurt?"

The female officer looked barely old enough to drive, let alone wear a System badge. She was shorter than Gretel, and couldn't have been more than three or four years older.

Her face was so smooth and pretty.

"Ma'am?" the office repeated. "I'm calling for an ambulance now."

Her injuries, Anika had forgotten about them. Hansel's blow to her head had been fatal—at least it would have been in most cases—and she had spent a considerable amount of time at the bottom of a lake where God only knew what had fed on the loose skin and muscle that had been exposed by the strike. Her eye had exploded as well, and despite the patch now covering it, it must have given a shocking first impression. And Anika, herself, had crafted a long, deep cut across the base of her neck. That injury had receded, but in the form of a rough scab that was in the process of scarring.

"I'm not hurt," Anika said. "It's...I'm okay. I was hurt, several weeks ago, but I've been for surgery since then. My bandages have gone bad and I've not replaced them. That's why I look so frightening to you. I'm sorry. I didn't expect to see anyone out here at this time."

"What happened to you?" the officer asked, her voice low and shocked. She was staring at Anika the way a child would have, barely able to hide her amazement at the battered person in front of her.

"A boating accident," Anika replied, suppressing a snicker at the abstract truth of the answer.

"Are you certain you don't need medical attention?"

Anika couldn't take this girl's life. She was not The System officer Anika had pictured when she first heard the siren beneath Pavel's porch. This officer looked like a teenager; she probably first knew about the story of Gretel and Anika and Marlene from the schoolyard, not from the files of her organization. "I'm fine. Really."

The officer stood staring, not quite convinced.

"May I ask how long you've been with The System?"

The officer looked at Anika plainly now, without judgment of her appearance, and then gave a bemused look that quickly evolved into a pleasant smile. "Eleven months."

Anika frowned and nodded, adding this number to her equation and realizing she could never carry out her plan. This woman was as innocent as any young girl in the Back Country, and she deserved to die at Anika's hands no more than they did.

But restraint was still required; the wind had shifted slightly and the smells of the woman's body were now wafting toward Anika. The officer had bathed this morning, and was soon to get her menses.

"I'm sorry, I must be getting home," Anika said, willing herself to turn and begin walking in the direction opposite the cruiser.

"Please stop, ma'am. I need to ask you a few questions first." The officer's voice had a sternness now that Anika wouldn't have believed she possessed.

Anika took a deep breath and turned back towards the officer.

The officer smiled. "If that's okay?"

Anika returned a weak smile and gave a pleading look with her eyes. "I really must be going. I've...I've got dinner to plan. Husbands, you know?"

The officer gave the upward tick of a nod, a resin of suspicion now forming around her eyes. "Sure."

Anika turned again to leave.

"Did you call in the sighting of a dog?" the officer asked, catching Anika in mid-stride.

Anika closed her eyes now, weighing her options, considering the consequences of simply running down the Interways or off into the forest. The woman would catch her in the cruiser of course, and the resulting physical confrontation would end either with Anika shot or feeding on the corpse of the officer. She could escape to the woods, but the attention she would garner by running seemed, in her mind, to negate the point of the effort.

But the longer she stayed talking with this woman, and the more the aroma from her body and the sight of her supple cheeks and arms and hands penetrated Anika's senses, the more difficult it would be to pull back from her instincts.

"A dog?"

"Yes, ma'am. Someone called in the report of an injured dog at this mile marker."

"I see. Well, I'm afraid that wasn't me."

"That's interesting then. At this stretch of the Interways, which is nothing but a sea of trees and grass and pavement, a woman calls in the sighting of a dog, and when I arrive, there is no dog, but there is a woman."

"That is interesting."

Anika could see that the officer's eyes were measuring her now, assessing the possibilities of the potential suspect in front of her, mentally running through the lessons of her training, trying to apply them now to the situation before her.

"What is your husband's name, ma'am?" The geniality in the officer's voice was now entirely gone.

"My husband?" Anika asked, realizing almost instantly the question was an attempt to trip her up on the lie she'd told earlier.

"Yes. You said you had to hurry home to cook for your husband. What is his name?"

Anika smiled, her eyebrows scrunched in confusion. "It's Pavel." Anika straightened her smile, now offering a look that said she was done with the conversation. "Good bye, officer. Good luck with finding the dog."

Anika turned and took two steps down the shoulder of the Interways.

"Freeze."

Anika took another step and then stopped, and a film of tears instantly formed over her eyes.

"Turn around."

Anika hesitated and then turned toward the officer, who now held a gun pointed straight at Anika and a radio up to her mouth, calling in for a support cruiser.

Anika wiped her eyes clear, feigning the tears were a result of her fear of imminent arrest. "What have I done, officer?" Anika pitched her voice up slightly, hoping to find the notes of mercy. "I'm taking a walk. That's all I've done. I don't know about a dog."

"That may or may not be true. To be sure, however, I'll just need to ask you a few more questions. In a more formal way."

"Why?"

The officer gave Anika a disappointed look, as if she truly wished their brief relationship hadn't ended up leading to this place of lies and distrust. "You said your husband's name was Pavel. That is not a very common name. In fact, the only person I have ever known with the name 'Pavel' is Pavel Delov. And it so happens Mr. Delov's house is just through these woods not a half mile. My family owns a restaurant on the outskirts of the Urbanlands. I worked there until I graduated from the institute. Mr. Delov has been delivering seafood to us my entire life. He's become somewhat of a family friend. And he's not married."

Anika was speechless, both from the trap she'd created for herself and from the feelings of desire brought on by the sweat that had now built up over the entirety of the young officer's body.

The officer put the radio back into the receiver and brought her other hand to the gun, wrapping her fingers tightly around the butt. "Please take a step toward me and get on the ground until you're lying flat with both hands spread wide."

Anika stayed motionless for a moment, her eyes narrowing slightly, saliva coating the insides of her mouth in a wave. She swallowed and blinked slowly, bringing her attention back to the details of the moment. "Is this necessary?" she asked, her voice chilly and strong.

"Had you told me the truth, it would not be. But now it is. And if Mr. Delov and his property are unharmed, and you've done nothing wrong, as you claim, then you will be on your way in a few minutes. But until I know that for sure, and until the support cruiser arrives, I'll need to detain you. Now, again, take one step toward me, lie on the ground, and spread your hands wide."

Anika took the step forward and got to her knees, suddenly recalling the night not so many years ago when she had found herself in a similar position, having escaped Marlene's cabin to these very Interways, exhausted and terrified of what awaited her beyond. Officer Stenson had found her that night, pretending to rescue her before bringing her to the warehouse where her father regaled the story of Anika's mother and his plans for Anika's demise.

The System, she thought. She was once again at their mercy, though this time Anika had instigated the scene.

Anika lie prostrate now, the tears she'd held back now falling silently to the pavement.

"I'm sorry ma'am. I'm not trying to scare you. I'm just going to reach into your pockets and the waist of your pants. Do you have any weapons?"

"Please stay away from me," Anika pleaded, now openly weeping.

Anika judged the officer to be only six feet or so away now and approaching. "Ma'am, relax. It's okay. No one is going to hurt you. I promise. I'm just going to do a quick search of your person. Please don't move."

The woman stopped and was now standing above Anika, her feet straddling Anika's body at the waist. She squatted and placed her hands at the small of Anika's back, mechanically patting her waist before shifting her palms down to Anika's buttocks and legs, slipping her fingers forward until they were between the pavement and Anika's thighs.

The touch of the officer's fingers sent shivers of ecstasy through Anika, and she began to recite a prayer of strength in her head, desperate to summon the god she'd worshipped at church most of her life, but whom she'd never quite believed in. If he was real, she needed him now; this was the moment to emerge and set Anika on her path to redemption.

The thought of god and the afterlife abruptly set forth a wave of peace within Anika, and although the scents and sounds of the woman were still producing a fire inside of her, her new focus on something higher was keeping the blaze contained. She nearly began laughing as the feeling of calm took hold, assuring Anika that she was capable of making it through this moment, and that this young woman with sixty years ahead of her would live beyond today. To see her mother and father again. To one day become a wife and mother and grandmother.

Anika smiled when the woman removed her hands and then stood tall. She was done with the search.

"I'm almost done here," the officer said, "I just need to check your torso."

Anika's panic resurfaced. "I've nothing on me," she pleaded, squeezing her eyes tightly, trying to harness every last feeling of god and spirituality.

Anika felt the officer lean forward, her crotch now on Anika's thighs. Her mouth was only inches from Anika's ear when she said, "Please remain still."

The soft wind of the officer's whisper exploded on Anika's ear, and all of the hairs on her body seemed to rise at once. Anika opened her mouth and licked her two front teeth, tasting the breath of the officer that still lingered in the air.

Anika's thoughts of god turned black, and, in an instant, she snapped her head to the left towards the officer's neck. The accuracy of the strike was acute, as was the silence that instantly befell the Interways. In a second, Anika had the woman's throat in the clutch of her mouth, her oversized canines pierced deeply into the officer's windpipe. She bit down with the force of a vice until she felt the tube of cartilage snap in her jaws.

Anika sat up slowly and scanned the area around her, perusing the road for any cars that might be approaching, or perhaps some other witness, an unlikely pedestrian who had decided to make the dreadful decision to walk the Interways this morning.

But Anika saw only the staring leaves of the red maples and douglas firs that blanketed the landscape, and quickly got to her feet, lifting the officer's dying body with her as she rose, drinking in the sensations of blood and skin and hair, as well as the sounds of the last gasping chokes of innocence. The officer's corpse dangled in Anika's bite, the toes of her boots barely scraping the gravel below as Anika stood trance-like, her jaws still clenched reflexively, unwilling to let up for even a moment until the last twitch of the young woman was a memory.

Anika finally let the body fall to the ground and stared at it blankly. She could feel the sting of regret build within her, slowly replacing the unstoppable ferocity that had momentarily besieged her. But the kill couldn't go to waste, and before Anika's guilt rendered her impotent, she grabbed the woman's hair at the crown of her head, gathering the thick brown tress in her fingers, and dragged the officer's body into the woods, continuing to walk until she was well off the shoulder of the Interways.

As she fed on the body, replenishing her energy for what she hoped would be the final time, she cried, her salty tears mixing with the bloody meat of her victim.

She was just beginning on the liver when the sound of an approaching siren wailed in the distance, and for a moment, Anika considered a default surrender. She could simply continue feeding on the officer until the System men came, and once they reached her, they would shoot her on sight. Even if they offered Anika the chance to surrender, she could rush them, not too fast, just fast enough that they could get their shots off.

Instead, Anika turned back in the direction of Pavel Delov's cabin and began walking, looking back over her shoulder one last time at the fresh kill behind her, silently praying the officers would find the body while it was still fresh.

Chapter 8

PETR PULLED THE TRUCK up to his rental house just before midnight, noting the absence of any other car on the street out front. His roommate was still out for the evening, damning his tomorrow through an infernal combination of alcohol and sleeplessness. Petr was relieved at the empty sight though, knowing he could now avoid the required tell-all conversation with Gil and immediately get to work.

The group project was due on Thursday, and Petr's portion of the assignment—a comparison of plants grown with nitrogen fertilizer versus those grown without it—had begun in earnest since before the school year was even underway. And he had maintained a strict schedule thus far; with the exception of yesterday, he had never allowed a day to pass without at least touching the assignment in some way.

But there was still a lot to do. He hadn't finished writing the final analysis of the overall experiment, and his final presentation, for which he would have to demonstrate and explain the outcome of the experiment to the group at large, still needed a lot of attention.

The group collaboration was almost half of the final Freshman Biology grade, and, not foreseeing that his lover and best friend would be abandoning him for the Old World just days before it was due, Petr had committed himself fully to his partners and the project.

But Petr also knew that any work he began at this hour would be done as much to distract his thoughts from Gretel as for preparation. He could still feel the puncture of her words, even so many hours later, and though he trusted her promise that they would see each other again, that didn't mean it would be any time soon.

Petr opened the front door and walked in slowly, taking his usual notice of the dark quiet that resonated throughout the house. He never assumed he was safe anymore, anywhere, even when entering his own home; the comfort and complacency most people settled into over the course of a day, he rarely found in his life. It was a symptom of Marlene's poison, of course. It was the thing he had tried to explain to Gretel.

Petr toggled the kitchen light on and, as if on cue, his stomach groused. The only thing he'd eaten since breakfast was a few bites of the orchard pear, and he was starving. Mrs. Klahr normally sent him home with a month's supply of rations, but this most recent visit had been a whirlwind, and under very different circumstances. Thus, Petr had returned home empty-handed.

He opened the refrigerator and stared lid-eyed at the paltry display: an unwrapped stick of butter, a nearly empty glass bowl that was coated with something resembling mayonnaise, and two separate mystery items that had been wrapped tightly in thick pieces of foil. The latter items weren't Petr's, and he suspected that whatever lurked within was well beyond the days of being edible. Using the fridge as an indicator, he didn't even bother with the pantry.

Petr sighed and walked to the living room, and then sat with a thud on the sofa that he and Gil had somehow managed to squeeze into the small cove that acted as their living room.

Petr was exhausted, and the thought of walking across campus to the all-night commissary was overwhelming. He gauged his hunger objectively, and soon reached the conclusion that food could wait until breakfast. As long as he could fall asleep within the next half hour, which, he thought, was about twenty-five more minutes than he would need, he could wait until morning to eat.

Petr's eyes closed once and then shot open instantly, but drifted down again just a second later, this time maintaining their shut position. He let his head fall back to the stiff cushion behind him, and then turned to his side, grabbing a stray blanket that had been left on the floor at the foot of the couch. He was asleep in less than a minute.

Thoughts of Gretel entered his dreams almost immediately, and for a moment, he relived their last moment together, her body pressed between Petr's legs as her lips brushed his. The kiss in his dream stretched longer than in reality, and Petr's sexual desire steadily rose as he slept.

And then the phone rang.

Petr sat up immediately, inhaling and holding his breath as he searched the room, not quite sure where he was for an instant. He quickly got his bearings and rose from the sofa like a bullet, turning and walking to the phone, hesitating before picking up the receiver.

"Yes," Petr croaked and then cleared his throat. "Yes," he repeated, this time speaking with affirmative clarity as he searched the room for a clock, having no idea of the time.

The caller gave no response, but it was obvious to Petr the line was live based on the ambient sounds in the caller's background.

"Hello?" Petr said, prodding.

There was a pause of several seconds and then, just as Petr was taking the receiver from his ear to hang up, a voice said, "Petr." It wasn't a question.

Petr became fully awake now, and he began to shake with fear. The feeling of hunger in his stomach was now replaced by dread, and his body began to quiver. He instinctively brought his second hand to the phone's receiver, steadying it against his mouth and ear.

"Who is this?"

"Help me, Petr."

The voice was a raspy whisper, slow and breathy, and Petr immediately envisioned Marlene as the speaker, standing bloody and wet in a swamp somewhere, holding the head of some young girl in one hand and the phone in the other; or perhaps in the basement of Gretel's house, the bodies of Hansel and Gretel and Mrs. Klahr shredded and strewn about the floor.

"Who is this?" Petr repeated, willing himself to hide his panic and sound angry.

"Help me, Petr!" the voice screamed, and then erupted into a fit of hysterical wailing.

Petr squinted at the volume and pulled the phone away from his ear, his fear suddenly turning to alarm for the woman, recognizing the sincerity of her distress.

"Where are you calling from?" he asked now, changing the focus of his question, figuring that if he simply continued asking who it was, it wouldn't get him any further in the conversation.

The crying on the other end of the line continued, now at a steady volume and pace.

"Miss, tell me where you are and I'll send someone to help you."

The crying stopped suddenly. "They're already coming. But not to help me. I need you, Petr."

"Anika?" The name escaped Petr's mouth before he could stop it, knowing the impossibility of what he'd just suggested. Certainly it couldn't be her, but something familiar in the way the woman on the phone had just said his name sparked a memory. It was the day at the Morgan cabin when Petr had asked about Anika's necklace, the one made from Marlene's teeth. She had made it, she told him, to memorialize the terror that had befallen them and as a way to never forget. That was the last time he'd had a real conversation with the woman, and Petr remembered now the desperation in her explanation of why she had kept the teeth. The way Anika had said his name that day seemed to be a plea for help, and Petr heard the same tenor on the phone just now.

Petr waited for a response, affirmation or denial from the woman on the phone, but instead he heard another voice, low and distant, as if it were coming from somewhere distant in the room from which she was calling.

"I've nothing here. What do you want?"

The voice was certainly masculine, and he was obviously distressed, as the words came out labored and dire.

Petr made the decision to simply stay quiet, to listen for any clues that could tell him what exactly was happening on the other end. There were sounds of a scuffle—thuds and such—and then a scream. Petr couldn't tell for sure whether it was from the man or woman, but based on the clues he'd already gathered, he assumed the man.

And then the line clicked dead.

Petr held the phone to his ear for a few more seconds, but didn't bother with the perfunctory "Hello" that normally followed this type of disconnection.

The caller was gone.

Petr placed the phone gently on the cradle and thought for a moment, and the blurred image of the human figure he thought he saw on Gretel's back porch came to his mind. He ignored it for the moment, and instead searched his mind for the steps to take next, reluctantly deciding he had to go for help. From whom he wasn't sure, but he had to do something; simply going back to sleep wasn't an option. There were people in trouble. Who or what the nature of the trouble was he didn't know, but some kind of action was required.

Petr walked quickly to the front door and pulled it towards him, and then raced in the direction of his truck, prepared to head off into the night to a place not yet determined. But before he was two paces onto the porch, and well before his eyes had time to adjust to the unlit night beyond the threshold, he ran head first into an approaching body, sending it sprawling out in front of him.

Petr knew the collision was with a man, both by the exclamation of the voice and the feel of his body, but as he bowled him to the ground, Petr caught the glimpse of another figure—female—in his periphery to the right.

"Pete!" the man said from his position on the ground, which was now several feet from Petr, nearly to the edge of the porch's top step. "What the hell?"

It was Gil, coming home for the night. Beside him was a small, brown grocery bag that he'd dropped upon impact. It was still intact, however, having been rolled tightly from the top to the level of its contents.

Petr, who had kept his balance after the crash and was still standing, opened the front door again and reached his hand in to flick on the porch light. "Gil?"

"Welcome back, buddy. Did you set the place on fire already?" Gil was on his elbows now, smiling back at Petr.

Petr quickly stepped toward his fallen roommate, stooping over and extending his hand to help him to his feet.

Petr stood back and looked Gil over, assessing if he'd caused any injuries, and then looked toward the girl. Petr had never seen her before, and she was no doubt Gil's prize for the night. He looked back to Gil. "I'm so sorry. Are you okay?"

Gil laughed. "It's okay, buddy. I'm fine. What's happening in there anyway?" He looked at the girl beside him and smiled. "Oh, sorry, this is Jenna."

The girl was tall and thin with a wild head of red hair. Her eyes were beautiful, though slightly unfocused at the moment. And her crooked teeth, Petr noted, somehow made her more attractive.

"Jana," the girl corrected, not seeming the least bit irritated by the mistake.

Gil winced and shrugged. "Jana. Sorry."

"It's nice to meet you," Petr said. "I'm sorry Gil, I have to go."

"Go? What are you talking about? You can't have been home for what, three or four hours at the most?"

"More like fifteen minutes."

Gil looked bemused, and then shivered his head, priming Petr for the explanation.

"I just got a phone call."

"Home for fifteen minutes and the whip is already cracking. My goodness. Gretel can't get enough, hey buddy?"

"It's not Gretel."

Gil raised an eyebrow and grinned.

Petr frowned. "I don't know who it was. It was very strange. I just have to—"

"Was it that woman with the shitty voice?"

Petr's eyes bugged.

"Yeah, she's been calling all day today. I told her I didn't think you'd be home until tomorrow. I asked for her name but she wouldn't tell me. Just gave these heavy breaths. But not, like, sexy. Like it pained her that you weren't here. Damn crazy. And I told her fifty times you probably wouldn't be home until tomorrow. I can't believe she called again. And this late. Though I guess now is technically to-morrow."

"What did she sound like?" Petr tried to stay calm, though he wasn't quite sure why; the bruises his roommate would be displaying tomorrow from Petr's frantic dash to his truck would be proof to the contrary.

"I don't know. Shitty. Like I said."

"Yes, but you said she sounded upset that I wasn't here. Did she sound in distress?"

"Distress? I don't know. Not really, I guess. Well, not at first anyway. But by the third or fourth call, now that you mention it, I guess she did sound a little harried. But she hung up almost immediately the last time I told her you weren't here. Yeah, though, it did get a little worse each time she called." Gil was measured now, momentarily sobered, intrigued by the story. "Who the hell is it?"

Jana was slowly becoming uncomfortable with their position on the porch and, Petr imagined, embarrassed by being there at all. Her body language indicated she was reconsidering the whole evening. Petr had clearly lingered too long and was now on the brink of short-circuiting the girl's decision, which was probably a good thing, since she was destined to rue it come morning.

"I don't know who it is. Look Gil, I didn't mean to interrupt you two. I'm sorry, I'll—"

"Don't know? Well then where are you going? If you don't know who's calling, why are you running off like a murder of crows is on your ass?"

"I...I don't know."

And Petr didn't know. The only women he really knew at all, besides Gretel, who was barely a woman, were Anika and Mrs. Klahr. Anika was, ostensibly, dead, and whoever was on the other end of the phone call he'd just received was decades younger than Mrs. Klahr. She may have had a shitty voice, but there wasn't the aged croak and cadence of Amanda Klahr.

So where *was* he going? He'd probably just end up back in the Back Country. And what then? Find Gretel and resume his pleas for her to stay?

"Listen Petr," Gil continued, sounding clear-headed and mature, "you look beleaguered, frankly."

Petr's stomach grumbled again, clamoring for the aroma coming from the brown bag.

Gil laughed. "And hungry."

Petr gave a defeated sigh as the exhaustion he'd felt earlier began to return.

"And I've got a giant bag of sliders. Bertram's Diner."

"I don't want to eat your dinner, Gil. You and Jana obviously had plans." The smell of the grilled meat made Petr's mouth burst with saliva.

"Dinner? It's after midnight. And look at her. Does it look like she eats hamburgers?"

Jana smiled and rolled her eyes, clearly taking Gil's words as a compliment.

"Besides, maybe she'll call again. The woman. And if you're out driving around aimlessly, you won't be here to take the call."

Petr accepted Gil's logic as sound, and within ten minutes he'd already eaten three sliders, lying and telling Gil he was full when his roommate offered him a fourth.

Jana decided to stay and hang out with the boys, but within fifteen minutes she was asleep on the couch, curled up like a cat.

"I'm sorry," Petr grinned. "I know this isn't how you were hoping the night would go."

Gil waved him off. "She'll rally."

Petr told Gil about the lakeside funeral and Gretel's plans to leave for the Old Country, and Gil listened with the attentiveness of a real friend, which, to this point, Petr hadn't really considered him. But it was nice to have someone to talk to that wasn't Gretel. He needed more male companionship in his life.

Jana stirred and asked the time, and Petr took it as a cue. He got up from the couch and thanked Gil for the food, and then headed to his room. As he grabbed for the handle of the door to his bedroom, the phone rang.

Petr stopped in mid-stride and lowered his head as if he'd been expecting the call, and then he looked over at Gil, who was wide-eyed and smiling, nodding his head. "I told you," he said.

Petr walked to the phone and paused for a beat, taking a deep breath before answering at the end of the third ring. "Hello?"

A voice on the other end answered immediately. "Hello, my name is Officer Zanger. I'm a System officer in the East Point District. Who am I speaking with?"

Petr instinctually stayed silent, taking his time before simply blurting out his name. It was his last name, in particular, that gave him pause. 'Stenson' was as infamous a name as any in the history of The System.

"Pete," he answered.

There was a second or two pause, as if the man was writing the information down, and then: "What is your last name, Pete?"

"What is this about?"

It was the officer's turn to remain silent now, and Petr could see him debating whether to press hard for an answer to his question, and risk being hung up on, or to come clean about his purpose for calling. Thankfully, he chose the latter.

"I'm calling you because this number was the last one dialed from a recent crime scene."

Petr said nothing.

"Did you receive any phone calls recently, Pete?"

Petr calmed his nerves, but answered immediately. "No. Not recently. I just got home...a few minutes ago. I've been away for a few days and I just walked in the door."

"I see. Well, perhaps someone else at the residence took a call. Do you live alone?"

"I have a roommate, but he's been gone all weekend too. I haven't seen him since the day I left." Petr looked over at Gil and put the tip of his index finger to his mouth.

There was another stretch of silence on the other end of the line and Petr recognized the technique instantly. His dad had always told him the easiest way to get information from people was to shut up and let them talk. He had said that people were naturally uncomfortable with pregnant pauses and glaring lulls in conversation, and the easiest way for them to fill them was with the truth. But Petr didn't bite.

"I see," the officer finally added. "Would you be willing to answer a few questions for us, if necessary? That is, if we need to talk with you about the nature of these calls?"

This request by Officer Zanger was obviously rhetorical, but Petr had no intentions of simply bending to the wishes of The System. He had sworn never to enter a System station again, and he planned to stick to that oath. If they insisted he come in and talk, they would have to arrest him. And if they detained him, Petr would offer them about as much information as a dead clam would.

But Petr was intrigued by the call and wanted to know more about the crime? And, more importantly, the woman who had been calling him. She had said his name on the phone, had asked Gil for him by name. Perhaps the officer already knew exactly who Petr was and was trying to catch him in a lie, something damning and convictable.

"I would be happy to talk with you, Officer Zanger, but I won't be available for a few days. I'm very busy with school."

"You're a student then?"

Dammit. Based on the location of the phone number, the officer probably knew that detail already, but Petr hadn't intended to offer any more information than he had already. "Yes, that's right, and I've an incredible workload this week. Perhaps next week would suffice?"

"We'll have to see where the investigation takes us, Pe-te..." The officer drew out the 'T' in Petr's name, waiting for Petr to fill the space with his surname. He had no choice now.

"Soren," Petr lied. "Petr Soren." He had now lied to a System officer, had given a false identity, which was, if prosecuted, a jailable offense.

"Thank you, Mr. Soren, we will be in touch. And please keep in mind, depending on where our investigation leads us, we may need to speak with you sooner. Possibly much sooner."

"I understand." Petr tried to sound casual, but he detected a crack in his voice. He was sure the officer noted it too. He hung up the phone.

"Goddamn, Petr. Who was that?" Gil asked immediately, the bell of the phone still ringing in the air.

"I'm gonna go." Jana picked up her bag and walked to the door. "I need a ride."

Gil didn't look at Jana, but held a finger up, indicating he needed another second.

"It was The System," Petr replied, and then added, as if to himself, "Who else?"

"Really? The System?"

Petr nodded.

"Why?"

"Something to do with the phone calls we've been getting. They said there's been a crime at the place they were coming from."

"Why did you lie? About us not answering them?"

"Gil, let's go," Jana called, standing at the threshold.

"Okay, go to my car. I'll be right there."

Jana threw the bag over her shoulder and stomped out, leaving the door open as she went.

"There's a lot about me you don't know, Gil," Petr said. "And I don't want to get you tangled up in my past. That's why."

Gil smiled. "Don't know? About Gretel? And Anika and Marlene? Are you kidding? Who the hell doesn't know about that?"

Petr was fairly certain Gil didn't know who he was until Gretel joined him at the university, but his roommate had a point: it was silly to have thought he didn't know the story by now. Everybody seemed to know now. Everywhere.

"Does that officer's call have something to do with all of that?"

Petr didn't really know and said as much, which caused Gil to shudder with fear at the possibility that the ordeal of the Witch of the North wasn't over.

As if reading Gil's mind, Petr said, "Marlene is dead. That much I do know."

"Then why do you think these phone calls have something to do with your...story."

"I don't *think* they do, I just said I don't know."

Gil rose and walked slowly to the door, grabbing his keys from the table as he went. He stopped at the open front door and looked at Petr. "That story used to scare the crap out of me," he said. "Still does."

Petr grinned. "Me too, buddy. Me too."

Chapter 9

THE ANCIENT BEAST BRUSHED her crooked index finger along the side of the sleeping girl's face, sliding it down and around the curve of her jaw, dropping it along her chin and throat until stopping just above her cleavage. The old woman groaned at the suppleness of the girl's skin, and then smiled when the source opened her eyes.

She always loved that split second of confusion, that fleeting moment when her source awoke and began to blink desperately, struggling to find her way back to the moment. It was as if they were trying to transform the memory of their imprisonment into a dream simply through the will of their facial expression.

And how she adored the look that followed that one, that flash of terror that erupted in their eyes.

The source for this current batch was slightly older than those the woman typically strode for—this girl had perhaps even reached the age of thirty. But she had the characteristics of a younger female, her olive skin unblemished, her eyes fresh and alive, and the shape of her body suggested that no children had yet to pass through her. This last trait, the woman concluded, certainly meant the girl was barren, though she had denied that directly. But the woman knew better. In this land, a girl as shapely and beautiful as the one lying before her was often a mother before her eighteenth birthday, and always after twenty-one.

And this barrenness was a potential problem. If her source was, indeed, infertile, it could affect the effectiveness of the batch. The hormone balance needed to be proper, ovulation normal. She chased a recollection of a time when one of her sources had this same lacking quality, but the memory was fleeting, beyond her ability to find it within her dark mind. If she had experienced such a source, however, it had been long ago, perhaps before Marlene and Gromus had ever been born.

In any case, she couldn't take chances, and needed to off-set the imbalance with something strong enough to recreate the quality in the potion. The bungaru venom was perhaps overkill, but it had been effective once before, in another blend, and she could always cut it with something inactive it was too much.

The source lifted her head and swallowed. "Hello," she said, the remembrance of her current situation now forming across her face. She attempted a smile, but the dread in her eyes emitted the opposite expression. "How are you today?"

This girl was following the pattern perfectly. At this stage of captivity—almost a month in—the source typically became desperate, often resorting to attempts at convincing her captor that they had become friends, that she, the source, was understanding of the woman's needs. Perhaps even a willing participant in the whole sordid ordeal, if a proper deal could be reached, of course.

It was a ruse, obviously, a fraught play by the source to establish some type of bond with her captor. The hope, of course, was that once the connection was made, the jailer would release her prisoner back to the world, the underlying goodness of mankind claiming another victory just before that final, fatal, extraction.

These sources, the woman thought. They didn't know her at all.

"I'm just fine," the woman said, playing along, "though I must confess, I'm a bit piqued by one of my vendors today. Not your issue to deal with though, dear."

The prisoner gave a sympathetic frown, and the old woman placed the tips of her fingers to her mouth to stifle a giggle.

"I am sorry for your displeasure. Perhaps there is something I can do to help. My father is a vendor in the marketplace. The Central Markets. He is quite respected. I am certain he would be willing to speak with this man, to help broker a solution to your troubles. He is very persuasive in that way."

The old woman scoffed now, both amused and slightly offended that this girl thought her that gullible. She appreciated grace and creativity in the attempts for freedom, and this girl had shown neither.

"Have I insulted you? I'm sorry, that was not my intention. I just thought—"

"My dear," the woman replied, the playfulness in her voice now a memory. "I am quite sure your father is not familiar with this particular vendor. He is, shall we say, somewhat of an outcast."

The prisoner lowered her head back to the gurney and closed her eyes, squeezing back what few tears must have remained. Her arms and legs were tied with leather straps to a stiff, metal gurney—her arms just above the wrists, her legs at the shins—but she managed to lift her right shoulder six inches or so, an obvious attempt to alleviate the pain of a sore that had opened recently just below her clavicle.

For the first three weeks, the time during which the woman had performed the majority of the extractions, she had kept the girl on a standard sleeping mattress in the spare bedroom, a place that was relatively comfortable and warm given the circumstances. But at twenty days, the woman had transferred her to the gurney, a relic from an old hospital that had been bought at the market and placed in the middle of the home's small laboratory.

The lab was impressive, the woman thought (if she did say so herself), as it was originally built as a den, and then later converted, by her, to its current specifications.

And this conversion was crucial. The woman had made several tweaks to the potion over the centuries, and for some reason she hadn't ever quite figured, this tweak—the abrupt change from coziness to discomfort in the last half of the process—seemed to enhance the overall effectiveness of the product. The shock to the systems within the body—most notably to the endocrine system, she guessed—left the final liquid broth more palatable. The batches went down smoother, without the usual stagnation or sting of rancidity, and even the effects of the potion seemed more significant, often occurring immediately upon ingestion.

And most importantly, it took less than half the time to prepare.

She had tested this new method on the last dozen or so sources, and was certain she had the timing just right now. But the open sores wouldn't do. That type of rebellion from the body had the potential to affect the batch, and she needed to tend to the wound immediately.

The woman turned on her heels so that her face was now only inches from a solid white wall that formed one of the long sides of the undersized room. She raised her hands to shoulder height, and then, with palms flat, pressed them against the wall and shifted them left, easily sliding the wall open to a width of about two and a half feet. She glanced back at her prisoner, who was now crying softly on the table, and then scanned the rest of the small room that had served as her prison for the last two years.

She exited the room and slid the wall shut, and was now in the front part of her home. It was a one-room apartment really, consisting of a kitchen, dining room, and tiny living area—rooms that were far more traditional than the hidden prison hiding beyond the back wall.

Private latrines were a luxury in the Eastern Lands, and for the two or three times a year when it became necessary for her to eliminate waste from her system, she used a floor toilet that had been built in the back room by the previous tenants.

The exterior of the house displayed a thin, squatty structure that sat wedged between a second-hand jewelry store to the left, and, to her right, a combination butcher shop and delicatessen, which also operated as a slaughterhouse in the rear of the building.

Her home was technically a two-level structure, but only the first floor was habitable, since the top floor was full of junk and debris left by the former occupants.

The living arrangement wasn't her perfect scenario, and the city in which the house sat was a mass of wasted souls and depression. It was nothing compared to the Old World. Nothing compared to the cool air and open space of the Koudehcuvals, the place of her birth and her home of a thousand years.

But she had learned to adjust to her environment. For example, she had long ago learned the schedule of the lamb slaughters, and now knew them like she knew the tenets of Orphism. Whenever she had a source processing, she adjusted her extraction schedules accordingly, coinciding them with the preparation of the young sheep. Her privacy was her most important possession, and though this section of the city went largely ignored by the authorities, the constant refrain of screaming women would bring attention eventually. That was where the lambs came in, their braying cries of death helping to mask those of the young sources.

The woman walked to a small refrigerator that sat beneath the front window and fished the ring of keys from her pocket, finding the correct one before stooping and opening the door to the cooler. She took out the plastic case of medicine and then stood tall, holding it in front of her like a warm cup of tea while she stared out at the city below her.

It was a filthy place.

She watched with disgust as the pedestrians and bicyclists flowed past her home, their desultory lives as meaningless as the girl she held in the holding room only a few feet away. But the meaninglessness of these people was even more absolute; the girl, at least, through the fluids of her blood and bile and lymph, would help to extend the life of another. Someone significant. Legendary.

The woman had once loved it here, those first few years after her arrival, when the source material seemed as endless as the sands of the great deserts. That part, of course, hadn't changed at all. The fact was, there were far more to choose from today than at any time in history. So many more.

But the woman had grown tired of her existence here. The Eastern Lands were as different from her home in the Old World as fire was from ice, and lately, the differences had begun to weigh on her. The crowds and bustle and heat and filth; they never slowed, never subsided. Most of her life had been spent in places where she could go days—even weeks—without ever seeing another person. Now she couldn't look out her window without seeing two dozen, at least. These multitudes made the acquisitions easier, but once taken, the effort to keep them hidden was far more difficult.

But her disgust at her surroundings only formed the foundation of her impetus to leave. There was another layer that had been added to the mixture, a more pressing reason had begun to lead her from this place: Marlene.

The woman had felt it strongly when she passed, just as she did each time any Orphist died. She couldn't have known it was her daughter, of course, not for certain, but there was a different pang at the moment of this passing, something she hadn't felt in almost three hundred years: sadness.

The feeling ebbed a bit, but lingered for over a year before her suspicions were confirmed.

She had been walking to the market, one of her rare monthly outings, when she saw a group of girls chasing each other in the street. One of them, the pursuer, held up her fingers in the shape of claws, screaming at the other two, baring her teeth.

The woman had been compelled to stop, curious at the alacrity of the game at first, but was then struck by something familiar in the hunting girl's re-enactment. "I'll put you in my soup!" she screamed, and then laughed at the ensuing shrieks of her friends.

The woman had walked up to the girls, stopping only a few feet away when they finally saw her. They froze on their marks, equal looks of terror on their faces.

The woman had little doubt these lass' parents had told them to beware the eater of children or some such thing, and to stay away from her at all costs.

"What game are you playing?" she had asked them.

The children had looked at each other, each catching the eyes of the other two, trying to agree silently whether to answer, keep quiet, or run. Finally, one of the girls who had been playing one of the hunted said, "We're playing 'Gretel.'"

Something rumbled distantly in the woman's brain at the sound of the name, lingering for just a moment before evaporating. "Gretel?" she had asked, keeping her distance, trying to remain frail and non-threatening. "What is Gretel?"

The girl again looked at her friends and then back to the woman. She shrugged. "I don't know. It's a story. She killed the Witch of the North."

The woman raised a hand to her chin, rubbing it in curiosity. "A witch?"

The girl nodded.

"And what was the witch's name?"

The girl shrugged again and then ran away without answering, her flight triggering the hunter girl to continue the chase, growling like a bear as she came this time.

But the woman didn't need an answer. She knew her name. Marlene. Daughter of Tanja.

It had taken her another day to confirm the children's tale with the men at the marketplace, and she continued to go there daily for the next few weeks, attempting to pick up different pieces of the story each time, sometimes offering money to those who had family in the New Country who might be able to provide more details.

But the old fools in the markets knew little, and Tanja couldn't risk hanging around children for details of some sordid tale from a distant land. But she did learn of the Back Country, and the names of Gretel and Anika and Hansel and Petr. And some authoritarian group known as The System. She had even made an anonymous phone call to The System, hoping to get a bit of first-hand insight into that operation, as well as the case involving her daughter. But the initial questions of the answering female had made Tanja nervous, and she had hung up before speaking with anyone else.

But as the months dragged on, Tanja became obsessed with the story, and had sworn to avenge her daughter, an oath driven as much by her need to leave her wretched city as by vengeance. She would first go back to her home in the Old World, and from there sail out to the New Country. It would be an adventure. A point at which to start again.

Those plans to leave, however, had stalled. It was the addiction, of course, that had kept her here, addiction not only to the potion of life but to the routine she'd so delicately cultivated.

But this moment, as she stood and watched the crowds below, was epiphanous, a sign that the time to leave had finally come. The animals she watched on the street below existed everywhere. It would take work to develop again all she had created here, but it could be done. She had time. She had eternity.

And Gretel had to die. As did Anika and Hansel and Petr. And anyone else who was still alive and had contributed to the death of her daughter.

She would finish this last batch of potion and then leave this soiled heap of disease. Escape in the shroud of night, leaving the building in which she now stood a raging ball of fire.

There were still several days until the bungaru venom would be ready, and she would need a few more after that to finalize the solution. After that, however, when her business was finished, she would be gone from here, ready to commence the hunt for the Morgans.

Chapter 10

ANIKA KEPT TO THE TREE line as she made her way north to the Urbanlands, ducking behind the curtain of leaves and branches as she went, hiding at the sound of any car that approached. Ideally, she would have kept to the cover of the tree branches for the entire trek, but there were road signs to be read that gave her direction and progress status.

The university wasn't close, but she was on the right path. Now she just had to go.

She thought of her phone call with Petr, and how deranged she must have sounded to him. Of course, she was deranged now, and she had only called the boy out of one last desperate attempt at redemption. He was the only person she trusted, the only person she knew really, outside of her own family and Mrs. Klahr. And if Anika was going to attempt this quest to kill Tanja in the Eastern Lands, she wouldn't be doing it with the help of any of those three. It was Petr Stenson who was meant to help her. It was he who the voice at the warehouse had been suggesting, he who could help her carry out the mission. As she strode the Interways in his direction, she felt almost positive of that now.

Petr's name had leapt into her head the moment she got back to Pavel Delov's home, with the body of the System officer still freshly killed in the woods not a half-mile away.

Thoughts of suicide had raged during her walk, and once again she considered her options to take her own life.

But some quality inside the man's cabin had triggered a peace in Anika, and the death grip that had been squeezing her chest and mind as she left the scene of her crimes, suddenly eased. It was a moment of clarity, she reasoned, and she had seized it, locating a phone book in the drawer beneath the phone, and finding the listing for the University of the Urbanlands, and the sub-listing for the Directory of Student Housing. The automated voice that answered had directed her to type in the first few letters of the last name of the person she was trying to reach. The first few attempts were unsuccessful—the letters associated with the numeric keys proved to be a bit clumsy—but on the fourth attempt, she heard the robot say, *Stenson, Petr,* followed by the phone number to his home on campus.

And had he been home when she called, things likely would have gone much more smoothly.

She knew she could have just confirmed he was a student and then headed towards the campus, but she needed to hear his voice, needed to hear the sound of allegiance.

The roommate had not provided that, and as the day wore on, Anika had become increasingly unstable, her moment of peace and clarity gradually slipping. By the time of her last call—which could have been her fiftieth, if she included all of the times no one answered—she felt the anger and desperation that had brought her to that place to begin with, and Pavel Delov had become the unfortunate subject of her aim.

Anika had hoped the seafood man would stay away for the night—perhaps on some overnight delivery—but, as Anika was sure he had done virtually every night of his working life, he came home right around dinnertime.

She had cut off his air for a time to render him unconscious, but there was no lust in her for his killing. The young female officer had sated her desire to feed, so killing Pavel Delov would have been unnecessary. It would have turned Anika from an instinct killer to a cold-blooded one, which, to her, would have placed her at a much higher section of the evil echelon. The man had seen her, that was true, but what matter was that really? She would be leaving for the Eastern Lands soon, in a day or two if she could arrange it, and she had no real intentions of ever coming home. Even if she wanted to she couldn't. She had murdered three people now and was believed to be dead herself. There was nothing left for her in the New Country.

And if her irresistible drive for human organs didn't wane soon, there would be nothing left for her anywhere.

Anika could see the top of a sign rising on the side of the road in the distance. She looked back to the road and then, seeing nothing, jogged in the direction of the sign until she was close enough to read the words **Univ. of Urban—110**. A hundred and ten miles. That was three days at least. Probably longer since she would have to take shelter far more frequently during the day.

But it wasn't really the walking that was the issue. Police from everywhere—not just The System, but local and regional police as well—would have flooded the area the second the body was found, which had certainly happened by now. And once they were set free, they wouldn't stop looking until they found the killer. There was a System officer dead, a police murderer on the loose, and despite their sordid reputation of late, this type of incident would not be taken lightly by New Country law enforcement.

Anika had created some distance over the last few hours since she left Pavel Delov's cabin, but not as much as she would have liked, and the dragnet would reach her soon. She had wanted to leave earlier, but she reasoned that if she was to take to the road, she would need to clean herself up. So that was what she did, and based on the reflection she saw in the mirror, she had done a fairly decent job. Her eye was freshly patched, and the rest of her wounds were now cleaned and explainable, not that they would be anyone's business.

But regardless of her appearance, no amount of foliage was going to keep her safe. The dogs would be set loose, and with the smell of the officer all over her body, she would be caught easily.

No, walking was impossible. If she ever hoped to make it to Petr, if she ever hoped to make it to the Eastern Lands to fulfill her destiny, Anika would have to flag down a car.

And she would have to do it soon.

Once the report of the murder reached the public, there wouldn't be many motorists willing to stop for a hitchhiker. The fact that she was a woman would make little difference; after all, women were the source of most of the damage done in the Southlands over the past couple of years.

Anika quickly devised a rudimentary plan in her head, and then retreated to the tree line where she waited for the sounds of an approaching engine.

Chapter 11

PETR TRIED TO STAY focused on his project, which was due in a couple days, but the memory of the woman's phone call from two nights earlier kept invading his mind. There was a recognizable crackle and pitch in her voice, a tone that Petr was now intimately familiar with and one he had come to believe was a characteristic unique to beleaguered and abused women. Mrs. Klahr had that pitch now.

And Anika had developed it as well.

Her voice had deteriorated to that of someone twice her age, a combination of her traumatic imprisonment, the poisonous potion, and the addiction that followed.

Marlene, of course, had the same qualities as well, but Petr imagined her warped voice had been formed since before the discovery of the New Country.

But that voice on the phone, could it have been Anika's? Was that possible? Was it she who Petr saw on the porch from the bank of the Klahr orchard?

It wasn't Mrs. Klahr who had called him, he was sure about that. Petr had spoken with her yesterday, ostensibly to inquire about Gretel and Hansel and the progress of their mourning. He was sincerely concerned about them, of course, but the real thrust of his call was to make sure Mrs. Klahr was home and safe. He hadn't truly been worried about her—if she had been the caller, phoning from some strange phone number where a crime had been committed, he would have heard about it from Hansel or Gretel. But still, he had to be sure. He'd seen too much over the past couple of years not to cover all of the bases. Besides, it was no guarantee that Hansel and Gretel weren't also victims.

But Mrs. Klahr was safe, and this fact kept leading Petr's thoughts back to Anika. Nobody had called The System to retrieve her body from the lake, a decision Petr thought to be a mistake at the time and now believed even more so. He understood the reasoning behind it, but there was so much that felt wrong in it.

Gretel had relayed to him the whole story of the death: Hansel's strike to Anika's temple with the oar, and the blood and glaze in her eyes as she finally collapsed over the side of the canoe into the water. And perhaps the most important detail: how Petr and Mrs. Klahr had seen Anika sink beneath the surface and never come up again.

But Gretel's was a second-hand account of what had happened. She hadn't actually seen any of it. And though Petr believed she had told the story as she knew it to be, maybe it was wrong. Maybe Hansel and Mrs. Klahr hadn't waited long enough. Watched long enough.

Petr had read stories of people surviving after prolonged underwater stints in freezing temperatures, and though temperature couldn't have been a factor in this instance, perhaps something else had preserved her. It seemed possible. Ever since Gretel and Marlene and the potion had come into his life, everything now seemed possible.

But if it was Anika, why had she not simply told him so on the phone. Even if she were in the grips of addiction, why couldn't she just tell him it was she who was calling? Tell him that she was alive and, in fact, had not died at the bottom of the lake? Maybe Petr wouldn't have believed her at first, that was likely, but it wouldn't have taken long for her to prove the story. There were so many details that only she and a handful of people knew; it would have been easy to convince him of her identity.

Instead, she'd screamed his name like a wild woman, the desperation in her voice absolute and chilling. Whoever it was on the other end of the line, Petr knew she was in real trouble.

Petr scribbled another note for his project and then closed his biology book. He walked to the kitchen, staring at the phone as he passed, and then stopped and turned back to it, picking up the receiver.

His thoughts turned to Gretel. *Was she gone yet?* She had still been there yesterday when he called to check on Mrs. Klahr, but what about today? She had told him she would try to wait, but Petr had his doubts about her commitment to that statement. He could see something in her eyes when she made the promise—shame perhaps—which suggested her plans had already been made.

Well, there was no harm on checking in on them again. He had called yesterday, that was true, but every day was different in the mourning process. And he wanted to reiterate to Mrs. Klahr that he would be back again this weekend, as soon as his presentation was finished, and would stay as long as they needed him.

Hopefully she would remind Gretel of that too.

He dialed the number to his Back Country home and listened to the phone ring four times. Five times. Petr brought the phone back down toward the receiver when he heard the faintest "Hello," come from the earpiece.

"Hello? Mrs. Klahr?"

"It's Hansel."

"Oh, hi Hansel."

Petr had never learned how to talk to Hansel, a truth that was due mostly to the fact that he'd never really gotten to know him. When he'd first met him, he was just the little brother of the girl Petr liked—and later loved—but in less than three years, Hansel had been thrust into manhood, a cynical orphan who was now burdened with defending what remained of his family.

And now he was the killer of his own mother, a mother he had lost and found once as a little boy, only to lose her again a few years later to the poison of a monster.

"It's Petr, Hansel. How...how are you doing?"

There was a pause. "If you want to talk to Gretel—"

"I want to know how you're doing, Hansel."

"Why?"

Petr considered letting himself out of this awkward conversation, giving an exasperated huff and moving on to Mrs. Klahr. But something compelled him to stay on.

"Is there anything you need? There at home, I mean. For the orchard maybe. I'll be coming home this weekend, so I can go into the city to pick up some supplies. Maybe even a couple of luxury items? Something you can't get back home?"

"Sure Petr. That'd be great. I had no idea you were so well-off these days. Maybe you can pick us up a couple of diamond-handled fruit pickers to go along with some golden baskets. Oh, and I heard Mrs. Klahr swooning over a new ball gown that she saw in a Blanton's catalogue."

"Hansel, come on. I just meant—"

"I don't care, Petr. We don't need anything. I'm glad you're coming home because Mrs. Klahr will want to see you, but we're fine. You're not my big brother or father or uncle. You don't need to take care of us."

Hansel's words stung more than Petr would have imagined, but he kept them in perspective. The boy was devastated, obviously, and now that Petr thought about it, his own words may have come across as a bit condescending. "Okay Hansel. Can I speak with Mrs. Klahr?"

Petr heard the phone being set down, and then the soft, weary voice of his adoptive grandmother. "Hello, Petr."

"Mrs. Klahr, are you okay?"

There was silence on the other line, and for a moment Petr thought she hadn't heard him. But then Petr heard her swallow. "She's leaving, Petr."

Gretel had finally told Mrs. Klahr of her plans. "I know, Mrs. Klahr, she told me."

"I'm so frightened for her. Alone in the Old World. It pains me to think about it."

Petr felt his chest tighten and a lump developed in his throat. He hated to hear Mrs. Klahr so distraught, particularly when Gretel was the source of the pain. "She'll be okay. You know her, Mrs. Klahr. You've seen how much she's...grown."

Mrs. Klahr was still uncomfortable with the whole notion of Orphism, and, in particular, any of the strange powers it spawned. It was black magic to her, heresy, and though she'd seen too much at this point to ignore it or dismiss it as myth, she avoided the conversation whenever possible.

"I know, Petr, but I don't have good feelings about any of it. My feelings are quite the opposite, actually."

What could Petr say to that? He didn't have good feelings about Gretel leaving either, and any attempt at consolation would have been forced and transparent. He should have simply asked a few perfunctory questions and started down the path to "Goodbye." Instead, as if some external force had taken over his body, he asked, "Are you sure she died, Mrs. Klahr?"

"What?" Mrs. Klahr's response was immediate, like she'd been splashed with a glass of cold water.

"Anika. Mrs. Morgan. Gretel's mother. Are you sure she died? Are you sure she's at the bottom of that lake?" Petr wasn't angry, but his excessive description of what he was asking left no doubt about the seriousness of his question.

"Why would you ask me that, Petr?"

The tone of Mrs. Klahr's voice was one that typically crippled Petr and robbed him of any vigor, but he maintained his authority this time. "Just answer me, Mrs. Klahr. Are you sure?"

"She's dead, Petr. I'm sure. And don't you ever ask that question again. To anyone. Do you understand me?"

Petr hesitated, but agreed with a soft "yes," knowing it wasn't a pact he could necessarily adhere to.

"I'll be home this weekend," Petr said, awkwardly transitioning to a new subject. "And I'll probably stay for a while. Once this damn project is finished."

"Don't curse, Petr."

"I'm sorry. Anyway, I'm going to let my professors know that I'll need to miss a few classes." And then, preempting Mrs. Klahr's question, Petr added, "It's fine, I can afford to. I want to spend as much time as I can with Gretel before she leaves for good."

"What do you mean, Petr? She's leaving. You said you knew."

Petr was confused. "Yes, I know. That's what I just said."

Mrs. Klahr sighed, now understanding the breakdown in communication. "No, Petr. When I said she was leaving, I meant now. Today. She's at the docks. Her ship is scheduled to leave in twenty minutes."

Petr felt like he'd been kicked in the stomach, and the only word he could manage was, "What?"

"I'm sorry, Petr. I'm so sorry."

There was nothing to be done now. Petr couldn't have made it to the docks in two hours, let alone twenty minutes. Gretel was leaving. She was leaving without seeing him again. He was right: Gretel hadn't kept her promise. She hadn't even tried.

Chapter 12

"WHAT BRINGS YOU TO the Urbanlands?"

Anika raised her eyebrows and scoffed, and then smiled without looking at the driver. With that reaction, she hoped to convey to him that her story was quite a yarn and would take some effort to tell.

"You don't see many hitchhikers in this part of the country. Not anymore. And certainly none as pretty as you."

Anika could smell the sweat building in the man's crotch and back, his musk indicating he was entering the early stages of sexual arousal. She couldn't decide whether to gag or laugh at the odor. He was sixty at least, and his teeth looked as if they hadn't touched a toothbrush in a decade.

She, of course, had seen better days as well, and despite her ad hoc clean-up job back at the cabin, was still quite the mess, at least as far as her face and hair were concerned. But Anika suspected this driver would take it wherever he could get it, and with a body that was still fairly thin and shapely, Anika would have proven to be a treat.

Or maybe it was the eyepatch, she joked to herself, and then giggled aloud.

The driver smiled, obviously thinking Anika's laugh was due to his compliment. "So," he pressed, "whatcha doing out here? Not real safe for ladies out here this time of night."

Anika gave a weary sigh.

Randall was her third driver of the journey, and, based on where he said he was headed, her last. With any luck she'd be on the campus of the university within the hour.

The first car to stop for Anika was driven by a young couple, probably early twenties, and Anika could smell the hemp immediately after the driver rolled down his window to ask where she was headed. But they were harmless and relatively pleasant, and, best of all, they talked about themselves the entire time—the girl mostly—never asking Anika about her injuries or even why she was out on the road to begin with. If it had been up to Anika, she would have ridden with them the entire way, but they were headed east to start a new life at the beaches. From what Anika could gather, they had only vague plans about where they would live or how they would survive once they arrived, but such were the movements of youth. They would be fine. In any case, it left Anika stranded at a diner about halfway from her destination.

At the restaurant, Anika sat at the counter and drank coffee until she met the person who would come to be her second ride: a long distance hauler who was headed directly through the Urbanlands en route to the Northern Tips. And, best of all, the driver was a woman. It seemed the perfect scenario with only fifty miles to go.

But it began to go south less than ten minutes into the ride when the woman turned the conversation to the story of the murdered System officer.

"Gruesome," she had said. "They're looking for the killer along the Interways. Better keep clear of them until they find him."

Anika could tell the woman was smart, inquisitive, and in the hour or so it would take for them to reach the Urbanlands, Anika was afraid the woman's questions would lead to the obvious conclusion that it was she who was killer. The driver had asked detailed questions about the injury to her eye and face, and why her clothes were so dirty and tattered. But the questions hadn't come tactlessly; she had asked them the way a forensic scientist would inquire about the details of a crime scene. Anika had to get out of there.

Luckily, there were several exits that began to appear as they neared the Urbanlands, and Anika had told her she was stopping first at her sister's house before heading to the school. *Hadn't she told her that? Oh, I'm sorry. Yes, my sister will take me the rest of the way.*

Anika had insisted the driver—whose name she never got—leave her at the ramp of the exit. It was only a mile or so off, and rigs her size weren't suitable for the roads.

When the rig was well up to speed and on its way down the Interways, Anika began walking behind it, headed in the same direction with her arm extended and her thumb pointed to the horizon.

In less than twenty minutes, a faded blue pickup truck sidled beside Anika asking her where she was headed, and she felt she had no choice but to take Randall's offer.

"It's my son," she answered. "He's a student at the university."

Anika had planned the my-son-is-a-student story before beginning her trek, and, to this point, had needed to say only that much. The young beachgoers hadn't asked at all, and the rig driver had only asked to be polite.

"We have only the one car and I told him that, as a kind of going-away present, he could have it with him at school. Just for the first semester though."

The man glanced from the road every few seconds, staring at Anika with a cold smile that contained not a trace of interest or humor. And each time he looked at her, just before he turned his attention back to the road ahead, he let his eyes drift down to Anika's chest and waist.

"Anyway," she continued, "his birthday is tomorrow, and I wanted to surprise him. His education is very expensive, which doesn't leave much money for a proper present. Or a train ticket, obviously."

The man was nodding, but Anika could see he wasn't really listening. His mind was working on other things

"So I thought I would just pop in and say, 'Happy Birthday.' You know, show up and be a kind of doorstep surprise party?"

"I like parties," the driver responded, implying some vague double entendre. His grin, which had never been quite friendly to this point, was now gruesome, menacing, and he was now applying little effort to hide his intentions. He wore the look of a man who would ask first, but if the answer was 'No'—which it almost certainly always was—would press the issue anyway.

And his scent was getting stronger.

But Anika was calm, peaceful even, and this tranquility left her with a powerful feeling of control, even in this situation, which seemed destined to devolve into an attempted assault.

She had come this far without murdering anyone else, and since, one way or the other, this ride was the last one of the trek, she didn't plan on starting with Randall.

A thin green sign read **Univ. 19.** Nineteen miles. Close enough. She could walk the rest of the way.

"I did just remember something, Randall."

"Yeah? What's that?"

"I can't show up to my son's house empty-handed. He's got a roommate. It slipped my mind before. That would be rude, yes? The next store or gas station or whatever you see, could you drop me there?"

"Thought you didn't have money?"

Anika narrowed her eyes now, and her patience with Randall suddenly went from manageable to paper-thin.

Was this how it was before? Was this how powerlessly she lived her life? When she was just a Back Country wife and mother of small children, was every encounter with a strange man some passive survival game? Was it one where she told little lies to avoid confrontation, or gave a wider, more inconvenient berth as she passed them on the street or in the store, hoping just to get in and out of every scenario without the threat of harassment or groping or worse?

"I've got some," she answered flatly.

"Yeah? How much?"

Anika stayed quiet now, allowing her silence to build the tension naturally. Randall kept his smile wide as he looked back and forth at his passenger, each of his movements becoming more frantic and intimidating than the last, the odor of testosterone growing inside the cabin of the truck.

"What happened to your eye?" he asked, laughing now as he spoke.

"Fishing accident. What about that store?"

"There's no store for eight miles," he answered dismissively. "Fishing accident? I think that's a bullshit story." He laughed loudly this time, seeming to delight in the current banter, the way a cat delights in the resistance of a mouse it has trapped in the corner of a dark basement.

"That will be fine. Maybe we could just not speak anymore for the rest of those eight miles."

"That's no fun. Don't you like fun? I think we can find something more fun to do than not speaking to each other. I don't usually need but twenty or thirty seconds!" Randall laughed hysterically again at this quip.

Anika looked calmly at Randall, her face a frowning mixture of disappointment and disgust. Her breathing was slow and regular, her heartbeat not the slightest bit elevated.

Randall met Anika's gaze, a wild mischief in his eyes now, a look that was meant to be both playful and threatening.

But Anika held his eyes firm, just the wrinkle of a curl now showing at the corner of her lips. And for the first time since they'd begun driving together, which was about forty minutes now, Anika detected a grain of fear in Randall.

"You're going to drive," she said, "and I'm going to ride. And that's all we're going to do. Otherwise, let me out now and I'll walk the rest of the way."

Randall opened his eyes wide now, fighting off whatever fear may have nestled into his mind. "That's not much fun," he growled, and the manic smile suddenly disappeared from his face.

"You know what, Randall? Maybe you're right then. Maybe I don't like fun."

"You'll like my kind of fun."

Randall checked his rear and side mirrors, licking his lips once as he did, and then steered the car to the right, gradually slowing until the car came to a stop on the shoulder, just at the edge of an endless row of wheat stalks.

Based on the most recent road sign they'd passed, they were only ten miles or so from the Urbanland limits. But Anika would never have known it based on the landscape. This part of the Interways was as treeless and flat as the Western Deserts, and the fields of wheat that framed the road fanned out forever in the headlights of Randall's truck. The lights of the city buildings shone brightly in the distance, but everywhere around them was as dark as space.

And deserted.

Randall turned the headlights off and gently pressed the automatic door lock button; the loud thumping sound of the locking mechanism filled the car in stereo, and Anika felt a pang of sympathy for the man beside her.

"How did you want to pay me for the ride?" he asked. "You said you had some money. Is that right?"

Anika's body was as still as a sunning gator, but she could feel the rush inside of her, the molecules of her serum and plasma, of her spinal and synovial fluid, all resonating in a way she'd never felt before. It was a different feeling than with the hunters, different than with the officer. And it was different than any memory she had of her life under the potion's spell.

It felt now like her body was militarizing, preparing for war.

It wasn't hunger that drove her this time. It was anger.

"I don't have any money."

Randall gave a sardonic frown, and followed it with a slow, scolding shake of his head, feigning disappointment. "Well, see now, that's a problem for a couple of reasons. First of all, you lied to me and told me you did have some money. And I don't like it much when people lie to me."

"Does anyone like that?" Anika couldn't help the wisecrack.

Randall ignored the comment. "And two, if you don't have no money, than I'm afraid you're going to have to come up with some other form of payment. Any ideas?"

Anika closed her eyes and focused the anger that was building further inside her, feeding it with memories of her own loss and abuse. There was a comfort in the pain, a satisfaction that mimicked the feelings she'd recently gotten from her feeding, though it wasn't exactly comparable.

She thought of her father and his betrayal, and the ease at which he'd come to his decision to kill her that night in the warehouse. She thought of the greed of Officer Stenson, which in many ways was the worst betrayal of all, as his was a betrayal of his power and country. She thought of Heinrich, who had also betrayed her, but at least had put forth a last effort at redemption. She thought of the potion. And Odalinde, the woman she never really knew but wished she had.

And she thought of the loss of herself, of Anika Morgan, a loss that robbed Gretel of her mother and Hansel of his innocence.

And she thought of Marlene.

"I'm going to leave now, Randall. When I say, 'Open,' you're going to unlock the doors, and I'm going to get out and be on my way. Thank you for the ride. If you give me an address, I'll send you money. Just tell me what you think is a fair price for this delightful experience."

"I don't want your money, matey." Randall squinted an eye closed and mocked a stereotypical pirate's voice. "I want your booty!" With this last line, he erupted into laughter, and, despite the harassing overtones of his words, for a moment Anika thought she saw a glimmer of harmlessness in the man. That perhaps he was more bark than bite.

"Sorry, Randall. That will not be happening. Open the door. Now."

Randall looked sideways at Anika, as if considering whether to go through with the evil in his mind, knowing there was still a chance to do the right thing.

"Now," Anika repeated, the burn in her flaring again, reaching a level that was almost uncontrollable. "Now!"

The louder Anika yelled at him, the more heavily Randall began to breathe, and the fear that she had detected in him earlier revealed itself two-fold. And just when she thought he was going to unlock the door, thereby saving himself from death while she fled down the Interways toward the city, he reached for his waistband and began to unbuckle his belt. "You owe me," he muttered, spittle coming down his chin, catching in his stubble like cotton in a spider's web. "You owe me."

Anika's rage reached an apex, and the pressure of her blood in her veins made her head throb.

And then her rage suddenly transmuted to instinct.

She shot her hand down toward Randall's crotch like the tongue of a chameleon, and before he'd pulled his belt from the first loop of his pants, Anika had crushed his testicles in her palm. Through the thick layer of cotton, she could feel the blood explode in a warm gush.

Randall's scream was deafening, but short-lived. Before he could unleash a second squeal, Anika whipped the belt out through the remaining loops and quickly tied it around the driver's neck, fastening the leather in a knot so that the bulge in Randall's eyes showed almost instantly.

Anika reached over and methodically unlocked the doors, and then exited her side of the truck and walked around to the driver's side. She opened Randall's door now and pulled the man out by the limp strap of his belt, dragging him off the shoulder and into the wheat field.

"It didn't have to be this way, Randall. You had chances. You had choices."

Randall grasped frantically at the belt with his fingers, finally gripping the leather strap with the full meat of his hands. But he was no match for Anika, and she brushed past the tall stalks without breaking stride, pulling her victim twenty yards deep into the field.

In contrast to the effort and tension Randall was giving to the belt, there was no noise coming from his mouth. Anika knew he was almost dead, and when she finally stopped in a small clearing, she made one last yank upwards.

Something inside of the man's neck made a grisly snapping sound, and within minutes, Anika was back on the road and heading back toward the lights of the city.

She lifted her head high as she walked, with her shoulders back and chest out, striding down the middle of the Interways for a full mile before oncoming headlights forced her to the shoulder.

She felt content, and best of all, she wasn't hungry.

Chapter 13

TANJA CAREFULLY CLEANED the wound and then dressed it with a square of clean, white cotton, one of the few that remained in the makeshift medicine cabinet that had been wedged into the far corner of her secret room. If her source's shoulder lesion didn't heal completely within the next two or three days, Tanja would be forced to venture back to the markets for more.

The thought of leaving for another shopping jaunt aggravated her, and not just because of the effort it involved. It was a change in the schedule. Her plans had been made, she had settled into them, and any deviation from that plan would be unnerving.

As things stood now, she would pick up the venom in ten days, finish concocting the potion, and then slit the throat of the source before heading to the docks, her ramshackle townhome in a blaze behind her. Once at the docks, she would purchase a one-way ticket to the New Country, rejuvenated and ready for the hunt.

Within two weeks, she would be gone from this wretched place forever.

But the potion couldn't be prepared properly if the source became unhealthy, infected, and the fact that her wound wasn't healing was a sign her immune system was beginning to fail.

Tanja slid the wall back and went immediately to the kitchen, turning on the burner of the stove before opening the refrigerator door, hoping to find some band of ingredients that she could whip together to try to get the girl strong. She had no antibiotics, as those were somewhat of a luxury in this part of the world, but she had learned of other, more organic methods over her years to stave off infection.

She had no silver flakes, which would have been her preference, but she did find an old bulb of garlic in the door and a bowl of honey on the bottom shelf that surely hadn't been moved in at least two years. The garlic didn't look too promising, as it was shriveled and browned and had likely lost its potency, but the honey, she knew, was magical in its ability to stay unsullied; it was, in many ways, as immortal as she was.

She pulled both items from the icebox and placed them on the counter to her left, and as she was closing the refrigerator, there was a knock on the front door.

Tanja froze, afraid even to complete the seal of the refrigerator door. Her eyes blossomed wide as she listened for the sound of voices, but there were none.

Another rap on the door came several seconds later, followed by, "Hello, ma'am. Are you home? We would like to ask you a few questions. It will only take a minute. We are canvassing the area today. We're looking for a woman who disappeared from this neighborhood recently. We're hoping you might have seen something that could help us. The woman, the one who is missing, she lives not far from here."

They didn't sound like the policeman she'd talked to on a few occasions since she'd been in this country, but Tanja supposed they were meant not to sound that way. They took on a more pleasant persona, in the hopes that people would open the door.

Tanja could ignore them, and then again a third time. But for what purpose? Whoever they were, be they police or some makeshift citizen troop, they would be back. And the more she ignored them, she reasoned, the more suspicious she would appear. She was the crazy old lady on the street, the one with the foreign accent who lived alone. The woman who had been known to talk to children in the streets on occasion, and who was rumored to purchase strange things at the markets. She fit a profile that was at least suspicious, particularly with the recent stories of witches and potions that had reached these shores recently from the New Country.

And Tanja knew that it was, in large part, her physical appearance that had kept her safe over the last several years. As old and frail as she looked, it would have seemed impossible for her to have kidnapped anyone by force and detained them; and thus, for those few disappearances that had been investigated, she had stayed off the radar.

The mistake they had made was that she'd taken no one by force (though it would have been easy); she had coaxed and complimented until they walked into her snares willingly.

"Madam? Please, just a few questions."

They knew she was home. They had probably already spoken to her neighbors who told them she almost never left.

"Yes? Hello?" Tanja replied finally, as if just hearing them for the first time. "I'm sorry, I don't hear well. I'm coming now."

Tanja opened the door, trying to manufacture a look of confusion and fright, one she thought would fit the stereotypical expression of an old lady who was being confronted by police. On the stoop, in a row, were a man and two women. One of the women wore the trappings of a police officer, like the man, and the other was an identical copy of the girl Tanja had bound in the back room.

Tanja could feel her eyes widen slightly and her throat seize, and she suspected the police officers would have noticed it too.

"Hello," Tanja said, "I'm sorry for the fuss and stunned look I must have shown. I don't recall the last time I've had visitors here."

The male officer, who was clearly the senior of the two, smiled politely. "It's fine, ma'am. I'm not sure if you heard what I said behind the door..."

Tanja shook her head.

"...but we are looking for a woman who disappeared recently. About a month or so ago. I am Officer Durani and this is Officer Noor." He pointed with his outstretched hand to the woman beside him. "And this is Jiya." He nodded past the female officer. "We are looking for her sister."

The young girl averted her eyes sheepishly and looked to the stoop, as if embarrassed to be harassing someone over her missing twin.

"My heavens," Tanja whispered, perhaps a bit too dramatically for what little she ostensibly knew about the disappearance. "I am so sorry dear." Tanja looked back to the officer. "How can I help?"

The officer shrugged. "We're just asking people in the neighborhood if they may have seen Prisha—that is her name. Any time over the last month or so. She is Jiya's twin. They look as identical as I have ever seen sisters look."

Tanja held her face still, not sure what reaction this revelation should elicit. "How would I know then if I just haven't seen Jiya?" *Shut up*, she thought. *You don't have to be clever just to boast.*

The male officer cocked his head slightly. "Have you seen Jiya recently?"

Tanja opened her eyes wide, sympathetically, and then felt the glisten of tears coat her eyeballs. She willed the moisture from her ducts further until one escaped down the middle of her left cheek.

"I don't know," she said, her voice cracking on the last word. "I wouldn't know. I don't even remember any of the names you've just told me. I..." she swallowed and took a deep breath. "I forget so many things now. I'm sorry."

The source's twin—who Tanja remembered very well was called Jiya—spoke. "I am very sorry to have upset you Ms. And I am sorry for your condition. I know it well. It has plagued my family too. My father has been consumed by it for over two years now. He is quite ill. No longer able to function much at all."

Tanja smiled weakly, signaling appreciation for the attempt at empathy. "I am sorry to hear about your father."

"Thank you."

"I wonder how he can function in the central markets with such a condition."

The two officers looked at each other and then over to Jiya.

"He no longer works in the markets, Ms., but he used to. He used to be quite prominent there." The pace of Jiya's sentences increased. "Why did you think he worked in the central markets? Do you know him? Do you know my father?"

"What?" Tanja began to shake now, desperate to cover up her grave error. She'd slipped—badly—it was the kind of mistake that she would have scoffed at had she heard it told in a story. If she hadn't been a suspect in the disappearance of this girl's sister a minute ago, she almost certainly was now.

"You asked how he could have worked in the central markets."

"What is your name, ma'am?" Officer Noor, the female officer, asked, disrupting any further attempts by Tanja to demonstrate her mental incapacities.

"I...why do you want to know that?"

"Please ma'am, just answer the question."

"It's um...I don't..."

Tanja placed her hands flat against her face and began sobbing into them, muffling the sounds only slightly. She waited for one of the three people at her door to say something, if not in consolation, at least words to indicate they would give her some time, perhaps come back later when she was more composed. But no one made a sound.

Tanja finally lowered her hands and immediately noted that the expressions of the officers had not changed. Jiya had returned her gaze to the pavement below, but the sheepishness in her expression had disappeared and was replaced by something closer to indignation.

"May we come in, ma'am?" Officer Durani asked. "And have a look around your residence?"

Tanja could sense the tension of the officers' facial muscles and the slight change in their body angles, which were now in a position slightly sideways and straddled. There was nothing left to be done in terms of deterrence. She had become sloppy, cocky, and was now only a word or two away from arrest. If she agreed to the search, everything was over. Once the officers passed through the front threshold, they wouldn't leave until they found the girl. And it wouldn't take long. Her source would hear them from behind the wall and would immediately begin to scream, and within seconds, Tanja would be face down on the floor of her living room.

But Tanja knew of her rights. She had been in this land far longer than any of the people standing before her had been alive. They had no right to enter her home without a search warrant, and as this was just a canvass, they wouldn't be able to produce one of those for at least another three or four days. This was the Eastern Lands, after all, and everything here, court matters included, moved like a glacier.

She narrowed her eyes at the male officer and flattened her distressed lips into a cold flatness. "No," she said. "You may not."

The officer held Tanja's stare for longer than she would have thought possible, and then nodded, looking over at his partner before returning his eyes back to Tanja. "We will likely be back before the day is done. I would suggest you not go too far."

Tanja bowed a half-nod. "Good bye, Officers Durani and Noor," she said, mocking them by her power of recall, showing that it was still fully intact. "And good luck finding Prisha, Jiya. I'll be sure to keep an eye out for her."

Jiya looked at Tanja, a combination of fear and surprise in her eyes. Tanja smiled at her, wide and full, showing the full breadth of her mouth and the jagged teeth bursting within.

Jiya covered her mouth with both hands and gagged. She looked towards the officers in a panic, but they were as transfixed as Jiya. The girl backed slowly off the stoop, her fingers now pressed against her lips, and shuffled rearward to the splintered road before turning and breaking into a full dash away from the house.

Tanja noted that Officer Noor had averted her eyes for just a moment at first, but the older Durani kept his head and eyes stern.

"If there's nothing else then," Tanja said, "I'll be saying goodbye."

She closed the door and stood motionless for a beat, and then put her eye to the peephole, watching the officers linger for a moment before finally retreating. Officer Durani looked back at her house one last time and scribbled a final note on his pad.

She was done here. The risks had now become critical. The officers wouldn't be back today, and probably not for a few days after. But they would come eventually. She would give herself the remainder of the week and then set out for the docks. She didn't know the ship schedules, but if she had to wait a few days at the harbor until the right liner was leaving, then that is what she would do.

But there was still some final business to attend to here. She had come too far with this batch to simply discard it, and she had no intention of foregoing the bungaru venom. It was the ingredient of the future, the portion of the recipe that now rendered her magical elixir palatable and ready in weeks instead of months.

The source.

Tanja was now armed with new information now about her. Not much, but enough to be useful. She had lied to Tanja about her father working in the markets. And it was a lie that had tripped up Tanja and nearly cost her her freedom.

For that lie, the source would help Tanja out of this conundrum. And if she couldn't, she would pay.

Chapter 14

ANIKA WAS NOW WITHIN a mile of the Urbanlands city limit, but she could smell her imminent arrival two miles earlier. And it wasn't just the garbage and filth of the factories that was the indicator—she could smell that several miles back, as, she was told, could everyone who entered the Urbanlands—it was the people.

There were so many people.

She hadn't fed since the young officer behind Pavel Delov's cabin, but despite the time that had passed and the effort she had exerted, her hunger continued to stay at bay. It was a good sign, she knew, and one that suggested the voice at the warehouse was being truthful. Her craving was subsiding.

Anika hadn't even considered using Randall for sustenance. Even if she had been in the throes of thirsting, the driver's blood smelled rancid, diseased, and polluted with chemicals and alcohol. But more than that, she didn't want him to be rendered useful in any way. She wanted his death to be as dreadful and unimportant as the life he seemed to have led.

Anika continued walking the shoulder until she arrived at an exit sign with a diagonal arrow pointing right, and the word "Urbanlands" beneath it. She followed the curve of the exit road for another half-mile until she was off the vast

nothingness of the Interways and in a more municipal setting, with homes and businesses scattered about. In the distance was an array of lights fanning off into the distance.

She followed the lights, passing several deserted buildings that sat on the fringes of the exit, until eventually she
came to a river and the abutment of an arch bridge. Anika
saw a stairway and ascended it, and then began walking
across the bridge on a walkway built for pedestrian crossings.
The walkway struck Anika as luxurious, amazed that there
was a population large enough to warrant its own special
crossing just for strollers.

Anika reached the crown of the bridge when something
in the distance, just to her right, caught her eye. She turned
quickly and was instantly met by a large billboard that had
been positioned atop an old warehouse. On the billboard
was the painting of a sprawling gothic building and two
young adults who both wore smiles of satisfaction. Next to
the picture were the words "**University of the Urbanlands.
Learn to *Live*.**"

Anika put a fist to her mouth, stifling any sounds of
excitement that might erupt involuntarily. She couldn't believe what she was seeing. The billboard didn't mean she was
at her destination, not quite, but she was obviously getting
close and was headed in the right direction.

Anika tallied the billboard as an omen and a triumph,
and the fact that she had reached this far in her journey was
an achievement. But from here she still didn't know how to
get to the campus or the surrounding housing complexes of
the university. She would find it eventually, she assumed, but
she would rather not spend the next day and half wandering

the streets like a vagrant. The Urbanlands wasn't the largest city in the New Country, but it was big enough.

She walked down the haunch that formed the far side of the bridge, and there she saw another, more specific sign that read: "*Welcome to the Urbanlands.*"

She had officially made it. Finally.

She let the tips of her fingers slide across the city limit sign as she stepped off the abutment, and then, intuitively, headed into a city park that had been constructed at the border along the river. In the moonlight, Anika could see a small strip of sandy beach stretching for about twenty-five yards along the water. Anika strolled down to the water's edge and then stood for a moment, clearing her head as she stared back across the water, her eyes focusing on the road from which she had just come.

She reflected on the last couple of days and on her journey from the Back Country. There had been one casualty along the way: Randall. Of course, that was one more than Anika would have preferred, but unlike with the young officer, Randall's death was an inconvenience, not a tragedy. The truth was, his death was a net gain for the Northlands.

As she eased her mind, the knowledge that she was in the Urbanlands finally set in fully to Anika's mind. There were people everywhere here. She was surrounded on all sides by them.

But there were none here in the park.

A wave of suspicion suddenly washed over Anika, paranoia that she was being watched. She looked around, expecting to see a System officer perhaps, his gun pointed directly between her eyes.

Instead, she saw a sign posted on the side of the bridge warning that the park closed everyday at sundown. There was no one in park because it was closed.

Anika took a deep breath and tried to relax again, inhaling the multitude of smells coming from the river, which she guessed was the Dreta. Anika noted the odor had a familiar resemblance to the lake behind the Morgan property, and a pang of wistfulness struck her.

She did miss her home, and Gretel and Hansel, of course, but there was also a growing exhilaration in Anika as she stood alone on this bank in the Urbanlands. She was suddenly flooded with memories of the Old World and the Koudeheuval Mountains, of Noah and Oskar and of her dire journey to the lost village of the Aulwurm elders.

Anika slowed her breathing, trying to lower her heartbeat, and as she went to take in another gulp of air, she heard a grunting sound coming from somewhere behind her, maybe twenty or thirty feet away. Anika pivoted toward the sound, which seemed to be coming from a small building on the border of the park.

"Hello?" Anika said sternly, having already narrowed her gaze as she walked purposefully toward the sound.

She was halfway to the building when a frantic shuffle accompanied the grunting noise, a shuffle that sounded like sheets of paper being gathered into a pile with a rake.

Anika slowed her pace only slightly, and within seconds she was standing in front of a building with the word 'Maintenance' written on the door.

Anika grabbed the door handle and turned it, but it was locked. "Who's here?"

Anika stepped around to the right side of the building and then craned her neck forward and to the left as she made her way to the building's rear. Her eyes took a moment to adjust to the darkness behind the maintenance shed, and in that moment, something tall and spindly sprinted away from her. Anika's eyes adjusted quickly, as if triggered by necessity, and she could see now that the sprinter was a man. He was trying to flee, running away from her toward the bridge.

Instinctively, Anika dashed in the direction of the man and caught him within seconds, grabbing him by the back of his shirt collar with her left hand. With the fingers of her right hand, she gripped the front of the runner's throat and then dug her feet into the soft, damp park grass, effectively braking her run instantaneously. The abruptness of the move, along with the runner's momentum, caused the man's body to become airborne, rising a few inches of the ground before slamming back to the turf.

Anika was immediately on top of the runner with a knee in the middle of his chest. She cupped a hand across his mouth and then scanned the area like a cheetah mother after a kill, looking for the approaching lion or cackle of hyenas.

"Who are you?" Anika asked, staring down into the man's eyes, which were wide and filled with terror. He was younger than Anika, though the lines on his face were those of someone who had lived a life of hardship, and judging by the build of his chest now pinned beneath her knee, he was emaciated.

The man groaned, shivering his head in a motion of denial, but which Anika soon understood was a signal that he couldn't speak.

"Don't scream," Anika said calmly, and then released her hand from his mouth. "Who are you?"

The man squinted in confusion. "What does that question mean? Who am *I*?"

Anika let the rebuttal linger in the air, saying nothing as she held the man's eyes firm. During this short interlude, she assessed her hunger and her desire to feed. If she did need to eat, she wouldn't get a better opportunity than this in the Urbanlands.

But the desire wasn't there. Despite the meat below her, literally in her clutches, her instinct to feed hadn't emerged.

"I am nobody," the man said, and for the first time Anika heard the accent. It didn't sound exactly like that of the people of Jena, but it was close.

"You're from the Old World."

The man nodded.

"Why are you here?"

"I sleep here. Just in the night. I don't bother no one. I leave before the day. You are police?"

Anika frowned and shook her head.

"Then why *you* are here? Is no one after dark allowed in here."

"I wasn't asking, 'why are you in the park?' I meant, 'why are you in the New Country?'"

The man snickered and shook his head again. "I don't know. Why is anyone here?"

Anika considered the question earnestly.

"Can I get up now? I am having trouble with my breath."

Anika took her knee from the man's chest and stood quickly, reflexively taking a step back, keeping beyond striking distance in the event the man suddenly went on the offensive.

But the man rose slowly from his back and dusted himself off, and then winced as he began rubbing the back of his neck where he thumped against the ground. He squinted at Anika, a mixed look of confusion and intrigue as he honed in the dwindling light of the moon. "You are from the New Country too."

"No. What? Why do you say that?"

"I can see it. It is in your cheeks and body. It is, how you say it? Lithe?"

Anika touched her tongue to her teeth and she felt a surge of blood rush to her face and extremities. She was prepared to tear the man apart if he moved an inch towards her. His observation didn't sound sexual, at least not in context, but Anika was hyper-poised now, and suspected she would be until the day she died. For the rest of her days, comments from strange men about her body would be met with readiness.

But the memory of Anika's strength certainly still stung within the man's chest and throat, and, seemingly oblivious to Anika's growing fury, he said, "You no sound like it, but you are from there, eh?"

"Aren't we all?"

"Yes, but you are close to that land."

Anika let the man study her eyes for a beat, and then she changed the subject. "The university. Do you know where it is? At least the general direction?"

The man held Anika's eyes for a moment longer and then nodded once. He turned and walked down to the beach and

Anika followed. When she arrived behind him, he turned down the river, away from the bridge, and pointed to the modest skyline that spanned the horizon. "You see that tallest building?"

Anika nodded.

"Is not that one, but is just on the other side. Maybe one mile past it. Other side of the city. From here is twenty blocks—maybe less—to that building. And then one mile past."

"Why do you know that?"

"I go there sometimes. Is far, but nice there. Sometimes I read books in the library."

Anika smiled as she held the building in her gaze. Twenty blocks plus a mile. She could do that. And in the darkness of the night and early evening, she could probably avoid having too many encounters along the way. "Thank you," she said. "What is your name?"

The man lifted his shoulders and chest proudly, standing as if addressing a superior military officer. "I am Adis. Adis Kokot."

Anika smiled widely now, and for the first time since meeting him, her eyes softened on the man. "Thank you, Adis. I want you to have this."

Anika pulled Randall's wallet from her pocket and opened the billfold, taking out the cash inside. "It isn't a lot, but it should buy you a few meals."

Adis looked at the money like it was fairy's gold, eventually taking it in his hands as gently as if he were receiving a newborn baby. "It should," he said humbly. "Thank you."

Anika walked from the park, leaving Adis sifting through his windfall, and headed in the general direction of where he had pointed, all the time keeping the river on her right. She walked a full four blocks, passing nothing but abandoned commercial buildings and run down apartments, before she eventually arrived at a wide street that was lined on each side with a variety of stores and restaurants.

The day had made the transition from late night to early morning—Anika reckoned it was not quite five o'clock—so most of the establishments had been closed for at least a few hours. But the streets weren't entirely deserted, and as she looked the length of the street and chronicled the sidewalks, Anika could see a few isolated groups of people still milling about.

The Urbanlands.

To this point, Anika's knowledge of the place was only conceptual. She had never set foot inside their limits until today, and almost all of what she knew about them had come from her father. Every month when Anika was a girl, he would take at least one trip into town. She had never really understood the purposes of the trips, but the ostensible reason given was "For supplies and things." It sounded reasonable at the time, especially since he always came back with treats and other little treasures for Anika and her brothers. But as Anika got older, she suspected the jaunts were mainly to do with a woman.

In any case, secret lover notwithstanding, her father's opinion of the Urbanlands was like that of most of the citizens in the Back Country: it was dirty, expensive, and the people were as ill-mannered as any on the planet.

Based on these opinions, Anika had never felt the desire to come and see the place for herself, and as she stood now watching the various groups of men loitering before her, she realized that had she not died and been resurrected by a witch's magic potion, she never would have made it. The funny twists of life and death.

A car passed Anika and she instinctively moved to her right and off the sidewalk, sidling through the row of border hedges that lined the pavement. Thus far in her short journey, she had been able to avoid any main thoroughfares, and the buildings and trees along the walking paths had provided adequate cover. Now that she had reached this shopping district, however, she was going to have to enter the fold of streets. She was going to have to cross the paths of other humans.

Ahead of her, Anika could see that, of the seven or eight cross streets in front of her, there were three that were still fairly well lit at this hour. This indicated to her that these were the busiest areas of town, and her instinct was to get to one of those areas as quickly as possible. Then, once she was past those blocks, she would have only a few more to traverse before finally exiting the downtown area entirely. Beyond those final streets, she would be in the clear of the city and, hopefully, make it easily to the university campus.

Between Anika and the illuminated blocks, however, were three under-lit blocks that still needed to be navigated. She choose the right side of the street, avoiding a small group of three men who had huddled on the corner on the opposite side and seemed to be in the process of finishing up some type of illicit business. They paid Anika little attention as she walked past them, and Anika let out a sigh of relief.

She reached the last of the dark streets, where, just around the corner, she encountered another group of men. This group was only a few yards from Anika, and they stared her down curiously as she walked past them. Anika didn't turn towards them, but she could tell they were older and probably harmless. Nevertheless, Anika picked up her pace just slightly to be sure.

Anika reached the first corner of the heavily lit streets, and as she looked down the length of the cross street, she saw several more people, late-nighters who apparently had found an establishment that had stayed open late, or else they had brought the party to the street themselves. Despite their obvious intoxication, the signs of life comforted Anika.

She passed the third and final illuminated block, but as she entered into the last of the downtown blocks, she nearly crashed into a woman who was in the process of ashing her cigarette, laughing as she was finishing what was some kind of funny story or joke.

The woman was one of four who seemed to be completely out of place in this setting, standing idly and talking.

But as Anika took in the full scope of the scene, she immediately saw that each of them was wearing grossly inadequate clothes for the weather. Or any other weather for that matter.

Anika stepped back and apologized for the near miss, and as she did, she further noted that three of the women were old enough to be the fourth's mother.

This wasn't her business, she thought, and turned to resume her walk, lowering her head slightly as she plowed ahead.

"Hey!" One of the women yelled, and Anika knew from the direction of the sound and pitch of the voice that it had come from the youngest girl.

Anika ignored the call and kept walking, but then she could hear the click of heels behind her, striding purposefully at first before transforming into a steady trot.

"Hey, lady! Come here a minute. I just want to talk to you?"

"Leave her alone, Bibi." The command of one of the older women was uninspired and perfunctory. "How many times do I have to tell you? Women don't need to pay for it."

"They do if they want me," the girl called back, playful and challenging in her tone. She was running now and was right behind Anika.

Anika stopped and turned. Instinctually, she placed her hand over her mouth, hiding the teeth that had erupted from her gum line. She waited a moment for them to recede and then asked, "What do you want?"

The girl—Bibi—grinned at Anika, and then dropped her eyes and gave a dramatic once over, dipping her shoulders back as she silently evaluated Anika's body. "I think you know what I want."

Anika felt the aggression building, but acted the role of the stern prude. "Leave me alone, young lady."

Bibi laughed. It was the condescending laugh of teenagers. "Why? Don't you like the looks of me?"

Anika sighed, as if regretful that she was taking the bait of the question. "You're very pretty. Too pretty for this, frankly."

Bibi shrugged. "It's just temporary."

Anika nodded and raised her eyebrows doubtfully before turning to restart her trek. Even this brief interlude was too much time. The sun would be rising soon.

"You don't believe me?" Bibi had stopped following Anika, and was now calling after her from behind. "Well you don't know me. You don't know shit. Piss off."

The girl's voice was becoming farther away with each step Anika took, and she was glad to have escaped the encounter having only sustained a moderate verbal barrage.

"You're pretty too," Bibi called, now yelling from a distance, "from the neck down."

Anika couldn't help but smile at that.

"What the hell happened to your face? You look just like that bitch witch that got her head blown off by Gretel!"

No conscious thoughts entered Anika's mind as she spun on her heels, stopping with precision so that her body was now facing Bibi in perfect alignment. She pushed her head forward just slightly, slowly, and then lowered it to shoulder level like a panther in a sea of tall grass. The measurements of distance and direction processed automatically, and Anika inhaled first before breaking into a full sprint toward the young prostitute.

In less than four seconds, Anika had Bibi's arms in her hands, gripping her at the biceps as she carried her for several yards before pressing the girl's back against the brick façade of a restaurant. The young whore's feet weren't quite touching the pavement as she dangled next to a large window with the word 'Coffee' painted across it.

"What did you say?" Anika whispered, her lips brushing against the girl's chin.

"Get off me you goddamn ugly bitch!"

"Why did you say that to me? What do you know about Gretel?"

"What? Gretel?" The girl sounded sincerely confused. "That's what you want to know? That's what's gotten you so piss mad? What the fuck is wrong with you?"

"Tell me," Anika growled.

"Let her go, patchy."

The voice came from Anika's right, and as she turned toward it, she instantly saw the gun. The three older prostitutes were now standing in a line, ten or so feet away, with the two on the ends just a step or two back. The middle woman, the one who had spoken the command, was holding the weapon.

"She didn't mean nothing by the insult," she reasoned. "She's young; you remember how we were." The woman gave an earnest grin after this quip.

Anika liked this woman instinctively. She hoped she wouldn't be forced to kill her, but the gun was a problem.

"I'm not insulted," Anika said. "I just want to know what young Bibi knows about Gretel."

The woman scoffed. "Everybody knows about Gretel, honey. Now let her go."

Anika lowered Bibi down and released her grip slowly. She took a step back.

The girl shook her arms out and grimaced at Anika, looking Anika up and down again, but this time with disgust. "What the fuck is wrong with you?" she repeated, though less rhetorically than earlier,

"I'm sorry. I...I am. I don't know why I lost myself like that."

Anika knew she'd erred in her reaction, but she hadn't much choice. Instinct had taken over. Still though, her goal had been to pass through the downtown area unnoticed, and she had certainly failed in that.

Anika apologized again, backing away slowly as she did, and then turned face and started on her path out of the center district. She was only a few steps on her way when Bibi called out, "I see her almost every day, you know?"

Anika stopped and closed and opened her eye in one long blink. She sighed and then turned around slowly. She stood in place this time, lowering her shoulders as she shoved her hands in her pockets.

"I don't know that much about her though. Other than the stories everyone knows. I don't think I've ever actually spoken to her other than to say 'Good morning.'"

"You see her every day? So you're a student then? At the university?"

Bibi nodded. "She's in two of my classes. I haven't seen her this week though."

"Do you know her friend Petr?"

Bibi grinned. "Friend? I'd say they're more than that."

"You do know him then." The adrenaline was firing in Anika, but she fought the effects, keeping her demeanor relaxed and loose. Adrenaline had its place, but it wasn't going to get her anywhere in this conversation.

"He's in one of the classes I'm in with Gretel. So, no, I don't really know him, but I know who he is."

"Do you know where he lives?"

Bibi shrugged. "No. Does it look like I'm active in the campus community? I have a shit-stained apartment down here with my sister and I take a shuttle into classes."

Anika frowned. "Sorry."

"But it's not really a mystery. If he lives in the student housing complexes, than he has to live in the Ferns."

"The Ferns?"

"It's what they call the boys' housing. That's not really the name, but everyone calls it that."

Anika was captivated by this revelation of Bibi's. She knew of Gretel and Petr. She had classes with them. This accidental encounter—with an Urbanlands prostitute—now seemed meant to happen. Still stunned by what she was hearing, Anika began walking towards her.

"Hey, hey, hey," the pistol-wielding woman warned, patting her pocket where, presumably, the gun now rested. "Take it easy there, Ms."

Anika looked at the woman confused. She had already forgotten about the gun and the recent aggressive encounter.

"There's too many men I'd rather shoot, so don't make me waste a bullet on you."

With her memory of the standoff now refreshed, Anika nodded and stopped in place, holding up her hands submissively. "I just want to know how to get to The Ferns. Is it close to the main campus?"

Bibi looked sideways at Anika, and a glow of suspicion clouded her eyes. "What do you want with Petr and Gretel?"

"I'm...I know them from the Back Country."

"Really? You're from the Back Country?" Bibi's eyes lit up with wonder. "Were you there when it happened? When the witch kidnapped and killed all those people?"

Anika shivered at the questions. "I...didn't hear about any of it until after. Just like everyone else."

Bibi studied Anika's face as if trying to judge the sincerity of the answer. "So why are you here again?"

"I was caring for Petr's grandmother. She's become ill and he needs to come home. I came to pick him up and, well, my car broke down. It got me most of the way though. It started puttering less than a mile to the exit for the Urbanlands, and then conked for good as I was getting off. Tow came, but the garage won't be able to get to it for a couple of days."

Anika feared she was over-explaining, but she had formed a version of this story over the course of her voyage, and so far, to her ears, it was sounding reasonable.

"Anyway, it's urgent he be at home with her. She's been calling for him. He should be expecting me; Anika was to have called him to let him know that I was on the way to get him."

"Anika? Really? You know Anika Morgan?" There was reverence in Bibi's voice that warmed Anika.

"Of course. That's Gretel's mother. I know her rather well."

"So you're walking to the college?" one of the other ladies asked. "From the Interstate? Honey, that is too far of a walk for a woman at this time of night."

Anika smiled, "I know that now. But I didn't see any cabs."

And you won't after midnight," Bibi said. "But it's a slow night. Like most. And I've got classes this afternoon, so I'm heading back to my apartment to sleep. If you like, I can take you by The Ferns."

Anika agreed to the offer with a nod, and within minutes she was out of the lights of the streetlamps and riding in the passenger seat of a small sedan. The car was clean and appeared to be new. Anika didn't know Bibi's whole story of how she ended up trading sex for money, but she was beginning to believe that it really was going to be only temporary. She would pray for it.

In less than ten minutes, the car crossed over the street that led into the boys' campus housing, and Bibi stopped the car about twenty yards down the road. On the horizon, Anika could see the orange burst of the sun flooding the clouds like lava. Morning had finally come and she had reached her destination.

"There's a guard gate that all cars have to pass through, but I don't have a placard. Otherwise I'd take you in."

Anika had already spotted several options along the perimeter where she, as a pedestrian, could enter quite easily. She'd need to get going though, before the sun rose fully. "I'll work it out. Thanks for the ride, Bibi."

"No problem."

Anika stepped out and began to close the door.

"When you find them," Bibi said, just as Anika was shutting the door. "Petr and Gretel. Please let know that, even though I don't know them, I...I don't know... I think they're pretty special. At least they seem that way. I think most of the students here think they're strange, but that's just because they're scared of them."

Anika smiled softly. "I'll let them know." And then she added, "And Bibi, I do think you should consider quitting your night job."

Bibi scoffed. "I consider it every day. It's the quitting part that's hard. But I'll consider it harder. Good luck...hey, you never told me your name."

"Tanja. My name is Tanja."

Chapter 15

PETR ARRIVED BACK AT his apartment just after ten in the morning, having wrapped up his presentation only minutes before.

He had left the house early that morning, just before sunrise, and had headed to the library to do some final work. The library stayed open twenty-four hours, and since he hadn't been able to sleep for more than twenty minutes at a time during the night, he had risen to leave at the earliest reasonable hour. There was no sense spending his time pouting about Gretel when he could be using it to complete his project. He wasn't scheduled to meet his partners at the library until eight to go over the final production, but there was still plenty he could do on his own to prepare.

And the presentation had gone well, at least according to what his partners had told him. Petr couldn't remember most it; it had seemed like his portion was being presented in some type of auto-pilot. He was there, of course, speaking and pointing to graphs and numbers on charts that he had created, but it was like it was someone else standing at the dais.

He didn't care though. Not anymore. Not about the project or school or his commitments. It all seemed pointless now. He had honored all of those things, letting his integrity guide him, and what was left in him was a feeling of emptiness and dread. Gretel had been right about him: he was different from her. He was different in the way he went about his day, how he cared about being a good person, honoring his duties and oaths and considering what others thought of him. But he saw now that these differences didn't equate to goodness, they equated to weakness.

Gretel was gone. She was somewhere over the ocean now, her eyes and focus on a new life in the Old World, one that would begin fresh and without him.

And here Petr was still, proud and responsible, stranded in the world Gretel left behind. He didn't have the right to be surprised. She had given him warning, insisted that she needed to go alone, and then had waited for him to dive back into his honor of weakness so that she could leave without saying goodbye.

But the truth, Petr knew, was there was nothing he could have said back in the orchard a few days ago, or on the phone yesterday, that would have made Gretel stay. She was too special for Petr. He knew it and Gretel did too. He wasn't strong enough to be with her.

He opened the door to the house and walked inside. Thankfully, it was empty, and Petr reflexively put on a pot of coffee, not really wanting it but knowing he would be asleep in minutes without it. And he wasn't ready to sleep yet. He wasn't ready for the dreams that would come.

He sat on the living room couch with a weary plop and said, "What are you going to do, Petr?" and then repeated the words, this time nearly screaming in frustration. "What are you going to do?"

The ting of his words hung in the silence of the empty room, and just as the echo dissipated, a voice came from behind him, barely audible and at a distance. "I have an idea," it said.

Petr shot up from the couch and spun towards the voice, which seemed to be coming from the rear of the house. He walked towards the back door which was slightly ajar, and then opened it wide, putting his nose to the screen. He didn't see anyone.

"Hello," he called, clearing his throat, trying to sound in command, starting to doubt what he'd heard.

There was no reply at first, and then a rustle came from the row of hedges that ran behind the woodpile. Petr opened the screen door and stepped gingerly to the back porch. He squinted toward the hedges, and could see the outline of a dark figure.

"Who's there? Who is that?"

"Gretel's gone. Is that right?"

"Anika?"

The figure pushed through the hedges, stepping to the barrier of the woodpile, positioning herself behind the tallest part of the stack of logs. Petr registered that her positioning was not accidental.

"Oh...my god," Petr whispered, stepping backwards and slamming his back into the screen door.

Petr felt dizzy, his knees weak, and he put his hand against the porch railing to keep from falling.

Anika frowned but said nothing, and now, seeming to sense that Petr was no threat, walked in front of the pile and stood exposed. Her hair was stringy and matted, and her dark, bloody clothes were so tattered that the skin of her torso was exposed. Petr thought she looked like a rape victim.

"It *was* you on the phone the other night." Petr steadied his legs, but his voice was still barely detectable.

"It was," Anika said, speaking for the first time.

"Why...why didn't you tell me then? And how is it that you aren't..?" The questions flooded Petr now, and his mouth couldn't keep up. "And that was you I saw on the porch. The day after...How—?"

"That's a lot of questions to answer at once, Petr. I'll talk to you. I'll tell you everything, including why I'm here. But first, I need to know that you're alone."

Petr nodded.

"And am I right about Gretel. Has she left?"

"For the Old World. How did you know?"

"I didn't know. But I felt she was leaving. I sensed it the other day when you two were talking in the house."

"You were watching us?"

Anika nodded. "I was in the basement. I had just...returned. And I didn't know where to go or what to do. I still don't. Not exactly."

"I feel like I'm dreaming."

Anika ignored him. "Terrible things have happened, Petr. I've done awful things over the past week. Very awful. Things I will hang for. And should. But I think there's a way for me to—not make it right, I can never change what I've done—but at least make other corrections to the world."

"Corrections? What have you done, Anika? What are you talking about?"

Anika took a step forward. "I smell coffee."

Petr was confused.

"Your roommate left here an hour ago, maybe less. Will he be coming home soon?"

"I don't know. I think he has classes all day today. How do you know when he left? You were here when he was?"

"I was here at dawn. I was surprised to find that you weren't. Late night?"

Petr mildly resented the implication. "I left very early, and I've had a busy morning." Petr was feeling like the obvious questions were getting away from him. "How are you here, Anika?" he asked quietly, mystically, like he was hoping to uncover an ancient secret. "And how did you find me?"

"The second question is easy. You and Gretel are well-known, Petr. More well-known than you probably know or are willing to accept. And I already knew you were at the university; from there it just required a little persistence and luck. Not all of it good."

"So how about the first question then. Let's talk about that one. How are you here?"

Anika nodded. "Okay, Petr, but let's get that coffee first."

"IT WAS THE POTION OBVIOUSLY, but I think it may have been more than that."

Anika took a sip from her cup and stared out the sitting room window of Petr's house. The street out front was empty, and the overcast gloom of the morning made the scene look sad and sterile.

"And I think whatever remedy they gave me in the village, when I was back in the Old Country, also played a part in reviving me. Or resuscitating me. But I can't really know. I just knew I was dead. I was underwater, bloody and blind. I was dead." She stopped and took another sip, raising her eyebrows. "And then I wasn't."

Petr couldn't help staring. "Your head and eye...my god."

"Hansel is a hero. I was going to kill them, Petr. Both of them."

"You can remember how you were that day? Before? How can that be? That must be amazing."

"I wish I didn't. I wish I could scrub my memory until the day my car went off the Interways and I stumbled into the woods in the Northlands. But I can't. I remember it all."

"I'm sorry."

"But there's more I have to tell you, Petr. A lot more." Anika paused and stared contemplatively into her cup. "I'm in trouble, Petr. As I said, I've hurt people." Anika paused and looked away. "The potion didn't just bring me back from death, it ruined me inside. Those first two days of my resurrection, I...I had to feed. I had no choice. It was a draw unlike anything I've felt. Like the potion, but stronger. If that's possible."

Petr leaned back automatically, his hands folding onto his lap as his eyes began to scan the room for anything he could use as a weapon.

Anika nodded. "I know, Petr. I understand. You should protect yourself from me. You saw me before, at home, when I was in the throes of the potion. I was awful, especially towards the end, and you probably can't imagine me being worse than that. My mind was completely fogged and sick then. But my mind is healthy now. It's just that..."

"That you're a cannibal?"

Anika didn't flinch. "I suppose that's right. But not exactly. And it's getting better. The cravings. They're waning. Or I'm learning to control them. I don't know for sure. But I was told they would diminish over time and they seem to be doing that."

"Told? Who told you that?"

"That's part of the very long story. But I can't start it now. And I can't stay. They're coming."

"The System?" Petr guessed.

Anika nodded. "I've left a bit of a trail."

"They called here. They know about your phone call. They told me not to leave."

"I'm going to need you to break that order, Petr."

"What?"

"I'm leaving the New World. And not just because of The System."

"For Gretel?"

Anika shook her head. "No. I'm going to the Eastern Lands."

"The Eastern Lands? Why?"

"There's so much to tell, Petr. Too much. And I'll tell you it all if you need that. But only if you'll come with me."

"What? When?"

"Now. Today if possible, but by tomorrow for sure."

"Tomorrow!"

"We probably don't have even that long. I've come across a lot of people along the way here. I tried to keep low but things happened."

"I can't go to the Eastern Lands. I have school. I..." Petr couldn't think of another reason.

"What if I was going to the Old World?"

Petr frowned. He knew if that if the Old World had been Anika's destination he would have been far more interested in the offer. "But you're not going to the Old World."

Anika swallowed and shook her head. "No, I'm not. But where I'm going has everything to do with Gretel. And Hansel. And saving their lives."

"How do you know any of this? Where did all of this information come from?"

"That voice that told me about the Eastern Lands, it told me exactly who I was looking for. Her name is Tanja. She's Marlene's mother."

"What? Marlene's Mother?" Petr could hardly fathom such a being existed. Could ever have existed. "In the Eastern Lands? Why?"

"I don't know, Petr. She's probably lived on every continent in the world by this point. But she's there. I believe the voice is right. And she's a danger."

"The voice?" Petr's tone was doubtful, suspicious.

Anika nodded.

"Listen Anika, I believe that you heard what you heard, but—"

"I'm not psychotic, Petr. My mind is as clear as it's ever been. I can't explain how I know the voice is real, but it is.

And I'm going to the Eastern Lands to kill Marlene's mother." She paused. "And I need you to come with me."

Petr let the gravity of Anika's words settle and then asked, "Why?"

"That was also part of the voice's instruction."

"The voice mentioned my name? *Go find Petr Stenson?*"

"No, not by name. But it *is* you. It has to be. I figured that part out on my own. You're the only one I trust who isn't Gretel or Hansel."

Petr paused contemplatively. "Gretel's gone, so I guess I understand that conclusion. But why not Hansel?"

Anika shrugged as if the answer was obvious. "How could it be Hansel? He killed me, Petr. At least he tried to and believes he did."

"Won't he be glad that he didn't?"

"I don't know, Petr, but I've already spoiled Hansel's life as much as I'm prepared to. How could I show up at the Klahr's house—alive and not quite well—explaining that I want him to come with me to the Eastern Lands? I wouldn't trust myself to do that under any circumstances. And Mrs. Klahr would greet me at the door with a shotgun. As she should."

"But you'll ask me?"

"I need you, Petr. I'll need help to get where I'm going. I barely made it here, to the Urbanlands, and that was only coming from the Back Country."

Petr agreed that Anika's reasons for not asking Hansel to accompany her to the Eastern Lands were sound. If they were ever to have a relationship again, it would take years of slowly building up trust, and that would likely just get them to a normal level. A great adventure across the Great Ocean—only days after her death—was probably a bridge too far.

But there was more to it.

Petr guessed Anika wouldn't have asked Gretel to go with her either, even if she hadn't left for the Old World. The risk was too high, and Petr now believed Anika had no intention of coming back alive. The only way she would have the spirit to confront and kill the mother of Marlene is if she had nothing to lose. Anika loved Petr, he knew that, but she was still willing to put his life at risk to save those of her children.

And Petr was willing to risk his life too, though he wasn't ready to commit to Anika's proposal just yet. Despite her own confidence, Petr wasn't completely convinced of the soundness of her mind.

But the idea that Petr's doubt might contribute to Gretel's death was starting to sway him. If Anika was telling the truth, and there was someone named Tanja in the world somewhere who had her teeth bared and her sights on Gretel, Petr could never avoid that battle.

A car slowed and then stopped in front of the house, directly in view and Anika and Petr. Anika stood and scuttled back toward the door at the rear of the house, pausing at the threshold between the living room and the mudroom.

"It's Gil," Petr said, not sure exactly what that meant in terms of next steps. Could he trust Gil? He knew he could trust him with the typical confessions of friends, but this was different. According to Anika, herself, she was a fugitive, on the run from The System for murder. Multiple murders, if

Petr was reading between the lines correctly. And if that was true, news of such crimes would reach the Urbanlands soon. Even if Petr didn't tell Gil outright about why Anika was alive and standing in his home, he may have already heard about the corpses between here and the Back Country and could figure out the rest for himself.

"Is that the roommate?" Anika asked from the shadows of the mudroom.

"Yes."

Neither Petr nor Anika moved from their positions, both tacitly allowing the scene to play out as it would.

"Pete!" Gil called the instant he stepped through the door. He didn't look up and thus didn't see Petr sitting alone on the couch. He turned his back to Petr as he wiped his feet on the mat. "How did the thing go?" Gil called to the sky. He remained at the door, which was still open, and poked his head out for a moment, surveying the porch.

"Gil."

Gil whipped his head around. His body was still facing the opposite way and Petr thought he looked a bit like an owl. "Hey buddy." He chuckled. "What are you doing?" He turned fully towards Petr. "Or do I want to know?"

Petr frowned and then said immediately, "I need to know I can trust you."

Petr realized his words were a bit dramatic, but Anika was standing in the shade of the house just off the living room, and if Petr was going to bring Gil into the fold, he needed to get some promises on the record. Gil took the giving of his own word very seriously, and Petr intended to use that integrity to his advantage.

"Know that you can trust me? Of course. I'm actually a little offended by the question."

"I also need to ask for a favor. A big favor."

Gil left the door open and started toward the couch, peeking back over his shoulder once before sitting next to Petr. "What's going on, Pete?"

Petr didn't really know where to start, and he certainly couldn't go all the way back to the beginning of Anika's story. That was too much to put on his friend. He decided to start from where Gil got involved. "Remember the call other night, the one I got from The System."

"Yeah, of course."

"Remember how they gave the subtle threat that they would be coming here?"

Gil nodded.

"Well that's almost a fact now. They're going to be coming here. And they're probably going to ask some questions about certain things that have happened lately."

Gil chuckled again. "Well that's pretty specific."

"I'm purposely not being specific. The details will only be trouble for you."

Gil didn't challenge this.

"If they come...when they come, just tell them that this conversation, the one we're having now, was the last time you saw me."

"What?"

"Tell them you came home, like you just did, and that when you talked to me I seemed down. Tell them I mentioned my project or something. Just make sure it's based on things that The System can verify. Don't tell them I had a falling out with the Chess Club or the Campus Birdwatchers, because they'll find out quickly I was never in those clubs and then you'll be in trouble."

"Okay. And then what?"

"And then tell them I told you I was thinking about taking a break from school. And I seemed serious. And don't underestimate them, Gil. I know them. I know The System well. They're probably working on a warrant now. They're going to come, so have the story straight."

"What are you talking about, Petr? Is that true? The part about taking a break?"

"It's true enough. By tomorrow, I'll probably be gone for a while. Maybe a long while."

"What is going on, Petr?" The first sounds of distress laced Gil's voice.

"Who is she?"

The three words squashed the last part of Gil's question, dominating it into submission. The voice was young and feminine, and came from the opening at the front door.

Petr looked up to see Jana, Gil's prize girl from the other night; apparently, they were evolving into an item. She was looking past Gil and Petr on the couch and was focused on the back room.

And Anika.

Petr turned, praying Anika had ducked back further into the house, perhaps silently sneaking out to the backyard, repositioning herself amongst the woodpile or behind the hedges.

But she had done the opposite, and was now standing in the light of the room.

"Goddamn, Petr? Who is that?" Gil asked.

"My name is Anika. Anika Morgan."

Petr started to intervene. "Anika—"

"I'm here, Petr. There's nothing to be done now. I've been seen. There's no point being cryptic anymore." Anika's voice was cold, controlling; it was the cadence of someone who had diagnosed the problem and was now ready to remedy it.

"I thought you were dead," Jana said, nearly matching the iciness of Anika's words.

"I thought you were asleep," Gil retorted. He looked at Petr. "I didn't talk about what you told me the other night, Pete. I swear."

"It's okay. It wasn't really a secret or I would have said so. And I wouldn't have talked so openly about it in front of her." Petr looked at Jana now. "I thought she was dead too, Jana. And so did she."

"So did *she*? What the hell does that mean?" Jana kept her eyes locked on Anika. "Though I have to say, looking at your face, you do look like death may have paid you a visit."

"Jana!" Gil shouted, standing up and walking toward the girl, his gait aggressive and daring. She held firm, never glancing Gil's way as he approached.

"It's okay," Anika said, "she's right. But so is Petr. I did think I was dead. I should be. But I'm not. So here we are."

"That story sounds familiar," Jana said. "But that's not so unusual with the people in your family, is it? That witch was related to you, right? And *she* came back."

"This isn't quite the same thing."

"Isn't it?"

"No, it isn't."

Jana scoffed and shook her head, now looking at Petr. "I knew she shouldn't have come here. Neither of you should have come, but definitely not her. Not to this school. I knew your little girlfriend would bring trouble eventually, I just didn't think it would be this soon."

"Jana!" It was Gil again, and he looked poised to strike the girl.

"I know the whole story. I know all about the creepy magic she practices. Orphism."

Petr saw Anika's neck twitch at the word.

"The university was poisoned the second she stepped on campus. Back Country trash is one thing, but Back Country witch trash is—"

Anika's body was across the room before Petr's mind could register what was happening. When his brain finally caught up, Jana was pinned against the interior molding of the door jamb, and the color in her face was fading. Her smug look was unchanged, despite having a one-eyed woman's fist wrapped tightly around her throat.

"Anika, no!" Petr's exclamation was breathy and crackling, one of disbelief. "Please. Stop."

Anika released the girl, and Petr could almost see the fire in her eyes smolder and then die. She took two deep breaths and then stared toward the ground, not looking at Jana again as she walked back in the direction of the back room. She continued walking through the mudroom and out the screen door to the backyard.

Petr was defeated. Any doubts he had about not going with Anika to the Eastern Lands were now erased. He would be leaving with her tomorrow. "Are you okay, Jana?"

"Fuck you," Jana whispered, rubbing her throat, trying not to cough.

Petr turned to Gil. "There are no more ships leaving tonight. She—Anika—will just need to stay tonight. We'll leave first thing in the morning."

"Ships?" Gil asked. "Petr, where are you going? What are you leaving to do?"

Petr was exhausted. The lack of sleep combined with the emotional stops during the week—now culminating with the arrival of some undead version of Anika—had broken him. "It's too much, Gil. It's too much to tell. I need to go to sleep for a couple of hours. And you should probably stay somewhere else tonight. It's probably not safe as long as she's here. Maybe stay at Jana's?" Petr didn't really care, he was just giving fair warning. "But it's your house too, so I can't make you go."

Petr didn't wait for a reply, and he didn't go check on Anika in the backyard, but he knew she hadn't left the property. She had come all this way—killed along the way—to reach him. She was obviously committed to her final destination in the Eastern Lands. He would be joining her there. He would kill alongside her if necessary. He was tied up in the Morgan story for life. He'd always suspected it was so, but now he knew it for sure.

Petr went into his room and crawled into his bed, and, within seconds, he was asleep.

He didn't wake again until five hours later when The System broke down his door.

Chapter 16

TANJA WAS NEVER MUCH for torture.

It wasn't the inhumanity of pain-infliction that was off-putting to her, it was the impracticality of it. Torture was best used for extracting information; as a punishment, it simply left the body of the tortured beaten and bloody. And since, for the sake of her concoction, she needed her sources to be healthy, she had rarely used physical torture for penal purposes.

But there were exceptions.

Tanja opened the lid of a large wooden chest that sat at the foot of her bed and removed the top layer of blankets. She pushed her hands down through the strata of knick-knacks and random garments until, at the bottom of the chest, she felt the coarse texture of a large burlap sack, one that had been tied at the top by a single piece of string. She removed the sack and untied the bag, and then sifted through it until she found the two devices she sought.

She removed the instruments carefully, and, with one in each hand, she slid the door to the chamber open with her hip and shoulder. She entered the room without looking up, letting out a loud, animalistic wail as she walked past the source to the countertop at the back of the room. She had no interest in studying the nuances of an awakening source today. There were more pressing matters.

Tanja now stood next to the bed and waited until the girl's eyes were fully open and focused.

"A problem has developed," she said, "one which was preventable and unnecessary and which you played a part in fomenting. And due to this newly developed problem, some adjustments to our routine must be made."

The girl swallowed hard and looked at the device in Tanja's left hand. "What is that?" she asked, the drowsiness of the morning's soup mixture still rendering her groggy.

Tanja looked at her hand inquisitively. "This?" She held up the metal instrument as if seeing it for the first time.

The girl blinked and nodded.

The device was about a foot long and designed like a teardrop. At the top of the teardrop was a handle in the shape of a shepherd's crook, and that handle was attached to a long screw that ran through the middle of the teardrop. The teardrop itself was made up of four separate leaves that, when the device was closed, folded in around the screw.

"It's called the Pear of Anguish," Tanja said, and as she began to describe it, she placed the other device, the one in her right hand, down on the shelf behind her. With her right hand now free, she grabbed the handle and began to turn the screw slowly. "As you can see, when I turn this half-ring at the top, these lovely metal leaves begin to open like the bud of a flower. It takes only the smallest of turns to start the budding."

"What...what is it for?"

"I think you know what it's for!"

Tanja hopped once and then landed in a stoop like a wild cat, her face pressed into the source's so that their noses were now touching at the tips. Her eyes were wild and taunting, her teeth bared, glistening from the saliva brewing beneath her tongue.

"You can imagine, right?!"

Tanja stood straight again and then began to turn the screw again, this time maniacally, giggling with each rotation until the four leaves were stretched out around the screw in the middle. The tear-shaped device was now open wide like the talons of a falcon.

"If and when this becomes necessary, I will allow your input as to which orifice you would prefer. It's a bit gauche, I know, but it is quite effective in its utility."

The source was crying hysterically now, and Tanja continued to screw the Pear of Anguish open and closed for a full minute, laughing the whole while before finally closing the leaves fully and placing the device on the shelf next to the other, careful to leave it in full view of the source.

Petting the other device she asked, "Would you like to know what this one is for?"

The source closed her eyes and shook her head.

Tanja picked up the second instrument with both hands, rattling the metal chains that hung from it the way one would to taunt a baby or a dog. The device was a skeleton of iron and was structured in the shape of an open-framed helmet. The thin frames seemed to run in every direction and resembled the bridle of a horse.

Tanja held the device over her head for a moment before lowering it down over her face. She was now looking at the source through the openings in the metal structure. In front of her mouth, on the inside of the frame, was a hinged piece of metal which, when lowered, folded down in front of her mouth. It was currently in its upright position.

"It's called a Branks. Painless for the most part, though it could certainly get uncomfortable within a few days, and anything past a week could drive a person to madness. This," Tanja tapped the hinged metal piece, "is definitely the worst feature."

She folded the flat piece of metal down and wrapped her mouth around it, the iron bit stifling an impromptu giggle. She made a few muffled sounds in a variety of pitches to demonstrate the speaking difficulties the feature provided, and then took her mouth off the metal and said, "Once the bit is lowered on the tongue and the bridle is tightened, it's virtually impossible to talk. Muffled groans is about the extent of the possible sounds. The truth is, however, I haven't had much use for this device in eons, so I can't really remember how effective it is. I suppose we shall see."

"Why?" the source cried. "Why are you...I haven't done anything."

Tanja lifted the Branks from her head and placed it back on the shelf. "Haven't you?" she asked, her voice absent of all mischief or levity. Her words were deep and thundering now, as if formed in hell

"No!" the girl cried, "I haven't! What did I do?"

Tanja paused a beat and then said softly, "Tell me more about your father, Prisha."

Tanja used the girl's name purposefully, tossing it casually as a threatening puzzle, one the girl would need to solve quickly before she spoke her next sentence.

It was also a tip off, of course, a forewarning that Tanja's knowledge of the girl was more than she realized. It wasn't a trick—with the hope the girl would string together a tale of lies so as to justify Tanja damaging her—it was a threat, a method of intimidating the girl so Tanja could get what she really needed: a connection in the markets.

"I seem to recall you mentioning that your father's position in the markets was quite elevated. 'Respected' and 'persuasive' were the words I believe you used."

The girl closed her eyes and sighed, and Tanja knew it was a sign of resignation. She was accepting that her only play now was the truth.

The source opened her eyes and stared at the ceiling. "He was. He worked there his whole life. His station was everything to him. He took a lot of pride in his wares. He treated his customers in a way that no one else did during that time. He was fair and calm with them, and never tried to swindle or berate them. It is common practice now to treat the customers the way my father did, but not back then. I wasn't there, of course, but I have heard these stories of my father for my whole life."

Tanja wasn't very interested in this girl's admiration of her father, but she stayed quiet.

"He made a lot of money because of his practices, and before I was even born, he had claimed one of the most coveted areas in the Central Markets."

"Before *you* were born? Just you?"

The girl closed her eyes again and a tear dripped down the side of her face. "Me and my sister. My twin sister, Jiya."

"Go on," Tanja encouraged.

"A few years ago he began to forget the names of some of his customers. That may not sound like a treacherous thing, but for him it was. It was devastating. His memory, particularly with names, was one of the traits that had brought him so much local fame and respect. He never had to work at it or use tricks to remember, it was just a natural ability. But then it began to slip. After that, the rest went quickly."

"So what happened? Did he lose his station?"

The girl scrunched her face as if the question were ridiculous. "No, certainly not. I have a large family. My uncle took over at first and now my brother has assumed full management. Prisha and I help too. At least I used to."

"Give me the plot number of your family's station."

The look of terror in the girl's eyes exceeded even the one she flashed when the Pear of Anguish was displayed. "No! No."

Tanja smiled. "Young Jiya, I have no interest in harming your family. In fact, I have no interest in harming you. If I knew you could be trusted never to speak of your ordeal, I would try my best to keep you alive after the extractions."

"I can! You can trust me! I swear I'll never speak of it!"

Tanja laughed and shook her head. "I've heard this promise from more girls than you've met in your lifetime, Prisha. But this is just survival, dear girl, nothing else." Tanja cocked her head and gave a long blink. "But you should always hang on to hope. Now, about that plot number."

Prisha closed her eyes and shook her head.

Tanja smiled. "If you were to never tell me, how hard do you think it would be to find out? 'I'm looking for the station of Prisha and Jiya's family,'" she said, mimicking the

cadence and crackle of an elderly woman. "'Those two darling twins. Do you know which one it is?'" She erupted into
laughter and then stopped abruptly. "Don't make me use the
Pear this soon."

Jiya frowned. "It's 12A. The third station on Block 1."

Tanja nodded. "Excellent. Now for what I really need."

"I gave you the number."

Tanja waved the girl off. "My vendor has been slow and
unreliable in procuring some of the...materials I need. I've
been patient in the past, but my time here in this village is
about to come to an end. If you can find it in your heart to
help an old lady like me, this may be very good news for you
and your family."

"Yes," the girl nodded quickly. "Of course."

"It's to do with bungaru venom. Is your family capable of
procuring it?"

"It is illegal. No respectable vendor would sell it."

"That was not my question."

The girl's eyes opened wide now, searching her mind
for possibilities, and then she nodded. "My brother would
know."

"A bad boy, your brother? And he is now in charge of
your family's station?"

"Not that brother. A different one. And he's not bad.
Not anymore. But there was a time when he was. Now he
oversees the station only during the final daylight hours on
the weekends."

Tanja thought a moment, calculating where they were
on the calendar. "So he will be there tonight then?"

"I don't know. I don't know the day. And I don't even know if the station is running any longer since I've gone missing. I assume they're looking for me and have spent what resources they still have to find me."

Tanja suspected money had been spent to find Prisha, and the visit by the police and the sister certainly suggested they were still hopeful and active in the search. But Tanja also knew from experience that time marched on. Life continued. The ability to compartmentalize grief was a skill humans had developed over time in an effort to sustain themselves after tragedy struck. Besides, any family that was still holding out hope for their loved one's survival would need a way to finance a sustained search, and that often depended on keeping a thriving business alive.

"Tell me what I would need to get the venom from your brother. I need it tonight, and then all of this will be over."

The source inhaled and sighed. "You'll need money mostly, but on top of that, you'll need to tell the truth."

"What does that mean? The truth?"

"About what you're doing. About why you need it?"

"What are you saying, girl?"

"For the potion."

"What?" Tanja felt a pain in her stomach that she vaguely recalled from another lifetime. She was truly stunned, perhaps for the first time in decades.

The girl smiled and wrinkled her brow line. "I know what this is. I know why I'm here. Did you not know that I knew?"

Tanja was speechless.

"I've had a lot of time laying here to figure it out. It's Orphism. The potion."

"How could you—?"

"Most of the old people don't know of the stories yet, or if they do they don't believe in them. But I always knew they were true. You're one of them. You're one of the witches who seeks eternity."

Tanja was speechless.

"I know I probably don't survive this, and I'm slowly accepting that as the truth."

"No one does." To her own ears, Tanja sounded forlorn, apologetic.

"If you want the venom, if you must have it today, you will need to promise Garal that you will allow him into the story. You must promise to tell him of Orphism and, more importantly, a taste of the potion."

"I could never."

Prisha nodded. "You will or you won't, that will be up to you. But you must make him the promise. I have heard of the men who couldn't resist. Heinrich and Marcel. Officer Stenson."

Tanja remembered the Stenson name, and she assumed the others were from Marlene's story as well.

"Tell him. Promise him immortality. He will get it for you. Just don't harm him. He is good now. His wicked days are behind him."

"Why are you telling me this?"

"If I'm not to survive this, then I want your word that no one else in this village will be subject to what I've gone through."

Tanja had quietly terrorized the poor, bustling city for years, but it was all coming to an end after she finished with Prisha. The well was dry in this land, and thus she had nothing to lose giving her promise. "You have my word."

Prisha looked away and closed her eyes. "And no torture. Allow me the dignity of dying without screams of agony."

"That promise is still dependent."

Tanja lifted the Branks from the shelf and placed it on Prisha's head. The girl shook spastically, trying to keep her mouth away from the bit. But there was nowhere for her head to escape, and within seconds the witch had the bit in place and was tightening the frame of the bridle. The sounds coming from the girl were as deadened as Tanja had hoped and expected, and by the time she left the chamber and reached the front door of the house, she couldn't hear the girl at all.

If Prisha's search party showed up again, even if they entered with a search warrant, they would never know the girl was there.

Chapter 17

GRETEL LOCKED HER ARM in Petr's and put her head on his shoulder, grinning widely as she nestled into his neck, sighing contentedly as the two lovers sat in silence on the back slope of the Morgan property only yards from the lakeshore. She closed her eyes and scooted her hip into Petr's, moving in as closely as his body would allow.

It was late afternoon, summer, and as the night approached, the whistling of the crickets began to replace the chirping of the birds. There was no more perfect moment than this that Petr could have imagined.

A frog leapt fearlessly from the bank, awkwardly splaying its feet wide as it belly-flopped onto the surface of the water. The wavelet from the frog's impact rippled out toward the center of the lake, dying just a few feet from where the amphibian had submerged. Petr focused on that last moving spot on the water, and from there he saw a small carp leap toward the sky and flutter back. But, just before it touched the water on re-entry, something reached from beneath the surface and caught it.

The fish gaped in agony, at first in a struggle for oxygen, and then from the long, stringy fingers squeezing the life from it, shattering its fragile skeleton as the carp's eyes burst from its head.

Petr released Gretel's arm and stood.

"Come back, Petr," Gretel pouted. "Where are you going?"

Petr took two steps toward the water. Then a third. "Anika?" he said.

The murderous hand was back beneath the surface and the water was now calm, the ripples barely detectable. Petr took three more steps until his bare toes were touching the edge of the lake. "Did you see that?"

Petr turned back to Gretel, but she was gone from the hill.

"Gretel?"

Petr felt his heart rate swell and his face flush to red. Suddenly another splash erupted behind him and he turned back toward the water where two hands were now breaching the otherwise serene lake, this time in a panicked display of splashing and grasping.

Petr tried to scream for help, but he could manage to part his lips only fractionally, and soon a second set of hands appeared on the water, mimicking the first, as they too reached for the sky, begging for someone or something to grab them and pull them to freedom.

Petr attempted to move forward into the full lap of the lake, but his feet were stuck to the ground, encased in the mud beneath him.

"I'm trying," he cried. "I'm trying."

He reached his hands forward toward the drowning figures, able only to bend at his hips while his legs remained rigid, stretching his arms in desperation as far as they would go.

"Petr?" a voice called from behind him.

Petr stood tall again, turning to the voice, and there was Gretel again, this time standing only a few feet away from him on the shore. The right side of her face had been ripped from her skull, revealing the gruesome, smiling underskin of blood, muscle, and skeleton.

"Petr," she said calmly, girlishly, as if they were still cuddled on the hill together. "I need you."

Petr's feet were suddenly unfrozen from the bottom of the lake, and he took a step towards Gretel. But as he lifted his foot to take another, he was grabbed from behind at the shoulder.

Petr tried to run, but both sets of dying hands and arms were now wrapped around his neck and head and torso, effortlessly pulling him down to the water.

Petr didn't try to scream this time, and instead listened curiously to the sounds of the woodpeckers in the distance, becoming rapt by the birds as they pounded away at the bark of the maples. He felt peace as the arms folded in around him, and only the increasing noise of the woodpeckers was keeping Petr from fully enjoying his certain death.

The pecking got louder with each repetition, and soon it was a deep, thunderous banging, like the beat of a large, snareless drum.

Petr opened his eyes and seized on the inhale of a giant breath, holding it until he recognized the nightmare was over and he was back in his room.

But the thunder continued.

The door.

Petr was still fully dressed from the previous night, and he leaped from the bed, ran to the threshold of his room, and listened for the next wave of banging, trying to gauge the exact source and meaning of it. But there was no further wave. Instead, the aggressive pounding on his front door reached a crescendo, finally detonating in an explosion of jamb and frame and hardware, spraying the foyer with splinters and wooden shrapnel.

Instinctively, Petr stepped behind the open bedroom door, his back against the wall now as he hid from view of the intruder. They came in quickly, and based on the initial sounds of footsteps and voices, he gauged that there were three officers now in his home, forming a perimeter.

"System officers present! Any and all occupants of this house, come out slowly with your hands shown and empty!"

Petr considered his options, which were few and fleeting. The officers would be in his bedroom in a matter of seconds, and depending on the moods of Officer Zanger and his friends, a second or two after that he would be face down, zip ties binding his wrists, sniffing up the dust of his bedroom floor. They had tracked Anika here, that was obvious, and once they had the proof that she had come to find him, he would be arrested.

He made another calculation that was also now obvious: it was Jana. She had called The System and told them of her encounter. It was the only way they'd have acquired a warrant so quickly.

The window at the far side of the room was open wide, but for him to reach it, he would have to cross the path of the open doorway. He would be seen, but an attempt to escape was still a reasonable play. He figured he had nothing to lose, since he didn't suppose the officers would fire at him, and even if he was caught, he could explain that he thought he was in the midst of a burglary and was fleeing for his life.

With his decision made, Petr sprinted for the open window.

"Hey!"

Petr reached the opening and hopped up, planting his palms firmly on the sill, careful to avoid hitting his head as he leaned forward out the window.

His chest was already fully outside, and soon his hips and right knee were as well. Impossibly, he was almost free.

As Petr swung his remaining leg out, he felt a hand graze his foot, and then a solid grip formed around his ankle.

"Freeze, Petr!" a voice said from the doorway, signaling it wasn't the same officer currently holding his leg. "There's an officer right below you."

Petr looked down to the outside lawn and saw a female officer standing just off to his left; her legs were wide and her gun was drawn on him.

"Dammit."

"Easy, Petr. We just have some questions. Bring it back in."

Petr sighed and, defeated, began to push himself back to the bedroom. But before even his freed leg was back inside, the grip on his ankle released, and he heard an ear-splitting scream explode behind him, followed by, "Oh God! Oh no, oh God!"

"What the...?" Petr was still halfway out the window, and the frame was preventing him from turning to see what was occurring behind him.

But the screams of agony continued, and he suddenly felt ill

"What's going on in there?" the female officer asked, focusing on Petr, her eyes wide and terrified.

"I don't know."

She stood in limbo for a moment longer, wavering in her decision about whether or not to leave her post. She swallowed nervously and then dashed bravely toward the front of the house.

Petr thought of taking advantage of this new opening, of continuing through the window and running to freedom in the darkness of The Ferns, perhaps escaping for good, reuniting with Anika at the docks and then off to the Eastern Lands.

But his instincts held him in place, and, reluctantly, he pushed himself back into the bedroom. He was now standing back on the wooden floor, looking out through the window ruefully, keeping his back to the room. He sighed once, trying to slow his breathing to keep from hyperventilating, dreading what he would see once he finally turned around in the direction of the screams of suffering.

Petr pivoted slowly, and on the floor, only steps away, he saw two male officers, one of whom was writhing in pain as he pressed his left hand against the empty socket where his right arm had been ripped away, the gory mass of the stump spewing blood in every direction like a rogue fire hose. His eyes were broad, disbelieving, his face had already turned the ashen color of death.

Petr moved his gaze to the second officer who wasn't stirring at all, and Petr could see instantly that his neck was at an angle unnatural to a human, his head twisted in a three-quarter turn like a barn owl's.

Petr was paralyzed by the grisly scene, and he suddenly felt as if he'd been thrust into another horrible dream, one more terrifying than the nightmare from which he'd just awakened.

Petr looked for Anika—he knew instantly this was her doing—but she was nowhere to be seen.

"Help, Petr." The one-armed officer's voice was barely audible, his plea as meek as that of a hungry orphan, though relatively calm given his condition. Petr assumed this was Zanger.

"I'll get you help. But first try to stop the bleeding."

Petr unhinged the fitted sheet from his mattress and balled it as tightly as possible, trying not to look as he pressed the fabric against the man's stump.

"Help *her*, Petr." Zanger took hold of the sheet and then made a drowsy motion with his head toward the living room. "The woman who did this, she's going after Dian."

"Who's Dian?"

"The other officer outside."

Petr moved hastily into the living room to see the profile of Anika kneeling on top of the female officer, her teeth bared and her bloody hand held high above the officer's head with the tips of her fingernails pointing downward like medieval iron spikes.

"Anika, no!"

Petr rushed Anika, preparing to tackle her off the officer, but when he was at just the precise distance, Anika swung her right arm out like a wrecking ball, almost effortlessly it seemed, thudding Petr against the couch and over the arm to the ground.

Petr was up instantly, breathing heavily. "You can't, Anika! You can't kill anyone else!"

Anika kept her eyes locked on the officer. "I'll kill as many of them as necessary."

"This isn't necessary!" Petr caught his breath and tried to steady his voice. "You don't have to kill her. Let me help you. Isn't that why you came to find me? To help you through this. To help keep you on the path to save Gretel and Hansel?"

Anika stared back at Petr, and he could see the rage slowly seeping from her eyes, just as it had done with Jana earlier.

"Killing her won't help with that." He paused, ensuring the fury was over. "I'll come with you. To the Eastern Lands, or wherever your quest takes you. We can be at the docks before anyone knows we're gone. But you have to let her go. She doesn't deserve to die."

Anika stood slowly, keeping her eyes on the officer. "Don't move," she said, and then walked past Petr to the bedroom threshold. She stood for a moment and studied the scene on the floor dispassionately. "I saved you," she said, not looking back at Petr. "I saved you from them."

Petr had moved to check on the felled officer—Dian—who was unconscious but appeared to be alive and unharmed. "They weren't going to kill me," he said.

Anika looked back at Petr and frowned. "How could you know?"

Petr met Anika's gaze. "I know. I do."

"Yes? You do? Could you have been so confident about your father? And his intentions toward me?"

Petr dropped his eyes, silenced by a mix of defeat and embarrassment.

Anika let the jab settle and then said, "What do you want to do then, Petr?"

Petr thought a moment and said, "We'll go, of course. Tonight. You have no other choices now."

"And what about you?"

"I haven't done anything. Nothing that will warrant charges. Not until I help you. And I owe you and Gretel at least that. But I want to return here one day, and if we do this right, no one will know that I was your accomplice. At least they won't be able prove it. As far as anyone will suspect, you will have abducted me."

Anika thought for a beat and then nodded.

"But that means you can't ever come back, Anika. You know that, right? You won't be hanged. You'll be burned for what you've done. Tied tightly to a stake and burned alive, just like they did four hundred years ago. The Witch Punishments are back, you know? Ever since Marlene."

"I'd heard." Anika looked away, and for the first time Petr saw compassion and regret on her face. "But I don't care about any of that. I have a mission, Petr. And as is obvious, I don't intend to allow anyone to stop me."

"I understand. I truly do. But you *can't* kill innocent people, Anika. Even System officers. You can't."

"I will kill Tanja!"

Petr closed his eye and nodded. "If what this voice has told you is true, that she is kin to Marlene and has made some vow to kill you and Gretel and Hansel, then she is not innocent."

Anika stayed silent.

"I know you think Hansel and Gretel's lives are more valuable than those of these officers, and whoever else's life you've taken since your resurrection, but they're not. An innocent life is just that, and it must be protected."

"Hansel and Gretel *are* more valuable." Anika's anger had returned, but Petr stayed steely.

"They're not, Anika."

"What?" Anika's voice sizzled with contempt for Petr's statement.

"I love Gretel. She doesn't love me, but I love her. More than I love anything on this planet. And not like a sister or a friend, like...love. But I won't kill innocent men for her. I won't, Anika."

"You aren't me, Petr. You'll feel differently when you have children."

Petr shrugged. "Maybe. But that's not how I feel now. I won't help you if you won't promise me."

"I sometimes crave them, Petr."

"I know." Petr did know. Anika had used her children as the excuse, but her desire to kill was driven as much by her newborn instinct as motherly protectionism.

"It's getting better, but it still...hurts. I made myself the promise that it would only be System officers from now on, but once we're out of the New Country that won't be an option." Her eyes were pleading with Petr now. "What do I do?"

A groan came from Petr's bedroom.

Anika nodded toward Zanger, whose ashen color had turned to purple. He was dying. "What do we do with him? With all of them?"

"We'll call for help from the truck. I at least want to give him a chance. The rest of the scene we'll leave as is. We should go. I'll gather as many supplies as I can and then we're leaving. Leaving for a while."

"To the docks?"

"To the docks. And then first thing tomorrow, we'll leave for the Eastern Lands."

Chapter 18

TANJA WAITED ON THE fringes of the markets, watching the people come and go from Station 12A, the lot of them laughing and shaking hands with each other, as well as with the tall, substantial man standing behind the long table and mountains of wares. It was late afternoon, and virtually every other station had been closed down for at least an hour; but 12A bustled in the center of the district, the bright green and saffron colors of its flags enticing shoppers from every direction.

Based on his age and mannerisms, the man helming the station was almost certainly Garal, and he appeared from Tanja's distance to be as charming and amicable as Prisha had described her father to be, a quality that had apparently been passed down in the bloodstream.

The whole scene riveted Tanja, and though she was eager to approach the station, she restrained herself, and instead stood watching and wishing the interactions would go on forever, so impressed was she with the efficiency and ease of the store's trading.

Another full hour passed before the crowds finally began to thin, and, after an additional thirty minutes, as the young man was finishing his collection of the gorgeous, delicate stoneware and had moved on to the mounds of golden necklaces and bracelets, beginning his meticulous placement of them into their special trunks, Tanja approached.

"I am sorry, my dear," the man said without looking up, a smile beaming across his face, "but we have—finally—closed for the evening. Rest assured we will open again tomorrow, and I will look forward to seeing your kind face the very first thing in the morning."

"I was told you work only at the end of the day," Tanja replied.

The man smiled again, this time quizzically. "Yes, well, someone who is very close to me will see you then." And then he added, "*Who* told you this?"

Tanja smiled and shook her head, dismissing the question. "What are you doing tonight, Garal?"

Garal looked up at Tanja now, his smile narrowing along with his eyes, and for the first time, Tanja saw a glimpse of the young, troublesome side to which his sister had alluded. "Why?" he asked, skipping another inquiry about how this old woman knew of him and his personal information.

"I was told you could get something for me. Something that is...well...shall we say, rather difficult to acquire otherwise. Thus, if you were to be able to spare a few moments once you're all settled here, perhaps you could facilitate another transaction, one certain to be beneficial to us both."

Garal turned away from Tanja and resumed the nightly, and obviously tedious, job of clearing the station. "Well, madam, as I said, we will open again tomorrow. Deals can be made then."

"The deal must be with you, and you will not be here then."

"What do you want?" Garal hissed.

"Bungaru venom," Tanja answered calmly, not at all put off by Garal's aggression.

Garal held his look of disdain for a beat, and then smiled the friendly smile from a moment ago. The smile continued to broaden before transforming into a bout of hysterical laughter.

Tanja allowed the humor to run its course, noting the meanness with which it was laced, all the while maintaining a steady smile upon her own face.

"Bungaru venom? Is that it? And what would an elderly woman—not to offend, of course—need from bungaru venom. It takes but one drop in an open wound and you are no longer."

"Those are the words of someone capable of its acquisition."

Garal pursed his lips and raised his eyebrows.

"I'll need it tonight."

Garal laughed again. "Tonight? Oh, yes, of course. Perhaps I have some bungaru venom hidden in the bottom of my pockets. Perhaps stuffed in my ass." The smile disappeared again. "Please leave, madam. I won't ask you again."

"Can you get it?"

"You can't afford it," the man snapped.

"Can't I?"

Garal stared at Tanja intensely now, seeming to measure her in full for the first time. "Who are you? I've seen you in the markets before. Always alone. Shuffling mysteriously about."

Tanja moved in closely so that the lashes of her eyes were touching the tip of Garal's chin. She reached around to the back of his head and pressed her palm flat against his occipital bone and then pulled his face down to hers, his resistance no match for her strength. She moved her lips past his cheek to his ear.

The words spilled from her mouth automatically, as if they had been scripted and planted in her memory without her knowledge. They were words of magic, there was no other way to describe them, and with each whispered sentence, Tanja knew that if Garal was indeed the man his sister claimed he was—that is, questionably moral, even if during some prior life—he would have no choice but to obey her. Even the noblest of men fell quickly under its spell; men of lower character were virtually helpless.

Garal pulled away from Tanja slowly, his face a canvas of fear and dread and awe. "Prisha," he said.

"She will be fine," she lied. "In fact, healthier and stronger than before. She was reluctant at first to be a donor, that is true, but now she embraces the process with alacrity. But listen to me, Garal, you musn't tell of our arrangement to anyone. Not until after."

"My sisters are worried. My parents. All of us."

"I can imagine, but not a word, Garal, or none of it will happen. There will be no potion without the preservation of this secret. Your chance at it will be lost."

"Immortality." Garal's voice was distant, and he still wore a look of astonishment, the residue from Tanja's earlier incantation still washing over him.

Tanja assented with a dip of her head.

"How is it true? I've heard the stories from the Old World and the New Country, just as many have, but how can it be true? How can it work?"

"It is a very difficult mixture to make, Garal, both in terms of ingredients and procedure, but it is true. It does work. My body is a testament."

"How old are you?"

Instinctively, Tanja looked to the sides and behind her, suspicious of any lingering ears. Her age was a thing about which she was both proud and uncomfortable, and though she didn't remember with precision how many years she had lived, her memory through the centuries had remained apt.

"Let us just say that I remember a time when the Eastern Lands had never been touched by anyone from the Old World, and the New Country wasn't even a conception."

Tanja could see Garal was no historian, and thus couldn't quite calculate her age based on these clues, but his expression suggested he understood generally the magnitude of what she was saying.

"Where shall we meet then, Garal? I must be going now, before the night falls."

"Meet?"

"To exchange the venom? You haven't forgotten my purpose already?"

"No, of course. When will I get ...?"

Tanja smiled. "A taste? Three days at the most. Three days from when I get the venom. I'll need to finish the blending. And test it, of course. I wouldn't want to poison you after you will have turned such a noble deed. And then it will be your turn."

Garal lifted his chin and puffed his chest, and was now staring down his nose at Tanja. "How can I trust you? Trust that you will uphold your end of this arrangement?"

It was a fair question, and one Tanja had been expecting. "Because you already know about Prisha. So if I default on my promise now, that means I will have defaulted her as well, and once she tells the lawmen the details of her or-deal—which she will no doubt falsely describe as impris-onment and torture—the authorities will be soon at my doorstep to arrest me."

"Unless you just kill her after."

Tanja frowned and bowed her head, a signal that Garal's words had stung her to the very marrow of her bones. She looked up again, her eyes as beady as a bat's. "And if I did that," she explained slowly, "would not my default with you still loom? Would you not go to the authorities with a tale not only of your sister's abduction and imprisonment, but of her murder as well? They're looking for her now; if you were to have your story land upon their records, a warrant to search my home would follow. And believe me, Garal, they would find evidence of Prisha."

Garal's face softened and the challenge in his eyes faded.

"I have no reason to renege."

Garal gave a nervous swallow. "I can't get it until tomor-row morning."

This news was a blow to Tanja's plan, but it wasn't an un-reasonable timetable. It would still be another week or so be-fore her regular vendor would have the venom, and even that seemed unlikely. The fact that this new dealer had emerged at all was a win, and so a one-day waiting period would suffice.

"I can bring it to you. To your home."

Tanja smiled. "I don't think so. That would look entirely too suspicious to the policemen in the neighborhood."

"Well it can't be here either. I don't work tomorrow, and my presence here would be questioned."

Tanja thought a moment and then said, "By the temple at the village entrance. I'll be there at dawn. I will wait until you arrive, whenever that is. But you will arrive." This last sentence was said with the command of a colonel.

Garal nodded. "I'll be there. Perhaps not at dawn, but when I can."

Tanja turned and walked from Station 12A without another word. She took her steps slowly, lightly, listening for Garal's footsteps behind her. She had revealed a lot, precious information about her source and the potion, about the truth of its magic and life-everlasting. These were secrets she'd told to only a handful of other humans during her long life, for it was this type of information that turned men into monsters.

But Garal didn't follow, and, for once, Tanja made her way through the streets to her home without urgency, taking in the sights of the vacant marketplace and the distant mountain ranges for what was likely the last time.

But the leisurely stroll proved to be a mistake.

Tanja finally reached her home and methodically unlocked each of the three locks that ran vertically down the front of her door, and then entered the foyer without concern. She closed the door and walked to her closet to begin her travel preparations, and just before she touched the knob of the wardrobe, a clicking noise stopped her in mid-reach.

She stood motionless, waiting for a follow up sound, which she now determined had come from the laboratory.

It wasn't unusual for Tanja to walk in on the sounds of screams and groans, indicators of agony and struggle that were inaudible from the outside, but muffled and detectable once inside the home. But this time she had placed the Branks on the source, an extra precaution in case the investigators had somehow obtained a warrant. The bridle would have ensured silence not only from outside the walls of the home, but outside of laboratory's walls as well. An apt detective may discover the moving wall anyway, but there wouldn't be audible clues to guide him there.

Tanja moved stealthily until she was standing in front of the moving wall, and then placed her foot at the base and pushed gently, guiding the rail to its track. She pressed the wall now with both hands and cracked it open until she could see the edge of the gurney. She should have been able to see the source's feet, but they were gone.

The source had escaped.

Chapter 19

THE NON-DESCRIPT INTERMODAL freight contain-
er formed the bottom layer of a six-container stack that rose
toward the sky in the right corner of the cargo ship's stern.
It had the same burnt red color that matched the hundreds
of other containers that were stacked in various heights all
along the ship's deck.

But the inside of this particular container had a small
8x10-foot section which had been isolated from the rest of
the container, cordoned off by a makeshift metal door and
customized for, by Petr's judgment, a family of five or six. It
was a relatively plentiful amount of elbow room for Petr and
Anika, since they were the only occupants of the space.

The carved out area was luxurious compared to what
Petr had expected. A small opening had been cut into the
metal wall, and an open window was formed which looked
out onto the ocean, allowing in both light and fresh air to the
stark steel compartment. And though the container was essentially a metal prison until they reached their destination,
bedding and seating were abundant. There was even a lidded
bucket for toilet purposes, and with the window, the waste
could easily be disposed off. Overall, Petr was pleased with
the accommodations, despite the fact they had cost him his
entire stipend for the school year, as well as a fake gold watch,
Petr's only piece of jewelry.

His knowledge of the "stowaway tents," which they were apparently referred to by those in the know, had come from his father, who had patrolled the shipyards and docks for years. He once told Petr that some of the merchant sailors—not all, but some—subsidized their salaries by renting out these specialized container spaces to seagoing travelers, most of whom either had few means to travel properly or were fleeing some pending legal trouble.

Obviously, Petr and Anika fit the former description, but in truth, it mattered little; the old men who attended to the transaction showed no concern with motive, and they spoke barely a word of expression or emotion throughout the deal. Once the payment was made, Petr and Anika were waved from the harbor docks onto the large cargo ship, and within the hour they were bound for the Eastern Lands. It was all very illegal, but quite effortless.

Once they had arrived at the harbor from the university, Petr had spent the good part of an hour scouting the docks for the proper ship. And he knew it the moment he saw it, judging its worthiness based on the large foreign characters printed on the side of the ship, as well as the racial makeup and language spoken by the men tending to it. With these clues, he had made the assumption that their particular ship was indeed headed east. He had confirmed the assumption, of course, before handing over his life savings to a band of strangers, but once he was certain of its itinerary, he wasted no time negotiating. He knew they couldn't waste time; The System certainly would be sending officers to the waters in search of a murderer.

But if officers had been sent, Petr and Anika never knew it. They had pushed off for the Eastern Lands unmolested, and once the ship was on the ocean and far from the sights of the New Country shores, Petr and Anika were alone to pass the time during their four-day trek.

Anika lie on her back on a floor mattress in the corner of the room; her eyes were closed, but the weariness on her face was evident. Two full beds, frames and all, had been arranged in an L-shape and buttressed along one corner of the container space, but Anika had chosen the lone mattress on the floor for her sleeping quarters.

"How are you feeling?" Petr asked solemnly. He was seated on a small single-seat bench that was made of wood and surprisingly comfortable. His question was, in part, a test to see if Anika was asleep. He hoped she was.

"I'm okay," she replied immediately, almost surprised by the answer. She opened her one eye wide and stared at the ceiling. "I feel relief mostly. I didn't think we would make it out of there. You've saved me. And maybe Gretel and Hansel."

"You got us out, Anika. For better or worse."

Anika closed her eye and then opened it again, the glisten of tears now evident, the memory of her kills once again resurrected.

"I got us on a boat, that's all, so I'll back off from accepting my medal for valor until this journey is over and everyone is still alive."

Anika closed her eye again, this time keeping it shut. "Are you afraid of me, Petr?" she asked.

Petr wasn't. Even in her former life, when she was in the throes of addiction and madness, Petr had never feared Anika, and in fact had never even considered the idea of it until the very moment of her question. It was probably naiveté on his part that he hadn't, especially now that he was captive in this ship-locked container for days. They would have a day-long layover on the island of Cupchin, a respite to get fresh air and to replenish their food and, more importantly, their water. But that wouldn't come until day three. If Anika decided to spring on him, if the instinct to feed became too strong, there was little Petr would be able to do to fight her off.

"No. Should I be?"

The trickle of a smile appeared on Anika's face. "I don't think so. But I *am* afraid. Afraid that you should be."

Petr let the gravity of Anika's words land and settle, and then he decided to redirect the conversation back to the purpose of their voyage. "What will you do when you find her? How will you even know?"

"I'll know. I don't know how, but I will. She's connected to me now. Somehow, through Marlene, or maybe the potion. Ever since the voice uttered her name in the warehouse—*Tanja*—I've felt the connection grow within me."

"And what about the answer to my first question? What will you do?"

Anika sat up now and rested on her elbows, staring at Petr. "I'm going to kill her, Petr. If I get the chance. And I won't hesitate. Nor will I worry about the preservation of my own life in the process."

The hate in Anika's eyes was instant and real, and Petr was thankful not to be the source of it.

"I'm sorry for dragging you into this with me. It was never fair of me to do that. But if your only role was to get me on this ship, something I could never have done by myself, than it was worth involving you. Worth it to me. And if you want to leave when we get to Cupchin, I'll also understand.

"I'll see this to the Eastern Lands, Anika, and help you as much as I can when we arrive. But I obviously can't stay indefinitely. I'll have to go back. Within the month. I have to clean up the mess we left behind. The authorities will be looking for us, and Mrs. Klahr will be frantic."

"Of course."

"But I have a feeling there may be more for me to do yet."

Anika smiled. "I have no doubt."

Petr stood from the bench and walked to the beds against the wall and reclined on the one directly under the window. The container space was bright and warm, and there were several hours of daylight still remaining, but sleep was coming hard.

"Good night, Anika. Hopefully we'll get the blessing of sleeping through until morning." He held up the flashlight he'd brought from his home on campus. "I'll put it here," he said, and then reached over and placed it in the center of the floor between them.

"Good night, Petr. And thank you."

Petr nodded and opened his mouth to reply, but he had already drifted to sleep.

Chapter 20

TANJA SLID THE LABORATORY door open quickly now, and was simultaneously relieved and horrified by the girl in the corner, hunched over and caked in blood, her eyes wide and threatening. With her hands behind her, Tanja slid the door closed again and stood still, waiting for the next move.

It was her source, Prisha, and the blood masking her face and hands was her own. Tanja studied the evidence of the scene for a few beats, and within moments had put together the details of the puzzle.

The skin on the top of Prisha's right hand and wrist was shredded, her tendons and bone exposed to the lab air, and it appeared by their disfigured form that two or three of the fingers on that same hand had broken.

But the damage had paid off.

The source had freed her right wrist from the leather restraint, crippling herself in the process through an unimaginable method of skeletal crushing and surface trauma. She had then used that free hand, and the two working fingers on it, to untie her other. After that, she easily untied the straps on her ankles and removed the Branks from her head. The effort was certainly difficult and painful, given the condition of her right hand, but she had managed it, and was now free of the gurney and standing on her feet.

The one thing Tanja couldn't understand was why the source hadn't fled, choosing instead to stay for the battle. In her hand was the Pear of Anguish, held out in front of her like a pistol, the claws of the torture device open like the jaws of a spider.

"Stay away from me! Unless you want *me* to choose which orifice to put it in!"

Anika smirked, twitching her head fractionally. "So it seems you're not the willing participant you suggested you were. I should say, that was quite the performance you put on. In fact, you had me feeling quite proud of myself. Like I was some kind of celebrity."

Prisha shrugged her eyebrows.

"Tell me though, you did tell the truth about your brother. About where he works and when his shifts were, his ability to get the bungaru venom. Why would you do that?"

"He's disgusting," the source answered quickly. "If you had returned to tell me he was dead, that you had killed him, I would have celebrated you. Just as they'll celebrate me after I kill you." The girl's dictum was calm, her whole demeanor contrasting the chaos of her appearance. "And I knew it would keep you away for a while, long enough to give me this chance."

Tanja cocked her head, struck by how badly she'd underestimated this woman, and wildly curious about the girl's resourcefulness. But she kept her expression flat and emotionless. "I assume you suffered some type of childhood ordeal at the hands of your brother? Am I far off? I know of these things, Prisha. All too well, I'm afraid."

The source kept her eyes fixed on Tanja, but the witch saw the lump descend in her throat, a suggestion that she had touched a nerve, though it was possible again that it was just an act.

It made no difference in the end. They would both die.

"We're to meet tomorrow morning. Garal and I. You should come with me. Confront him about the mistreatment he gave to you, whatever that may have involved."

With this last sentence, Prisha dropped her gaze.

"I will get the venom, and then we can bring him here. As your...replacement."

Prisha's eyes softened and a beam of hopefulness sprung. "How could there be...? How is that possible? I thought it was only *my* fluids that could make it work. It's what you've told me."

Tanja shrugged. "Perhaps there is another way. I don't know it for sure, but it is possible. Since he is your brother, perhaps that genetic link is enough."

Tanja was out of her element here, negotiating with one of her sources about possible modifications to the ancient potion. But as she spoke, the ideas formed quickly behind the words, and notions that were intended only as stalling methods began sounding plausible.

"It is from the liver where the last of the extractions come, and the mixtures have always been of the same source. But I've been experimenting with it. With the bungaru venom. Perhaps that additive will be enough."

"What are you saying?"

"The final surgery is quick but gruesome, and I would rather the suffering be inflicted on someone who has made others suffer. If it be viable, of course that is my preference."

Prisha's face looked defeated now, and the spiked tips of the pear of anguish began to dip. At this point, Tanja was confident she still had the speed to overtake the girl, to apprehend her and avoid any damage from the makeshift weapon. But she was intrigued by her own suggestions, and wanted to hear herself out about the prospects of using sibling bile as a replacement.

"I can live? Is that it? And you will use Garal to complete the mixture?"

Tanja would never let her live, and she had no intentions of chancing the potion at this late stage for this particular source; there simply wasn't time. As it was, she would be lucky to flee the village before a warrant was obtained and the police returned.

"Perhaps," Tanja answered. "But you must trust me now. We'll clean you up. Get you a proper meal and send you to rest. Tomorrow we'll make things right. Right with everyone."

Prisha assented with two blinks and a nod, and then lowered the pear of anguish to her side. "Okay."

Tanja would kill her here and take her chances with the infected bile. If she performed the extraction immediately, while the cells were still fresh, she should avoid any infection. But first she had to know the answer to one question.

"Why didn't you leave?" she asked, smiling bemusedly at the girl who had retreated to the corner instead of simply fleeing.

"It was locked. I tried to leave but I couldn't open the wall."

Tanja turned to see the blood prints on the side of the door.

"It wasn't locked," she said, "you just needed to line up the track and slide." Tanja demonstrated by turning and facing the door, and then pressing her toe against the base and sliding it open once again. She started to laugh uproariously. "It's quite simple actu—"

A sting of electricity flashed through her lower back and Tanja's breath seized, leaving her face frozen in horror. The pain felt like she'd been stung by a swarm of metal wasps. She bellowed in pain, reaching her hands around to her back, groping for the source of the attack and an assessment of the subsequent wounds. But as her fingers touched on one of the four lacerations that were now open between her kidneys and ribcage, another four-point stab landed, piercing her to the bone, this time in the area between her head and neck.

One of the jabs had smashed her cheekbone, while another of the metal points drilled down into her eardrum.

It was the Pear of Anguish, and the blows to her back and face had rendered Tanja stunned and nauseous.

She listened absently to the weapon hit the floor of the laboratory, and as she held the side of her head, squeezing her eyes tightly as she tried to keep her blood and brains from seeping out, she collapsed to the floor beside the ancient torture device.

As she writhed in pain with her back against the legs of the gurney, she saw her source step over her legs and then jog toward the front door.

Tanja closed her eyes in defeat. It was over.

Chapter 21

ANIKA OPENED HER EYES in time to see the slice of light form beneath the container door. She held her body still, but listened with interest to the rusty creak of the metal door swinging upwards, opening like the jaws of some giant reptile. It was day two of the voyage, which meant the layover at Cupchin was still a day away. No one should have been letting them out of the container yet.

She knew from their breathing that two men stood outside the box, and as they clicked on their miniature flashlights and entered the space, that number was confirmed.

Anika's instinct was to speak, to confront them about their purpose for being there, but instead she waited, curious. Maybe there was a problem with the ship and they had come to alert them, to prepare them for a catastrophe, or possibly a sea rescue.

But it was only seconds until she heard the laughter. It was a laughter devoid of merriment, one she had heard many times throughout her life, almost always from men, objectification in their minds and abasement in their hearts.

They spoke in whispers now as they moved toward Anika, approaching the mattress slowly and quietly. The language they spoke was foreign to her ears, but the words they voiced had a cadence of conspiracy and plotting.

She closed her eyes and waited for the first touch to land, at which point she would murder these men with the ferocity of a jaguar.

But the touch never came, and she heard the men move past her and over to the beds against the wall.

Petr.

Anika rose to a sitting position and saw the men standing at Petr's bed, their backs to Anika now, the moonlight from the makeshift window illuminating them like criminals in a courtyard.

One of the men grumbled and sniffled, and then began to remove his belt. The second, seeming to take his cue from his friend, followed suit. As if planned, they both let their pants fall to their ankles, and then slipped their feet out so that they were both standing at the intersection of the L in their underwear.

"What are—" Petr started, but he was immediately muzzled to silence by the man standing closest to his head. Anika could see that the man was bent over Petr now, his hand pressing down on Petr's face.

The second man removed the lone blanket covering Petr's body, and then climbed on the bed and began to pull of his underwear.

"You're going to die today."

The men turned toward Anika's voice in unison, as if they had practiced the routine for days, the looks on their faces identically fearful and shamed. Anika's first thoughts were about how old these men were, and it added to her disgust. They were fifty if they were a year, attempting to gang rape a child, which Anika still considered Petr to be.

She thought of Randall, and of how pleasurable his death had felt in her hands. And of Bibi, and of how many times that poor, young girl must have experienced a scene similar to the one currently playing out in front of Anika.

Anika rose from the mattress in a single motion, like a beagle at the sound of a doorbell, and stood with her legs slightly splayed. "Get off the bed."

The man on the bed looked to his friend and then back to Anika, smiling now as he scanned the length of Anika's body. "Is part of the price to sail, see? You will be tomorrow night, yes?"

Anika felt as if every ounce of serum and hemoglobin and adrenaline flooded her inner body at once, and the energy that the deluge produced was no less than supernatural. Her chest expanded, and the muscles in her legs warmed and tightened, as if they'd been turned to rubber and wound for explosion.

She took another deep breath, letting the oxygen flow across the breadth of her lungs before dispersing to her cells at large, and then, without a sound, Anika pounced.

In two steps, she grabbed the flashlight from the floor and was inches from both men before they could blink. The man on the bed still had his arms by his sides when Anika smashed the tailcap across the side of his neck, cutting off the blood flow to his brain and sending him unconscious to the floor.

The first man, who must have watched the attack as if it were happening on a movie screen, suddenly made a move for the door, but Anika whipped out her left foot and caught him at the shin, sending him sprawling to the floor next to his accomplice. Almost in the same motion, she unscrewed the tailcap and removed the large cylindrical battery from the tube, and then flung it down, landing it squarely on the back of the rapist's head. He was immediately motionless from the strike, and Anika was sure she had killed him.

She walked to the second attacker, whose filthy underwear was still halfway down his buttocks, and placed her foot on the back of his neck, measuring the strike. She lifted her heel high and slammed it down.

Her boot landed flush, and the satisfying sound of snapping vertebrae and cartilage was surpassed only by the gagging noises of the rapist choking on his own blood, a result of his now obliterated carotid artery.

Anika stepped to the other predator, straddling him at the waist. She kneeled now, and after further inspection, as she was wrapping her hands around his throat to ensure the kill, she felt a pulse. He was only unconscious.

She slid the fingers of one hand across the man's Adam's apple, drumming the lump lightly with the tips, and as she wedged the blades of her dagger-like nails into the loose skin beneath his chin and tensed the muscles of her hand, poised to pull the life from the man, Petr shouted, "Anika, no!"

Anika twisted back to Petr in a motion of fear and fury, like a hyena disturbed at a feeding. She felt outside of her body, but she regained her composure quickly, and took care to keep her lips wrapped around her teeth, which were unsheathed and braced to bite.

"Don't kill him, Anika. He didn't do anything."

"They were going to—" Anika's breathing was heavy, her tone pleading.

"I know." Petr looked away, the fear on his face morphing into something close to shame. "In know, Anika. And you prevented it. But you can't kill him. Not both of them. I just..." Petr tented a hand above his brow, rubbing his forehead in astonishment at what almost happened to him.

The fury in Anika dissipated, but the strength and energy in her body remained. Her urges were unbearable, and spanned the gamut of human emotion and instinct. She was hungry, aroused, though in a way indescribable, one that seemed to transcend sex. She felt the need to run and fight, to climb a tree and swim a river. The container room suddenly felt like a fishbowl, and she a marlin.

"Fine," she said, "but that means we have to abandon this space for the rest of the trip. We'll lock him in here and find ourselves other arrangements until we arrive."

"He'll die in here."

"Did we die?"

"We had food and water."

"Then we'll leave him our food and water, but it means we'll have to be scavengers for the next few days."

"And people knew we were in here. How will anyone know about him?"

"When we reach port he'll have the window to call from. If he's lucky, someone will hear him. Otherwise, I don't care."

"So allow him to starve in here?"

"And what do you think they were going to do with us, Petr? Do you think they were going to come find us the second the ship arrived and greet us with leis and roses and kisses on our cheeks? Or, based on the two men in charge of our accommodations," Anika waved a hand through the air over the felled sailors, "do you think they had no intention of unjailing us at Cupchin? And that our raped and ravaged corpses would only be discovered when the container was finally unpacked a week later, somewhere in the Eastern Lands?"

Petr looked away in defeat.

"We'll give him the courtesy of removing his friend. We'll wrap him in a tarp or something." Anika shined the flashlight in the long section the container, outside of their cordoned off space. "Look at all this stuff and space. The rats will certainly be pleased."

Anika walked back to the man on the floor and flipped him over, slapping him across the face. He grunted once, sleepily, but he didn't open his eyes.

Anika lifted him by his shirt and thrust him on the bed against the wall. His eyes sprang to life and he instantly began shaking his head and pleading. "No. No, please."

"Give me the keys to this container," Anika said, and the man motioned to his pants on the floor, a shameful reminder of how it all came to this point.

Anika fished the keys from the pockets of the stained pants and then grabbed the leg of the dead man, dragging the corpse behind her as she walked into the main part of the container. With Petr beside her, Anika turned the beam of the flashlight to the sailor, who remained on the bed.

"What is your name?" she asked.

"Kiet," he answered.

"What does it mean?"

The man closed his eyes and lowered his head. "Honorable."

There was no need to point out the irony. "What do you do here on the ship? What is your position?"

"I work the deck. Maintenance and cleaning."

"Will you be missed?" Anika held the man's eyes, hypnotizing him like a python with a rabbit, daring him to lie.

"I would have been missed by Balot, that is all. He was my super."

"I take it Balot is this piece of debris at the end of my arm?"

Kiet nodded.

"Where are your sleeping quarters? Give me a direction or a number? Who did you share them with?"

"All of the quarters are centralized, aft and port side. We are 1C."

"We?"

"We bunk in pairs."

"And who was your bunk mate?"

Kiet stayed quiet, and the silence meant he was folding the last of his playable cards. He wouldn't be missed for days, if at all, since his supervisor and bunkmate were one in the same.

"You have no memory of any of this, Kiet. You don't know what happened to your boss, or how you ended up in here. And if I or my acquaintance is ever asked about an incident on the *ESC Mongkut* traveling on these dates from the Old World to the Eastern Lands, I will know who reported it. His name is Kiet. A crewmember and a rapist. And everyone he has ever known will die."

Kiet's eyes were like globes now as he listened to the threat, and he pushed his back against the container wall, pressing it as if he were trying to break through and send himself to the sea below.

"I don't need to ask if you understand, correct?"

Kiet shook his head wildly.

Anika held the flashlight on the man's face for a moment longer, and Petr realized that Kiet couldn't see them in the darkness, and that Anika's words must have sounded like the voice of God.

Anika nodded and Petr slammed down the makeshift container door, sealing in Kiet for the next few days. They stood and listened for screams from the room, cries for help, but ten minutes of silence passed without a whisper, and within another five minutes, Petr and Anika were outside the larger container on their way to find room 1C.

PETR AND ANIKA MADE their way toward the center of the ship, the narrow paths forming a giant maze, the stacks of containers rising above them like skyscrapers. The redness of the steel was like the color of some distant planet, and the uniformity of them made it difficult to maintain direction.

They had intended to find Kiet's accommodations during the night, but it had simply been too dark to navigate the metal corridors, so they had camped in an empty, open container not far from their original quarters. By dawn, they were back on the deck, using the newly risen sun as a guide to find the proper room.

"Where are we going?" Anika asked, following Petr, who had taken charge of this portion of the adventure. "You can't possibly know."

"I *don't* know."

"Wait," Anika whispered. "Do you hear that?"

Petr didn't

"Stop here. There are men coming."

Petr eventually heard the approaching voices. They were coming from the opposite side of the container, over the maze wall where he and Anika stood.

They watched silently as two crewmen entered the intersection, speaking loudly and laughing as they passed through and continued to walk toward the port side of the ship. Within minutes, a dozen more men followed, spaced out in groups of twos and threes.

After the last group passed, Petr and Anika waited another minute, and, hearing no one else approaching, they crossed over onto the path the crewmen had just walked. They stared down the corridor in both directions. It was all clear.

"I could smell food coming off of them," Anika said, "and you could hear the glee in their voices. They've just eaten. The mess area must be this way." She nodded to her right.

Petr and Anika followed the reverse path of the crewmembers, and soon they came to a white, two-story box of a building with a metal stairway leading up to a second floor. There was a round, eye-level window on the first floor that looked into the building, and through it Petr could see the room inside was a kitchen—the galley. He took a step closer to the window and could now see that a pair of men were washing dishes and wiping down counters, obviously in clean-up mode.

"We'll need food," Petr said, and then hesitated, scanning the length of Anika. "At least I will."

"I will need to eat food too, Petr. The other...the other cravings have waned. They're almost completely gone. I promise. I had no desire to feed on those men back in the container room."

"Just a desire to kill them?"

Anika paused, considering the question. "Yes. I did. But that would have been my instinct before. Before the potion and Marlene. I would have wanted to kill them both.

The difference is, before I would have restrained myself. Out of fear. But that part is gone now, the fear. Because I'm strong. Stronger than most of the predators of this world—predators like those crewmen—so I no longer need to temper the instinct. I can simply kill who needs killing."

Petr understood. She was right. Her new strength had changed her behavior. It was probably the way all animals were wired, he thought, and humans were certainly no different. Over millennia, people had developed weapons for defense—guns and tanks and the like—but the body was also a weapon, and when one had been transformed into a killing machine like Anika's, it was meant to be used not only to hunt, but to protect. And sometimes protection meant killing.

"Here's what we'll do," Anika said flatly, shifting back to the matter at hand. "I'll inspect the mess hall upstairs. If everyone has left, I'll check the plates for any leftovers. If there's nothing worthwhile, I'll create a distraction for you.

Some type of noise. If and when those two in the kitchen head up to investigate, you get into the kitchen. You'll have to move fast. The door is there. Raid the pantries and try to keep it non-perishable."

This rapid-fire thinking was also part of the new weapon, Petr thought, the ability to clear away any ambient cloudiness of the mind and simply focus on the immediate problem. It was the type of mind everyone aspired to but few ever reached.

He watched Anika scale the stairs, and within seconds he heard the sound of crashing metal. On cue, the men abandoned their tasks and followed the sound, and Petr was immediately through the deck door and in the kitchen collecting bread loaves and cans, using one of the trash bags that had been laid out on the counter.

The bag was half-filled when he looked out the window and saw Anika coming back down the steps, frantically waving her hands toward her, signaling Petr to hurry. He nodded and held up the bag to indicate his current stock, and then took a step toward the deck door.

"Hey!" a voice called.

Petr stopped in his tracks, and then closed his eyes and sighed.

He heard the man pause for a moment before leaving the bottom step, beginning his approach slowly from the stairway. "Drop the bag, fare-dodger."

"I paid my fare," Petr replied, opening his eyes. He was facing the wall of the galley, standing directly in front of the window, about six feet from the man now. "But we had some trouble with our rations. It's a bit of a story."

"We?"

Petr winced at his mistake, but didn't answer.

"I suppose '*we*' is who broke two of my plates upstairs?" The cook stepped in front of Petr, hands on his hips, studying the intruder from foot to head. He was at least six inches taller than Petr and a hundred pounds heavier. "I am correct in my supposition then?"

"I'll pay for the plates and the food."

"Will you? And how do you plan to do that?"

"When we get to Cupchin. I'll sell some of the things I've brought from home. You and the crew probably wouldn't find value in them, but the locals there might."

The cook creased his face in confusion. "Cupchin? We're not stopping at Cupchin."

"What?"

The cook shook his head slowly, unblinking.

"When was this change made?"

"It was never part of the itinerary. I'm not quite sure why you would have thought that, seeing as you say you paid your fare to sail and thus would have been informed about the schedule."

The men who Petr paid for the container space had lied to him. They had told him they would have a chance to restock their supplies along the way, on day three at Cupchin, and he and Anika had planned to ration the food and water with that understanding. Two extra days without food would have been manageable, but water was something else. They may not have died, but it was a possibility.

Petr stood before the cook in a quiet rage now, disgusted not only with the cook and the rest of the crew of the *ESC Mongkut*, but with his fellow man generally.

"Trevor!" the man called, leaning his head toward the stairway. "Come down here. We have a fare-dodger."

"I paid," Petr replied flatly, waiting for the other cook, presumably the steward, to come barreling down the steps with interest. But he never came.

The cook was now completely blocking Petr's view of the deck window, so Petr inched to his left, trying to catch a glimpse of Anika.

She was gone.

Petr assumed she had something to do with the steward's absence in the galley, and he didn't press his thoughts for another answer. Whatever had happened, he knew she was fine and he was glad she had fled. He could figure his way out of this. He could work the kitchen maybe, pay for the remainder of the trip washing dishes and sweeping floors. Certainly young men snuck onto these cargo ships all the time in search of work and adventure. There had to be a precedent for the situation in which he found himself currently.

Anika, however, was not likely to fare as well if she were caught, not with the character of men that seemed to be a part of this ship. Petr's hope was that she would find 1C and settle there for the remainder of the trip, locked inside, quiet, emerging only when the voyage concluded.

There was no longer a layover in Cupchin, which meant the trip would be cut by a day from their original estimation. If the weather held, they should be arriving in the Eastern

Lands in two days. And with Petr working the kitchen, he could find a gap in the day to sneak Anika food and water.

"Do you know what we do with stowaways?" the cook asked, unsheathing a large butcher's knife and holding it beneath Petr's chin. "Trevor!" he called again to the steward, but still no reply.

Petr swallowed. "Put me to work?"

The cook smiled back at Petr. "Not exactly. We don't like putting criminals to work on our ship."

Petr frowned. "So what then?"

"It's an old law of the sea we call overboarding. I'm sure you can imagine what it involves."

Petr shook his head.

"No?" The cook gave Petr a look of mock confusion, as if moderately surprised that Petr wasn't familiar with the practice. "Well let me explain. First, we tie your feet with a long piece of rope, and second, we throw you off the back of the ship."

"That's not very creative."

The cook shrugged. "You'll get dragged along for a while. Drowning slowly as you go. Pirates made a practice of this a few centuries back. Surprised you haven't heard of it."

"And your ship's master approves of this? Pirate punishments from the dark ages?"

"He's a by-the-book man. And the overboard punishment is technically legal and still on the books."

The cook laughed and then took one more check of the stairway leading up to the mess hall. He frowned at the empty well and then nodded his head forward toward the deck door.

"Let's go."

The cook grabbed Petr by the collar of his shirt and pulled him forward so that Petr was now in front of him, and then repositioned the blade of the knife to the base of Petr's skull. He pushed him out the deck door and began leading him aft, toward the stern of the ship.

"This punishment seems a bit antiquated," Petr said. "I feel I have to say that. Perhaps there is another, more reasonable punishment for stealing a can of hash and a half loaf of bread?"

"Antiquated, yes, but still applicable today. Haven't done one in years, though, I'll admit that. Most of the fare-dodgers caught word of the practice years ago and it's become somewhat of a deterrent."

"I've told you three times now, I paid for my space. It was a stowaway tent. In one of the cordoned-off containers."

"Well then why aren't you there now? You can't get out from the inside."

Petr stayed quiet.

"That's a big secret, is it? Well then, with whom did you make these arrangements? Or is that a secret too?"

Petr sighed and shook his head, still being pushed along quickly toward the ship's rear. "They were two deck ratings, I think. I don't know their names. They didn't say much. If you can find them, I'll point them out to you."

"Find who? You think anyone I find will admit to these payments? And risk their hanging in front of the master?"

The cook had a point. This was always the risk with under-the-table arrangements.

"We've only got four deck ratings in total, anyhow, and they're all four bastards. You'll be wasting your breath. And if it's between you and them, the master's gonna believe his crew. Anyway, stow, they're all at work now, busy with the operations and earning an honest day's pay. Maybe when they're done tonight, coming back to the hall for supper, they'll take a look out the rear and see you bobbing off the stern and then fess up about the whole transaction. Though it'll be a little late by then."

"Only four?" Petr asked, struck by the small number of deck ratings.

"Ship runs itself. Most containers do. Only got twenty-two crew total, including me and Trevor."

Petr thought of the dead rapist's body in the container and of Trevor's absence. "Twenty you mean." Kiet was incapacitated but still alive, so Petr included him in the count.

The cook raised the blade slightly against the back of Petr's skull, piercing the skin and drawing blood. "What did you say," he growled.

Petr winced and took a deep breath. In the distance, maybe a hundred yards from where Petr and the cook now stood, a scream of torture rang, followed by silence.

"I'm sorry," Petr said, "I meant nineteen."

Chapter 22

GET UP AND GET OUT.

Tanja opened her eyes and could see clearly the left side of the empty laboratory; the right side, however, was clouded and pocked with stains of brown. She tried to swivel her head right, to locate the source of the voice that had just spoken, put the pain in her face and neck was unbearable.

If you stay, the voice whispered, *you will die. Just like Marlene.*

Tanja thought of her daughter in a way that she hadn't for centuries. The memories couldn't be real, she understood that, it had simply been too long since she'd last seen her.

But they felt real.

She remembered Marlene as a little girl in the Old Country, ten perhaps, travelling with the village families, nomadically wandering the countryside every few years, trying to find a new home where they could settle permanently, away from the seemingly endless hordes of raiders and looters. Those were difficult times, she recalled, helpless for women, though the idea of helplessness was no longer a concrete one.

Yet, in spite of the tribulations of that ancient life, there had also been joy. She could no longer capture that feeling in her waking hours, but she dreamt of it on occasion, waking to a tightness in her heart so gripping it felt like death itself.

But it wasn't death, obviously, it was something less tangible, something she understood before the blackness had overtaken her heart. The smoldering remains of love, perhaps.

It's not time.

Tanja brought her attention back to the lab, and then tested the limits of her pain with first a shallow breath, and then, feeling the elements flow easily into her lungs, another, deeper gulp of air. The oxygen felt cool, medicinal, and she raised her arms straight, directly above her head, stretching them toward the ceiling as she shrugged the tightness and throbbing from her shoulders.

So far, so good.

Her face was a problem, however, and she knew by the faded ambient sounds around her that she had lost the ability to hear in her right ear. She could still see on that side though, mercifully, but the blood from her wounds had dried thickly and was clouding her vision at the moment.

She wasn't mortally wounded, she knew that much now, and, more incredibly, she was still free. But that wouldn't last for much longer; her source had escaped, and that meant she was likely reporting all of this to the police at that very moment.

Her source had escaped.

It had never happened before. Never. Tanja had taken hundreds of human sources during her life—maybe a thousand—and she had never allowed one to leave. Neither out of mercy or through escape. There had been occasions when she'd had to kill her sources before the potion was finished, either because the locals had become too suspicious or the source had proven too unruly. But death was different—they all died eventually—for escape she had no precedent to learn from, no plan to deal with it.

Go, Tanja! Get the mixture, get the venom and go.

The venom.

She looked to the window and saw that night was still in full darkness, but internally it felt as if morning was arriving soon, and when she checked the clock on the table beside her bed, she saw she had only an hour or so until dawn.

The details of the night were fuzzy—the specifics of the attack and the subsequent escape—but Tanja remembered her meeting with Garal. It was at the temple. Sometime after dawn. There she would collect the venom, finish the mixture, and leave for the docks.

Tanja tried to push herself to her feet, but the right side of her head felt as if it had been weighed down with concrete, and she toppled back to the floor. She adjusted for the mass of blood that had hemorrhaged from her head and was now dried in her face and hair, and then tried again, this time succeeding in the rise. She grabbed both sides of her head and twisted gently, as if fitting her skull back onto her shoulders. There was a dull crack somewhere down her spine, and with a few more cocks and turns of her neck, she began to feel restored. She took a heavy breath of relief. She wondered if the injury would have been fatal in her previous life, but it was time so distant now that she couldn't really be sure.

Tanja looked at the Pear of Anguish on the floor beneath the gurney and shook her head ruefully. She had gotten sloppy with the source. She never should have left the device in the room for the girl to access, but if she had simply strapped her properly, the Pear would never have been an issue to begin with. The girl had disfigured herself in order to escape, that was true, but Tanja should have factored that possibility into the equation.

She was getting old. That was the truth. Too old to continue this life for another fifty years even. Her only daughter was dead now, murdered in the New Country by some lowly country farm girls. Her one son Gromus was presumably still alive, but she had no real way of knowing that for sure, and he was no doubt the monstrosity that she and Marlene were. Perhaps worse.

Maybe it was time for her to die, to cycle through this final blending before allowing the natural world to intervene. And once she avenged her daughter, she could make one last journey to the Village of the Elders, a last pilgrimage to return her copy of *Orphism* and let death take its rightful place in her story. The religion was an abomination—she never pretended otherwise—and it couldn't be chased forever.

But it was also a gift, and its draw was irresistible.

Still, Tanja had heard of Orphists who had given up the sickness of immortality, who had simply decided the time had come when they no longer felt the need to fight off death, and, in fact, had welcomed the unknown that the afterlife held. Perhaps she, too, had arrived at this place.

But there was one more goal to achieve first, and one more potion that needed to be blended and consumed, this one containing the poison of one of the most deadly snakes in the world and the bile of a source's sibling.

Chapter 23

SIX MORE SCREAMS ERUPTED from nearby on the ship, and Petr knew that Anika was purposely signaling to him that she was now in control. She was forcing them to yell before disposing of them, bringing them close enough for Petr to hear; and that meant she was tracking him the whole time.

Six screams. That meant thirteen crewmembers remained. Subtract the cook and Kiet, and that left eleven, including the ship's master and chief officer. Petr prayed she wouldn't kill them all. Not just for the humanity of it, but because they would need the engineers and captain to get them to the Eastern Lands.

Another scream. Ten left.

Chapter 24

TANJA SPENT THE NIGHT at the temple and was awake before dawn, waiting for Garal, just as she had promised, watching for him from behind one of the several large columns that lined the entrance. In her hands she held a narrow steel container, tightly sealed and filled with the incomplete concoction of eternal life. It needed two more ingredients, which she planned to get this morning.

Within the hour, Garal appeared on the grounds of the lower courtyard, the sun shining on the entrance steps as if it had been anticipating his arrival. Tanja was pleased and impressed with this show of punctuality, and a dusting of disappointment fell over her, knowing that he would have to die in the end.

He had also come alone, thankfully, a hopeful sign that he had kept this meeting secret, despite Tanja telling Prisha that a meeting with her brother was planned. But perhaps he hadn't spoken with her and hadn't yet heard of her escape, which made this encounter potentially catastrophic. An ambush might be accompanying Garal, unbeknownst to him.

But Tanja needed the venom, and the bile, so the risk had to be taken. If all went well, she would need to spend only a few more hours in this wretched village and then she would leave for the docks, bound for the Old World and then the New Country.

Tanja peered down to the courtyard and could see in Garal's hand what looked to be an old leather bag, weathered and holed, about the size of a small duffel. The tote seemed a bit excessive for transporting the small amount of venom she needed, and, she thought, was even likely to garner unnecessary attention. But, she reasoned, the toxicity of the poison was not to be trifled with, and Garal's caution was yet another characteristic Tanja found appealing.

She tucked herself further into the shadows, wedging her body between a gap at the front temple wall and a large bulbous column that ran from the floor to the ceiling. Behind her, in the center of the temple, was a large stone statue of some god, long forgotten no doubt, invented millennia ago and likely credited with certain good elements of the world but none of the strife.

Garal reached the bottom of the first set of stone steps, and then scanned the area around him, rotating a full turn, checking his surroundings for anyone who might be interested in his movements.

But Tanja knew his suspicions were unnecessary; this part of the village was always deserted at this hour, and the temple itself had been virtually abandoned by the locals for the last thirty years or so, existing now only as a tourist attraction, and a lightly visited one at that. But, again, Tanja took Garal's caution as a sign that he hadn't spoken of the meeting. He was coming for the potion in earnest. He was already hooked before ever tasting a drop.

Garal ascended the topmost flight of steps and then stood still on the temple platform, small and alone, directly in front of the divine statue. To Tanja, he looked as if he had come to offer himself in sacrifice.

"Garal," Tanja hissed, her speech sounding like it had been filtered through gravel. "I'm here."

Garal whipped his head toward the voice, searching for its source in the darkness, and then gave one more look over his shoulder before moving towards it.

Tanja remained shrouded in the shadows, invisible from where Garal stood, but the merchant stopped well short of where he would have had the ability to see her. That was intentional, Tanja knew. He was keeping his distance.

"Have you brought it?" Tanja asked

"They're looking for you," Garal replied. His voice was rushed and breathy, fearful, a complete contradiction of the polished vendor from the previous night. "And Prisha has escaped. You are aware of that, I assume?"

"I watched her flee, helpless to stop her." Tanja paused. "But there's more to the problem. She knows I'm to meet you today. Not the time or place, but that we are to meet."

"I'm aware. She came to me first. Before the police. She told us everything, Jiya and I. Prisha thought you might be...dead."

"And yet here I am."

"I knew it already. It's why I've come. Prisha told me where you lived, so I went there first. To see for myself. I was pleased you were gone."

"You went without the police? How could that be?"

"I convinced Prisha to wait before telling the authorities, that you would disappear if the word spread. It wasn't easy convincing her or Jiya, but they agreed at last. I told them our meeting was this afternoon, and that there you would be arrested."

Tanja realized now the girl had been lying about her brother, at least as it concerned any abuse he may have inflicted on her. She, in fact, seemed to love the man, if not to fully trust him. It was a smart maneuver by the source, to play up the evil of men.

But she had also been right about his lust for the potion, about that she was insightful. His presence at the temple this morning meant she knew him quite well in this regard.

"But she told me something else."

Of course there was a catch.

"She also told me the venom would do you no good without the final extraction. That you kept her alive until you had this final ingredient."

He held up the bag, which he seemed to do with some effort.

"It's true," Tanja said, not finding any point in lying. "What she said was true."

Tanja stepped from the shadows and Garal winced and turned away.

"This is what she did," Tanja snarled. "This is damage that could have killed a bear. Look at it!"

Garal turned back and fixated on the holes in Tanja's face, and the dried blood that now caked the entire right side of her head.

"But I will recover. I will heal. I will have life for as long as I wish. Just as you can." Tanja held the steel flask at eye level and waved it once, a hypnotist with a pocket watch. "With this."

Garal raised his chin and cocked his head sideways, looking at the container distrustfully, with a narrow gaze. "But what of the final ingredient? The extraction? How can it work now?"

Tanja stared into Garal's eyes, trying to convey the answer through a look. Prisha had no doubt told him of her possible plans to use his liver, a genetic relative of the source, for the final extraction. Yet she could sense his longing for immortality was stronger than his reason, and hope of another possibility emanated from his face.

"What is in the bag, Garal?" Tanja said finally, rerouting to another subject.

Garal blinked and looked down at the satchel he held. "It's the bungaru."

"It's a rather large bag to carry venom."

Garal shook his head. "It's not the venom."

He set the bag on the temple floor, keeping his eyes on Tanja as he did, and then unclasped the buckles on either side at the front, lifting open the leather flap. He hovered his hand over the opening for a moment, concentrating, and then shot his wrist down into the opening like a spear into a shallow fishing hole.

Tanja gasped at the motion.

Garal smiled proudly, and then lifted his hand slowly, bringing up the diamond-shaped head of the banded krait—the bungaru—and then snatched the tail of the snake with his free hand.

"What have you done this for?" Tanja asked. "I've no use for a snake. I need the venom. I need the process to have been completed."

"I caught this snake last night. In the jungle. I haven't slept. I've gone through great pains to bring it here by dawn."

"This wasn't our agreement, Garal. I need the venom milked and isolated."

"That takes great skill and time."

"You told me you could do it."

"Well this is the best I could do!"

Tanja settled, careful not to push the man too far. He was large, aggravated and irritable from a lack of sleep. And he held a snake with the potential to kill even her, especially considering her already weakened state.

An unexpected tear suddenly streamed down the left side of Garal's cheek. "It was the best I could do with the time I had. And I've nothing to go back to now. I've betrayed my sister. The only person that ever loved me. Even through all of my struggles." He began crying in full now. "Prisha."

"You have done well, Garal," Tanja consoled. "We shall make this work."

Tanja's voice was feminine now, young and sweet, and Garal looked at her like a boy to his mother.

"But the day is arriving and commuters will be passing here soon. Let us go to the altar in the back and work this out. We can do it, I'm sure. We are two minds against a serpent." She smiled and then grabbed Garal's chin, bringing his face inches from hers. "You have sacrificed too much for us not to, yes?"

Garal nodded, and wiped his eyes. "Yes."

"Good then, let us go"

Tanja nodded once and then turned and faced the massive statue. Directly behind it, hidden from the front view of the temple, was a large stone altar. She had mapped the entire complex during the night, leaving nothing to chance. "We have god on our side," she said, and then walked with purpose to the rear of the temple.

And Garal followed.

Chapter 25

ANIKA STOOD ATOP A three-stack tower of containers at the stern of the ship, staring down at the sadistic cook, who had laid his butcher's knife at his feet and was in the process of tying a thick hemp rope around Petr's ankle. Petr was lying on the deck holding the back of his head, and Anika could see blood puddled behind him.

Anika scoffed and shook her head in disbelief. The cook had heard the screams of his fellow crewmembers; she had picked up Petr's whereabouts midway through their journey to the rear of the ship, and she had seen the man's look of terror when two of the cries rang through the air.

The purpose of the screams had been to scare the man into submission. She had forced the crewmembers to howl in agony, had ordered it, threatening them with torture and death if they didn't comply. They had all felt the strength in her hands and the seriousness of her voice, squeezing them against her body as she made her way through each section of the ship, picking them off one by one. Only three of the eight had complied as directed, and those three she had detained by converting one of the empty containers into a makeshift brig.

The other five men had refused to comply, and each of them heard the snap of their own vertebrae just before their deaths.

"Petr!" Anika called down. She stood tall on the container, her chest out, her anger fierce, and she wanted nothing more than to fly down on the wretched cook like a falcon on a bunny. But she was twenty feet above them, too far for even for her to jump.

Petr writhed and attempted to find her voice, but he was dazed from whatever blow had been rained upon him.

The cook finished off the knot around Petr's leg with a flurry and looked up to the container roof , but before he could locate Anika, she had disappeared from view and had already started scurrying down the cargo ladders that linked the metal boxes together. Within seconds of announcing her presence atop the roof, she had already reached the ship's deck, the cook in her crosshairs, Anika, herself, just out of his sightline.

Anika watched him toss Petr's roped leg to the side and step away from the rear wall of the ship, and then move cautiously toward the middle of the stack of containers. He held the butcher's knife in front of him like a torch, with the point piercing forward.

Anika stood at the corner of the bottom container, her one functioning eye peeking around it, watching the man as he moved closer to the metal boxes to her left. He came quietly, taking each step delicately, listening for the next sound that would give Anika's location away.

Anika had to restrain herself from attacking. She didn't necessarily think he would be a difficult kill, not with her strength and leopard-like movements, but he was a large man with a knife, and thus he had to be considered a serious threat. And if she were injured—or killed—it would mean Petr's life too, and perhaps those of her children.

She pulled her head back from view and placed it flat against the container, standing with her back pressed to the metal. She took a deep, silent breath and then slammed her heel back against the bottom of the large metal crate.

Anika heard the cook scuttle, but by the time he had reached the place around the corner where the noise had originated, she was already gone, having dashed around to the opposite side of the box. She now had an open view of Petr.

She ran to Petr's side and lifted his head off the deck, examining the wound.

"Anika," he groaned.

"It's okay," she whispered, untying the knot around his ankle. "There's a lot of blood and I'm sure you have a concussion, but you'll live."

Petr opened his eyes and lifted his chin. "Look," he said groggily, as if doubting that what he was seeing was real.

Still holding onto the rope, Anika stood and turned in the direction of Petr's stare. The cook was again standing in front of the container, having made a full revolution in search of the mysterious noise.

"A woman?" he said, shaking his head, confused. He took a couple of steps forward, casually, and then stopped, examining Anika more closely, as if disbelieving his eyes. "I thought I heard it in the voice, but...a woman?"

"There's a prison waiting for you. Midship. Some of your friends are there now." Anika paused and lowered her head. "Some others had less luck, though the same opportunity.

Drop the knife now and I'll take you there. If there is no resistance from you, your only punishment will be a couple of days in a container. It's better than you deserve, but I've got other things to do."

"Aye, matey!" he replied, squinting his eye and covering it with his palm, mimicking Anika's patch and her resemblance to some pirate from a child's story. "Thank you for the offer, but I think I'll pass."

"Think long and hard before you do. It is the only deal you'll get, and you will only get it once."

The cook lowered his chin and scowled, his eyes focused, glaring at Anika like a bull toward a matador. "I've got some business to finish first with your thief friend. He's a fare-dodger, as I suppose you are. But I've got him to deal with first. Drop the rope and step to the side."

Anika's adrenaline was like lava, and the burn in her veins was real, visceral. Containing the eruption bubbling inside her took every bit of her will.

The cook took another step forward, and then began a steady walk, increasing his speed with every pace. He had lowered the knife to his side during this first part of his approach, but when he reached a point only ten paces or so from Anika and Petr, he raised the blade high and started to run.

Chapter 26

TANJA PLACED THE TIP of her index finger on the mouth of the flask and tipped the flagon sideways, moistening her skin with the potion. "Open," she said.

Garal closed his eyes and opened his mouth, taking in a long breath as if preparing for some kind of meditation. He sat cross-legged on the altar, his back facing the back of the colossal statue that overshadowed the altar room.

He held the head and tail of the serpent tightly in front of him, not yet prepared to trust Tanja entirely, despite her insistence that she meant him no harm.

Tanja pressed her wet fingertip under Garal's top lip and rubbed the potion over his gum line, moving her finger slowly toward the back of the merchant's mouth. She held it on his cheek for a beat and, reflexively, Garal raised his tongue to meet her crooked digit, fondling the finger before wrapping his mouth fully around it. He suckled what trace of potion remained into his body, groaning as he took the finger deeper into his throat.

Tanja laughed, gently pulling her finger free. "Easy," she said, "I'm not sure we know each other quite that well yet." She could see his body relax for a moment, as if on the verge of sleep, and the head of the snake began to dip to Garal's lap.

Garal shuddered and opened his eyes wide, regaining his rigid posture and repositioning the bungaru back to a safe level. "I could feel it," he said, his face a mix of awe and disbelief.

"It's not ready," Tanja assured, "but I know you can feel the potential. Soon though. It will be perfect. If you will trust me, I can complete the extraction with little damage to your body."

"That's not what I've heard," Garal replied. "I've heard it to be fatal."

Tanja kept silent for a moment, searching for the proper cadence and look that would pull off the lie. "Fairy tales," she said, scoffing and waving a hand toward Garal.

"Except for in the story of Marlene," Garal said casually. "In that story, the bile was spared, and yet the potion was still effective."

Tanja stared at Garal for a few seconds, processing his words, searching his face for a tell of dishonesty. "What did you say?"

"That is how it was told to me. How the children on the street tell it. That the woman, her source, Anika, she escaped before the final extraction, and yet Marlene was rejuvenated by the potion nevertheless."

"Rejuvenated?"

"Yes. It's said that her life—Marlene's—was not only sustained by Anika's blood, but reversed, revitalized. This is the newest part of the story that has emerged only recently."

Tanja was stunned by the merchant's words. "Why?"

He smiled, bemused. "It is strange that you don't know this story. It is about you."

Suddenly it did seem strange to Tanja that her daughter, whom she had seen off to the New Country centuries ago, was now spoken about by people of the Eastern Lands, and yet she knew so little about the tale. But disconnection from the world at large was one of the costs of this existence. She could afford no relationships, and life in the hermitage had rendered her an uninformed pariah. "Me?"

"Not you exactly, but you are one of them. The stories say there are only a handful left in the world, and here you are, living in our village all these years. You must have one of the books then as well, yes? *Orphism?*"

Tanja rarely thought of her copy of the book any longer, other than when she fantasized about its return to the village. The text had all been memorized long ago, and it was now as much a keepsake as anything, since she had moved on to more experimental versions of the recipe inside. "Why?" she repeated. "Why does the story say she was made younger?"

"They were of the same blood. That was the key. The potion rejuvenates when kin are used in the blending." Garal looked at Tanja quizzically. "Why else would I have done this to Prisha?"

Tanja was beyond caring about the motives of men, other than to use those motives for her own ends. But it did make sense now, how easily Garal had been swayed to participate in this intrigue. "You are not old," Tanja noted.

"I am with dropsy. The doctors believe my kidneys are failing. I was hoping..." Garal looked away, as if disgusted with his attempt at rationalization. "Prisha didn't know. If she had, she wouldn't have trusted me. She wouldn't have waited to contact the police."

Tanja was still absorbing the revelation Garal had told her about Marlene, and she was delayed in processing the words Garal had just spoken. "Dropsy?"

Garal nodded.

"I can't use a dropsied source in my potion." Tanja scrunched her eyes and shook her head slowly, confused and sickened. "Your organs are no more useful to me now than those of a cow."

"It can still work. I'm sure."

Garal may have been correct in his hope; there was no data as to whether a bit of dropsy had any effect on the potion either way. But Tanja didn't care. Proof, or at least evidence, of the legend she had heard about her whole life had suddenly reached her ears, and now her aspirations were altered, her plans changed.

Anika. Her kin. Was alive somewhere in the New Country. As were her daughter and son, Gretel and Hansel. And their blood contained the greatest medicine imaginable. This changed everything. It was time to start a new quest, one based not on vengeance, but to create a new blend.

Anika felt a surge of focus fill her head, and she looked at Garal, studying every cell of his face. She smiled, opening her mouth wide, jutting her large teeth forward, and then shot her hand out and snatched Garal's left hand.

"What?" Garal was momentarily stunned.

With her second hand, Anika grabbed the body of the bungaru, just below where Garal's hand held the snake at the base of its neck and fangs.

"No," Garal said. "No, it can work. It can still work."

"Then let me try," Tanja replied, her eyes wide and shifting, madness boiling beneath them. "Give me the snake." A stream of saliva dripped from her upper teeth.

Garal swallowed, and with a final pleading look, he released the head, but continued holding the serpent by the tail.

"Let it go."

Garal released the tail, and it was only Tanja who held the snake now, dangling the five-foot reptile as it swung aggressively sideways, twisting its body in a blind mixture of escape and attack.

She brought the serpent to her face now, an inch away, and the krait stuck its tongue to the tip of her nose, tickling it with the fork. She locked in on the snake's pupils, searching the onyx, lifeless marbles. "Do you see?" she asked, not taking her gaze away from the bungaru. "Do you see it?"

"See what?" Garal asked.

Tanja slowly moved her hand toward Garal, holding the scaly diamond skull in front of his face. "Study its eyes and you will see it."

Garal looked at the black pools of the eyeballs, and within seconds, he was spellbound. "I do see it," he said, his voice distant and wispy. "Thank you."

Tanja smiled. "Thank *you*, Garal. Thank *you*."

With the skill of an expert fencer, Tanja thrust the snake's head toward Garal's throat, pressing on the skull by the serpent's ears, aggravating its temper and priming its venom.

The snake's fangs sank deeply into Garal's neck, and within seconds the poison was ravaging his bloodstream. He convulsed for a moment, and Tanja laid him down on the altar, laughing hysterically as the pain and paralysis set in, and finally the last spewing coughs before death.

She placed the krait on the ground at the base of the altar, and the snake slithered away to the far wall of the temple and then out to the forest, and Tanja followed it, watching it until it disappeared in the camouflage of the trees. She looked at the flask in her hand and then twisted off the cap and poured it into the red dirt.

It was time to leave for the docks, and then off to the New Country.

It was time to find her family.

Chapter 27

THE COOK, NOW WITHIN arm's reach of Anika, swung the blade like a squash racket, hoping to stripe the thin metal across her face or neck, perhaps catching the jugular and killing her in seconds.

Anika dropped the rope to the deck and dodged the knife easily, tilting her body slightly to her left, bobbing her head back as the knife swooshed by short and to the side of her chin, missing it by at least a foot.

"It didn't have to be this way," she said as the cook stumbled past her, crashing into the guardrail and nearly toppling over the side of the ship. Anika took several steps forward now, essentially switching positions with the assailant.

The cook leaned over the railing, staring down at the dark, purple water for a beat before pushing himself off, grunting as he turned, holding the knife high again, poised for a second attack.

"You had better make this count, cook," Anika said, "because the deal I offered to you earlier is now off the table. I die or you do, that's the only way this ends." She clenched her jaw. "And I don't die."

The cook was devoid of all cockiness now, his swagger having been transmuted into aggravation, rage, and fury.

Anika studied the man, detecting the inhalation through his nostrils and gradual lean of his back against the railing. She rotated her body a quarter turn, loosening her fingers and shoulders in the process, making sure her muscles were limber and prepared for the impending attack. She felt unstoppable, invincible, and she regretted now that the cook hadn't taken her offer, as he was all but dead where he stood.

The cook's pupil's dilated, and then he shot his body forward like a missile, the knife the warhead. But Anika knew by the shift of his eyes and twitch of his neck how he would come, speed and direction, knife positioning, and she had calculated her counter before the cook made a step.

He was halfway to Anika, and just as she unsheathed her fangs from the depths of her mouth, ready to disarm the cook and then sink them into his throat, he stopped suddenly, as if grabbed from behind by some invisible force.

Anika watched the cook fall face first to the deck, his eyes terrified, confused. He looked down to his legs and Anika followed his eyes, and there at his right ankle, was the rope that was around Petr's leg earlier, and Petr standing above it. He leaned down and began knotting the rope furiously, tying it over and over again.

The cook made a move to stop him, but Anika was upon the man in an instant, one foot on top of his hand, forcing him to drop the knife, the other wedged between the deck and his neck, ready to crush his spine, if necessary.

Petr walked behind the cook and grabbed him by the back collar of his shirt, forcing the man to his feet.

The cook staggered up, all the while keeping his eyes on Anika. His breathing was labored as he smiled and said, "I guess you were wrong, madam buccaneer, about my dying fate. You and I may have the same instincts—that is, to kill our enemies—but not everyone does." He looked at Petr. "Isn't that right, boy?"

Petr stepped in front of the cook and stared up at him, holding his gaze with the fearlessness of a badger. He shook his head once and said, "No, it isn't."

Petr grabbed the cook at the middle of his chest, gripping the dirty white lapels of his jacket into his fists. And then, as if launching a bobsled, Petr ran toward the guardrail, the cook still in his clutches, now backpedalling, horrified, staring over his shoulder as they approached the rear of the ship.

Six feet from the edge, Petr released the man, allowing the cook's momentum to carry him the remaining few steps to the edge. The cook slammed his back against the railing, and his body tipped backwards, leaving him horizontal across the guardrail for a full two seconds before a nuance in the twist of his body or a fraction of a turn in the movement of the ship sent him over, the rope around his ankle trailing behind.

Anika heard the splash and ran to the back rail, looking over to see the rope trailing taut, indicating the cook was still attached. He bobbed his head up once, his body still submerged, but it quickly dropped back under.

Anika looked over at Petr. "I thought no killing."

Petr shrugged.

"I know I've violated the rule, several times over now, but I didn't want this for you."

"He's alive," Petr replied. "Look at him."

The cook had managed to grab the rope at his ankles, and he was now attempting to hold his head up above the boat's wake.

"He'll last only minutes attached to the boat."

"It's the same thing he was going to do to me," Petr snapped. "And he was going to enjoy it."

Anika stayed quiet, knowing she was in no position to advise or judge. She was a murderer now, no different than an animal, and it was for this reason she felt compelled to counsel Petr. She only wanted—needed—him to maintain his humanity, for the sake of both of them.

"But you're right, Anika."

Anika looked over at Petr, who was still staring down at the body being dragged behind the container ship.

"I can't resort to the same torture. How does that make me any different?"

Anika sighed and nodded, and then watched in horror as Petr raised the butcher's knife, twisting it slightly, the metal reflecting the sun's rays at Anika, winking at her, as if letting her in on the joke.

With one swipe of the sharp blade across the tight, twisted hemp, the rope snapped with a pop, sending the loose cord to the sea below. Anika put a hand to her mouth as she watched the tether drift impotently to the water, marooning it with the cook of the *ESC Mongkut*, who would be sinking beneath the surface within the hour, or perhaps taken by sharks before then.

Petr stood watching the cook drift from their sight, and then he spit once over the side before turning and walking toward midship. "I assume you left the master alive," he said, his voice now commanding and with purpose.

Anika followed Petr, nodding at the question. "I've not been to the bridge. I don't know if the officers are aware yet about the rest of their crew."

"Let's pay them a visit then. If we can reach them before they discover a problem, we can keep them off the radio and us on track for the Eastern Lands. We're close Anika. We're going to make it.

Chapter 28

"GET OUT OF HERE! THIS isn't a hotel! You can't sleep here!"

Tanja opened her eyes and was staring at a thin, frail-looking man whose skin looked as leathery and beaten as an old saddle. The backlight of the sun illuminated him like the subject of a Rebirth-era portrait, though with none of the youth and beauty common to those paintings. He was wretched, and looked old enough to be Tanja's father.

Tanja touched the back of her head lightly against the eastern wall of a squatty brick building and sighed. She acclimated to her surroundings quickly, feeling the cold pavement of the dockyard beneath her, smelling the pungent odor of fish and salt and oil in the air. She had made the voyage here yesterday, walking quickly through the night, covering at least fifty miles, maybe more, and when she finally arrived at the docks, it was at the point of exhaustion.

She had chosen the maintenance building for her sleeping quarters, largely for its positioning away from the robust shipyard activities and unlikelihood of human interaction. On this last point, she had obviously misjudged.

"Vagrants," the man continued, "I'm sick of it."

Tanja cocked her head and batted her eyelids. "Va-grants?"

"Vagrants. Job seekers. You're all the same to me. There is no loitering here, and no work." The dock worker scrutinized Tanja for a moment. "Especially not for decrepit old women." He chuckled. "What would you do here?"

Tanja sighed and lowered her head, as if about to fall asleep once again, and then, with movements more akin to experts of the martial arts, hopped to her feet, spreading her arms wide like a spider as she landed in a crouched stance. With equal speed, she stood tall, her oversized robe flapping behind her, making the fluttering sound of a bat.

The old man gasped, his face now bloodless and panicky, unable to comprehend how this woman before him, whom he had just suggested was too feeble for basic work, had just moved like an assassin.

"I'm no vagrant," Tanja said, "and I've no desire to work alongside the weakest sperm of humanity, present company included. I am, however, looking for a ship that will take me to the New Country."

Tanja wasn't quite sure how sea travel worked these days; it had been two hundred years since she'd been on the oceans. But the boats still came and went from the docks, she knew that much, so the docks were where she came.

The man swallowed. "You're in the shipyards, ma'am. The docks are across the bridge, bay side. It's two, two and half miles from here across that bridge." He pointed to a narrow suspension bridge in the distance.

"When do the ships leave?"

The man shrugged. "I work in the shipyards," he stammered, the sheen of fear returning to his face, as if his lack of knowledge about shipping schedules might trigger another spasm from Tanja.

Tanja let her stare linger and then turned in the direction of the bridge and began walking. Fewer than ten paces in, she heard the dock worker open the door to the maintenance house and quickly close it behind him. She wanted to get to the docks as quickly as possible, but her intuition told her to wait, to check back on the man who had just fled to the building. And one thing she never ignored, not for centuries now, was her intuition.

She stepped quietly to the stoop of the building and placed her ear flat against the metal door, closing her eyes in concentration

"She was just outside sleeping," the muffled voice said. "I told her to leave, and she did, but...there was something wrong about her."

Tanja gripped the knob and swung open the door, and the man immediately dropped the phone to his desk, the receiver smacking the wooden top violently and then bouncing once to the floor as the accordion cord hung on desperately to its attachment. Tanja could hear the voice on the other end asking follow-up questions, and then there was a long pause before the voice asked if the caller was still there. He was, Tanja thought, but not for much longer.

She placed the receiver on the cradle and asked, "Who were you talking to?"

"It was, uh, my supervisor, my boss. It is...I talk to him. On the phone. About the shipyards."

The lies were terrible, and Tanja stifled a laugh. "The police?"

The man held his hands up, palms forward, demonstrating that he was coming clean. "Yes," he nodded. "But I wasn't—"

Tanja stooped down into a crouch, as if preparing to jump, and then opened her right hand wide in front of her face so that she was now staring at her own palm.

The shipyard worker parted his lips to speak again, and as he did, Tanja erupted upwards, driving from her thighs and hips, twisting with energy as her daggered fingers pierced through the bottom of the man's mouth.

The result of the impact was an explosion of teeth and blood as Tanja's middle and ring finger impaled the man's tongue and lodged into the hard palate at the roof of his mouth.

The maintenance worker gagged, his eyes gawking as Tanja stood tall and faced him. She could see her own fingernails through the opening of his mouth and thought it a bit funny. "You have too much to say," she said. "And you are rather rude."

The man quivered his head, pleading to be spared, and, as if granting his wish, Tanja wrenched her hand downward, freeing her nails from the man's tongue and mouth.

He grabbed for his face, spitting and crying as he collapsed into the chair at his desk. His tongue and chin were shredded; the top of his mouth spewed blood like a geyser.

"When they get here," Tanja said, her voice deep and serious, "which I'm guessing won't be for several hours yet, you tell them I've gone to the New Country." She flicked her eyebrows and said more lightly, "Though I suppose you'll have to write it down."

Following this last sentence Tanja paused a moment, and then began to cackle hysterically.

When the laughter subsided, Tanja turned to the door and opened it, pausing in the doorway. "And if you follow me," she held her nails up high, "I'll put these in your heart."

Chapter 29

ANIKA AND PETR STOOD in the pilothouse, flanking the ship's master on each side. The chief and deck officers sat behind them, strapped to their seats by steel cable seals.

"How much longer until we arrive in port?" Petr asked, standing only inches from the captain.

The captain didn't look at Petr, and silently pointed to one of the many electronic screens that formed a low wall between him and the long front windows of the bridge. A little over seven hours according to the display.

"There is money. In a safe, back in my quarters. It can be yours. All of it. Just tell me what you've done with my crew."

Anika didn't hesitate. "Some of them are dead."

The captain closed his eyes for a beat, processing, and then opened them again, regaining his stoicism.

"And some of those who are dead deserved to die," Anika continued. "They were rapists and murderers, both in their hearts and in their actions." She paused and took a deep breath. "About the others, I had little choice. They were unable to follow my orders."

"Perhaps because they were not your orders to give."

"Your crew was rotten, sir! God only knows the abuses they committed over the years."

The master closed his eyes and frowned, and Anika couldn't tell if it was disappointment about the character of his crew or the loss of their lives. Or a third possibility: that he knew of their character and had done nothing to correct it.

"And the others? Those whom you didn't murder?"

"They are locked away. Imprisoned in one of the containers. They are safe and unharmed. And so you're aware, I did nothing to the engine ratings. I never entered the engine room at all. They should be unaffected by any of this, though they're probably wondering now where lunch is."

"You?" the captain asked.

Anika was confused. "What?"

"You said 'I never entered the engine room.' This was all your doing? How could that be true?"

Petr began to speak but Anika interrupted him on the first word. "It is a story too long to tell in the hours we have remaining, sir, but it is true. Other than tying your officers to their chairs, which I forced him to do, my companion has done nothing wrong. He is innocent."

"Anika," Petr pled.

Anika shot Petr a look and shook her head, cutting him off again. "I'll face whatever punishment comes to me, though it will have to wait. I have business when we arrive, business that I won't abandon for any reason. But when it is concluded, I will turn myself in. I will not leave you to pay the full price for what's happened aboard your vessel." She paused. "Do you trust me to return?"

"How long?" the captain asked, his voice stern, detail-oriented.

"I can't say. Not exactly. I'm on a quest to find someone, and I don't know where she lives."

"In all the Eastern Lands? You can't be serious that you think you'll find her."

"I have a name. And an instinct. But I have more than that. I have a connection. A connection to the woman I'm looking for. By God or the universe, I don't know exactly. But we will meet soon. I can't say the time or day even, but sooner than perhaps I would even guess."

The captain shook his head, not giving Anika's mystical talk any time or consideration. "I can't make any promises, certainly not to someone who has murdered my crew, even if justified in some cases. And I'm a man of science and duty, thus I don't believe in knowing things through feelings or other magical nonsense. That said, I do believe you when you say you will return, though I have no choice but to alert the authorities the moment we arrive and have been released. If, indeed, that is to be our fate. It is my sworn duty, and I won't abandon it."

Anika respected the captain's candor, especially considering his captive position beside a powerful killer of men.

"And I believe you about the boy as well," the master added. "So if the surviving prisoners can confirm your story, that he was not a part of what took place here, I'll make no mention of him." He gave a backwards nod to his officers seated behind him. "They will follow my lead."

Anika nodded. "Thank you, sir."

"You'll hang for this," the captain said calmly, staring out at the vast blue of the open water. "Murder on the high seas is punishable by death in almost every scenario."

"I understand that."

"And this doesn't sway your promise to return?"

Anika followed the captain's gaze, looking forward to the vastness of the cerulean world before her. "No. If after my business is finished and I am still alive, and this ship is still in port, I will return to it. You have my word."

Anika could sense that the captain wanted to follow up on the cryptic 'still alive' part of her statement, but he held his tongue.

"As long as you keep your word about him." Anika nodded toward Petr. She had a good feeling about the captain and his honor, but, in case, she was careful not to use Petr's name.

The captain twitched a nod. "You do."

Chapter 30

TANJA REACHED THE HALFWAY point of the bridge and stopped, jarred to attention by a feeling of recognition and knowing. She sniffed the air and then looked behind her, checking to see if the maintenance worker had indeed followed her. But there was only the bleak landscape of the shipyard, a concrete world encased in iron and rust, and the few people who now populated the grounds were already hard at work, barking out orders and tallying figures on clip-boards, manning cranes and driving forklifts.

On either side of her, over the sides of the bridge, Tanja saw only the cool blue water of the inlet over which the bridge spanned, placidly reflecting the sun's rays, waiting patiently for the hulls of the boats that would be polluting it in a few hours.

But the knowing feeling still blazed inside her, and as she looked directly out in front of her at the bay in the distance and the horizon beyond, she saw a jagged pattern of gray against the blue and white of the sky, as if a portion of the atmosphere had been jigsawed out. But it was no gap in the atmosphere she was seeing, it was the outline of a large container ship, and she knew instantly that it was the source of her feeling.

The ship she was looking at currently wasn't the specific one, it didn't feel perfect, but it was the kind that would be arriving soon, eventually to take her to the New Country. To Anika and Gretel Morgan.

There was no need to rush, though, she thought; the ship that would lead her to her destiny was on its way, but it wouldn't be arriving until closer to dawn. She couldn't have said how she knew it, other than to say she could now see the ship in her mind, as clearly as if she were floating above it over the ocean, watching from the sky as the vessel skidded the ocean toward the port that was now only a mile from where she stood. The vision in her mind created such a flood of adrenaline and joy within her that it felt almost like a hallucination. But no drug had passed over her tongue, no powder up her nose or poppy in her veins. It was an intoxication of truth. Of revenge. Of life.

Despite her bliss and certainty, however, there were still logistics to work out. Tanja could feel the boat was on its way there, but there was no telling when it would be launching again once it arrived. It had cargo to unload, surely, and then it would likely be anchored for a few days after that.

And a call had been made to the police about a strange woman sleeping in the shipyards, and soon the body of Garal would be discovered. And once his death was announced, Prisha would reveal her tale to the police, and it wouldn't be long after that the docks would become flooded with authorities, asking questions and searching shipments.

But it didn't matter. She had come too far, discovered too much about her life and daughter and descendants. It was going to work out. It had too. She would slip on to the cargo ship soon after it arrived, and there she would wait. She barely needed food anymore, and there were more than enough places to hide on those massive ships, even after they'd been unloaded. She had, perhaps, in her wrath, made a grave mistake in telling the shipyard worker her desire to find a ship for the New Country while also allowing him to live. But even if he were courageous enough to expose those details, Tanja had implied she would be taking an ocean liner for her voyage, not a ship filled with steel containers.

She reached the far side of the bridge and then walked toward the terminal, scanning the entire area at once, allowing this world of container storage hangars and semitrailers to offer up its clues. Eventually Tanja's eyes settled on a small, house-like structure that looked as if it had been built for a child and sat just at the edge of the wharf.

She walked to the miniature house and peered through the only window, a tiny, single pane of glass that was chest-high to Tanja. Inside, sitting at a desk, was a boy of about fourteen, and he was reading a book that looked to be at least a thousand pages long. She wrapped a knuckle on the glass and the boy looked up, catching Tanja's eyes. The instant fear was obvious, but she smiled anyway, which likely made her look even more frightening.

The boy looked away for a beat before turning back toward the window, as if testing whether the woman was really there. Tanja waved again and pointed at the door. He rose slowly and walked to the front of the structure and Tanja followed. She kept her nails sheathed. What she needed now was information; after that, whether he gave it to her or not, she would make sure the boy disappeared. No more witnesses. That was a promise she had made to herself. There were far too many scattered around the Eastern Lands as it was, and she certainly couldn't afford another.

"Can I help you?" The boy called through the door.

Tanja was caught off guard, expecting the boy to open the door. "Um, yes you can, young man. I hope you can. I've been...I am expecting my son to arrive here. At this terminal. Some time today. Are you the person I should be speaking with about such things?"

"No. My father is the wharf master. But he's been called away for a bit. An emergency with his wife. I'm manning the station until he gets back."

Tanja saw this as an opportunity, though she couldn't see exactly where it was. "I see. Well I hope your mother is okay."

"She's not my mother," the boy replied quickly. "My mother is dead."

"Oh, well, I'm sorry. I shouldn't have made that assumption." The dialogue was off to a rocky start, but the boy had offered intimate information to Tanja, which, she knew by now, was always a positive sign.

"It's okay," the boy said, as if appreciative that Tanja hadn't overdone it with the condolences. "What was it you wanted to know?"

"Do you know if there is a schedule of ships? And a manifest of some kind?"

"Of course."

"Would you mind opening the door...uh...I'm sorry lad, what is your name?" Tanja was making progress, but she wanted full control of the situation.

There was a pause behind the door. "I'm Gerard."

"Yes, well, Gerard, could we speak face-to-face? Would that be okay?"

"No, ma'am."

Again, Tanja was thrown. "No?"

"I can give you the names, times, and places of origins for the ships that will be arriving today. But only from behind this door. That's my father's rule when he's gone."

Tanja closed her eyes and sighed. She took a deep breath and opened her eyes, and a thin layer of moisture had formed over them. She smiled at the reaction, almost embarrassed by it. But she understood where it had come from, however deeply. She had no reason to kill this boy, and yet she was prepared to without hesitation. It was evil, and the traces of humanity that still remained within her had emerged for just a moment.

"Of course," she said. "This way is fine. But I don't know any of the details you've just laid out. I was just told that he would be on a ship that will be headed next to the New Country. That is, after it delivers its cargo here."

"That's a strange detail."

"Yes, I...I don't know. As I've said, that's what I was told."

There was another long pause and then, "Just a moment."

The boy was sharp of mind, and Tanja was now even more pleased that he hadn't opened the door.

Less than a minute passed when the boy returned to the door and said, "None of the ships arriving today are scheduled to leave for the New Country."

"Are you sure?"

"Yes, I'm looking at the manifest now. But that's not unusual. Many ships have direct routes from the New Country to the Eastern Lands, but rarely is the reverse course true. Most of them go to the Old World first, or the Southern Continents, and then to the New Country."

Tanja felt the sting of disappointment resonate throughout her entire body, followed by a burn in her chest and seizing of her throat. She felt defeated, betrayed, lied to by the gifts of the universe that had arrived like angels so often in times of crises and need. But they had abandoned her this time. Orphism had abandoned her, and her belief that the time had come to let this eternal life end was reinforced.

"But," the boy continued, "there is a ship scheduled to arrive today that is *coming* from the New Country."

Tanja stayed silent, processing this news.

"We haven't heard any updates on their status as of now, but as it stands, they should be arriving around dawn."

Tanja turned and placed her back against the door and then collapsed to the pavement in front of the wharf master's door, sitting now with her legs extended in front of her. She covered her hands with her mouth as the meaning came to her all at once, in an instant.

She was never meant to go to the New Country to find Anika and Gretel Morgan.

They were coming to her.

"Ma'am, are you still there?"

"I'm still here," Tanja said, rising to her feet again, staring at the welcoming waters of the wharf with wide, weary eyes. "This ship you speak of, the one from the New Country, what time does it arrive?"

THE *ESC Mongkut* appeared on the horizon, and judging by its distance—ten miles out, perhaps—it would be gliding into the harbor as scheduled. And when it did, Tanja would be waiting for it, exactly as she was now, standing atop the girder of the wharf's container crane under which the ship would dock.

After receiving the ship's schedule from the wharf master's son, she had climbed the crane ladder that led to the top walkway, ascending unseen behind the empty operator's cabin. She now stood at the edge of the long steel jib, a narrow girder that extended out of the massive machine over the water of the harbor.

She had been in this position for hours now, but her legs felt lithe and prepared. The lifeforce streaming through her blood made her feel solid, her muscles twitchy and strong, her body like a supple statue of iron and steel.

"It's here," she whispered. "They're here."

Chapter 31

"WHAT IS THAT?" ANIKA asked, pointing into the distance at a crane rising from the edge of the wharf.

The ship had begun its docking procedures and was pulling in port side along the quay. The captain followed the direction of Anika's finger. "It's a crane. It's what they use to unload the containers."

Anika frowned and shook her head. "There I mean, on the top of the crane."

The captain squinted and shivered his head, clearing his eyes. "I don't know."

He called for one of the two deck officers, whom Anika had agreed to unbind from their cable restraints, to come take control of the wheel, and then he walked to the door on the side of the bridge and out to the open-air bridge wing.

Anika followed and now stood beside the captain. The crane was massive, rising above the wharf like a dragon, but the ship was still far enough away that the top beam of it was still visible. From the distance at which they were now, approaching it from the side, the object at the top looked like the profile of some type of giant perched bird.

"It's a statue," Anika said. "It has to be. But why would they build a statue on top of a crane? It must be some sort of religious symbol. For protection or safety or something."

The captain stood with his mouth open, his eyes narrowed, trying to hone in on the figure. "They wouldn't."

"Wouldn't what?"

"They wouldn't build a statue on top of a crane. I've been to this port dozens of times. That's a person up there."

Anika walked up to the railing of the bridge wing and leaned across it, trying to get as close and as clear a vision as possible. If it was a person, he was as still as stone.

And then he moved. The figure turned toward Anika like a giant, motion-detecting camera. She was still too far away to make out any features of the person, but she could tell it was looking down at her. "Oh god," Anika said, putting a hand across her mouth.

The figure then extended its arms straight out on either side of its body, its feet still together so that it appeared as if its legs were one. It looked like the silhouette of a cross, Anika thought, a black shadow against the backdrop of a white sky.

The figure then tipped its head backwards, bowing its back so that its face was up to the sky. How he kept his balance, Anika couldn't have imagined, so fearless was this person, daring death to show its face.

"What is he doing?" the captain asked.

But as the ship drew closer to the wharf, Anika's eyes began to center on the person, and she could see that it wasn't a man at the top of the crane at all. It was a woman, and there was something in her movements that was now beyond just terrifying. It was familiar.

"Tanja," she whispered.

"Who?"

Anika couldn't take her eyes from the woman, who had now regained her erect position on the crane and was staring back towards Anika.

She was watching her. Anika was certain about that.

And then with the movements of some giant insect, the woman pivoted on the crane, away from the water, and sprinted the length of the enormous steel jib in the direction of the frame.

Anika's adrenaline seethed. She kept her eyes fixed on the woman until she was out of sight, mesmerized by every step of her movements.

"Did you see that?" The master hissed, staring over at Anika. "What..? What did I just see?"

"How much longer until we dock."

"I..." The captain was still numb with amazement and disbelief.

"How much longer!" Anika screamed.

"Just minutes."

Anika ran back to the main bridge and confronted Petr, grabbing him at the shoulders. "I saw her! I saw her just now!"

"Who?" Petr asked, and Anika could see Petr questioning her state of mind.

Anika composed herself. "Tanja. I saw her. She was on the crane, and...and she saw me. I think she was..."

"Was what?"

"I think she was waiting for me.

"It's impossible," Petr said, "how could she know you were coming?"

Anika shook her head and shrugged. "I don't know. How did I know to come?"

Petr lowered his gaze to the floor, considering the logic of Anika's statement—or, perhaps, her lack thereof—and then nodded, accepting that anything was possible. He looked up again. "What are we going to do?"

"It's going to take a while to fully bring the ship in and for the captain to register with the harbor. So in the meantime, I'm going to the deck. I want you to wait here. No matter what, Petr, don't come. The captain has promised to allow you safe passage back, no charges, so you can't get involved in any way. No matter what. Is that clear?"

Petr nodded.

"And I love you Petr. Like you were my own. And I wish I could tell you to tell Gretel and Hansel how sorry I am. And how much I love them. But I can't. And you can't ever tell them about this. About the Eastern Lands or Tanja or, most of all, that I lived beyond that day on the lake. I fear it will be too much for them to hear, and they'll never forgive you for keeping it secret. And you need them Petr. You're going to need them. They're your family. Along with Mrs. Klahr. And I always want you to have each other."

"Gretel is gone." Petr said flatly, nullifying Anika's words.

"She'll be back, Petr. Or you'll go there. One day. I know you'll be reunited. Have faith."

Petr let Anika's last words stand and then brought them back to the moment.

"I don't think I want to know what your plan is, but I'm asking anyway. What's up on the deck? What should I ignore no matter what?"

Anika took a deep breath and then stretched her neck to one side and then the other. "She was waiting for me to come and now I'm here. Now I'm going to wait for her."

Chapter 32

TANJA COULD SMELL HER childhood arriving on the ship, drifting over the harbor like a pungent mist. Or perhaps it was the childhood of her daughter, Marlene. Or son, Gromus. All three were so distant now that, for Tanja, they had merged into one muddled abstraction from which she could find few tangible visual memories. Smells were different though. Through some miracle of olfactory evolution, she could still detect the aroma of past days, days so old they'd been forgotten by time itself.

"Anika," she whispered, the glowing sound of the name tingling the drums of her ears.

Tanja stood inside the wharf master's house behind the boy who had supplied her with the container ship's origin and name. He was in her grasp, though not clutched with aggression, her arms motherly draped across the boy's chest with one hand circling back to his shoulder, her nails tickling the side of his neck. She tapped the skin below his jaw every few seconds, a constant, dull reminder of their potential.

The boy's father lay on the floor beside the desk, decapitated. Unlike his son, the wharf master hadn't possessed the same instincts for survival or distrust of his fellow man.

Despite the violence and gruesome scene, however, the boy didn't struggle under Tanja, and, in fact, he seemed relatively calm. Tanja figured the boy probably hated his father and was, on some level, relieved of his sudden demise.

"We can do this, can't we Rolf?"

The boy frowned and nodded. There was no other answer to give.

"Then let's recapture what we've discussed. When the captain comes to pay his port dues, what will you tell him?"

The boy swallowed. "That there has been an incident," he said. "That there have been reports of a sighting. Of a person atop one of the cranes. And that the Port Authority has begun investigating. And I will ask if he, himself, saw anything while coming in."

"And then what?"

"When he says that he did see something, if that is what he says." The boy paused, not confident in this portion of the plan.

"It's what he'll say," Tanja whispered to his ear.

The boy nodded. "When he says he, too, saw a person on the crane, then I will inform him that he will need to wait here until he can be questioned, and that his crew will need to stay on board until given clearance to debark."

"Very good."

"You must understand, this is not how it would work. The ship's master will question my knowledge about these procedures. He'll ask for my father. He is an experienced captain and will know this isn't the protocol."

"Did you not tell me he didn't radio you about his position while en route? As per nautical law?"

The boy nodded.

"And thus you will tell him that you reported this dereliction to the authority, and they have identified his ship as suspicious and subject to inspection."

"But—"

"Why did the captain not radio the harbor?" Tanja asked, already knowing the answer. Knowing that the Morgans aboard were somehow responsible. "Why would such an experienced captain not follow such basic protocol?"

The boy shook his head. "I don't know."

"Then it is enough to warrant questioning from the authority. And combined with the sighting of a deranged person scaling cranes around the wharf, there will be no bending of the investigative protocol. Besides, his suspicions are unimportant to me. I only need a moment to get on the ship, to see them up close. I only need to touch them. Smell them. Taste them."

Tanja lifted her chin and closed her eyes, inhaling the stale air of the wharf master's house.

The boy seemed to realize that questioning this mad woman's displays and rants would be a grave error. Tanja had strayed off into her own story, one about which he knew nothing and would be wise to leave alone.

She looked over the boy's shoulder now at the emptiness of the air before her, her eyes wide, as if asking some invisible being for understanding. "I know at least one Morgan is aboard that ship. I know it. But I'll need to see them for myself."

Tanja released the boy from her grip and motioned for him to sit down at the desk, and then she walked from behind him, striding absently past the boy's fallen father, whose blood had pooled back into a shadowy corner near the back wall.

She reached down and lifted the head of the corpse and walked to a tall trashcan in the corner of the office and dropped the skull in, pushing down on it until it touched the bottom of the bin. Next she grabbed the headless corpse by the collar and hoisted it to its feet, lifting and carrying it easily to a front corner, wedging the body between the trashcan and one of office's four filing cabinets that lined the southern wall. She then moved another one of the cabinets in front of the body and stacked yet another on top so that the corpse was now entirely hidden from view. The setup wasn't going to fool any hounds on the hunt, and the office itself wasn't going to win any decorating awards, but the covering was sufficient for now, at least from the captain who would soon be entering, presumably sitting on the visitor's side of the desk during his visit.

Tanja took a seat against a sliver of space on the interior wall that faced the quay, across from the desk between the entrance and the structure's lone window. She turned and looked out the window every few minutes, following with interest the process of mooring the ship, calculating when the captain would be arriving at the door.

The boy sat across from her, staring at the space where his father lie hidden and headless. "He was bad to me," he said. "And to my mother. She killed herself because of it, I think. He beat her. And then left her for another wife."

Tanja followed the boy's eyes and then looked back to him. "I didn't know that. Not those details, of course. But I could guess he wasn't a good man."

"I'm glad he's gone."

Tanja hadn't planned to get into this much depth with the boy; she was confined here until the ship was fully moored and was just waiting for her moment to board.

"If only it was my stepmother too."

Tanja smiled. "Perhaps that can be arranged."

The boy finally looked away from the burial site and back to Tanja, narrowing his eyes, understanding her implication. "What do I have to do?"

"Do you have a gun?"

TANJA RAN HER FINGERS over the face of the captain of the *ESC Mongkut* as she walked from the wharf master's house, ruffling his hair as she did. He shuddered at her touch, but didn't turn to look at her, focusing instead on the wharf master's son and the revolver pointed at him.

Tanja had planned to fall in behind the captain after he entered the wharf house, and then with his back to her, sneak off while he conversed with the wharf master's son about port dues and waybills.

But there was no guarantee she could pull off the trick without being seen, or that the boy would have followed the plan at all. For all Tanja knew, once she had left the house and the boy was alone with the captain, he would have told him the whole story and immediately phoned for the authorities.

But then the gap had opened, the universe had made its offering, and she, in turn, had made the promise to the boy to kill his stepmother as payment for holding the captain hostage. She had no intention of ever fulfilling the promise, just as she didn't expect the boy could keep up his end of the deal, at least not for long. The captain would eventually talk the boy out of going through with the plan, or perhaps trick him somehow, forcing the boy to drop his guard while the captain secured the gun.

But a few minutes would be enough, Tanja thought, as she walked the length of the wharf to the water's edge, approaching the giant ship port side. She had waited for the stevedores to finish tying the ship off and then scatter before approaching, knowing that, according to Rolf, there would be no unloading of cargo until tomorrow morning.

She looked at the sky once and the darkening clouds that were bringing the night early, and then stepped up on the large bollard that rose from the harbor like an iron mushroom. She stood in perfect balance on the bollard as she gazed up the length of the thick mooring rope that led to the bow of the ship. The climb wouldn't be the easiest thing she had ever done, but her will was never stronger.

She gripped the rope with both hands, as tightly as her muscles would allow, and then dropped her body off the side of the wharf so that she was hanging over the waters of the harbor. She took a deep breath and then swung her legs up to the rope and wrapped them around, pretzel-like. She said a prayer of thanks to the Orphic gods, whom she'd all but forgotten over the centuries, and then began her climb to the deck of the container ship and the blood that would bring her eternal youth.

Chapter 33

TANJA WAS HALFWAY UP the mooring rope when Anika spotted her again, moving quickly, like a robed beetle escaping from the jaws of some large, predatory insect.

Anika had positioned herself at the top of a small stack of three containers, and now had a panoramic view of the harbor. She had watched the captain enter the wharf master's house, and then, minutes later, watched the same woman she'd seen on the top of the crane exit.

Tanja.

Anika prayed the ship's master wasn't dead—he had shown her kindness and dignity, in spite of the horrors she had brought to his ship—but she also had to assume the worst. It was too late though, she thought; whatever had been done was done. There was only the future to deal with now. The future—the realm where punishment existed.

Tanja dropped out of Anika's view soon after beginning her ascent up the mooring rope, but now, seconds later, she was visible again, working her hands steadily over each other as she progressed toward the ship.

Anika prepared her body for the fight, tensing her muscles and slowing her breathing, and then dropped down from the top container, finding a foothold and grip on the top of the middle one, focusing now on the forecastle of the ship where Tanja would, presumably, be emerging any minute.

She stared at the empty rail at the front of the ship, hearing the breathing as the woman below it drew closer. She fell from Anika's sightline once more for four of five seconds, and then she saw the first hand grip the railing. The other one followed a second later, and moments after that, the woman was standing on the bow, smiling.

Tanja's breathing labored, and Anika could see the sweat pouring from her twisted, mangled face, but she seemed to be regaining her stamina quickly.

"You are no girl," the woman shouted, fighting the words through the wind, "so you must be Anika Morgan. The mother. I would love to meet your daughter, the one whose fame is equal to yours. Where is young Gretel? Have her come to meet me."

"You'll never meet her. You'll be dead in minutes and she'll live a long happy life. And when she eventually dies, she'll live in peace in the glory of heaven while you burn, stretched on the racks in the depths of Hell."

Tanja laughed, and Anika could see, even from a distance, that her teeth were formidable still. She tried to imagine her age and the thought boggled Anika's mind.

"So you're alone then. I must say I'm disappointed. But not completely. It will make things easier for me, certainly. I am curious though, Mrs. Morgan—or is it Ms? I believe I heard somewhere in your story that your husband was one of my daughter's victims."

Anika didn't waver. "She killed many people throughout her treacherous life. As I'm sure you have. And most of them were more innocent than my husband. I don't cry for him anymore."

Tanja looked intrigued by Anika's hardiness. "And how is it that you managed to escape the wrath of Marlene. How is it that you're still alive?"

Anika jumped down to the top edge of the lower container, and then down once again until she was standing on the forecastle less than ten yards from the ancient monster.

She glared at Tanja. "I didn't escape it. The torture and villainy that Marlene inflicted on me, I feel it still. But you should also know how Marlene felt our wrath, the wrath of the Morgans. And there has been no sight in my life that I've enjoyed more than watching your daughter's head explode."

Tanja's smile lingered for a moment and then slowly faded, her face gradually turning to tension and anger.

"And as it concerns your last question: I'm not alive anymore, Tanja. I died already. Just as you will today."

There was hardly a pause between Anika's final word and Tanja's eruption toward her. The old witch's hands were held high above her as she ran, clawed, the nails facing toward Anika like the spikes of a morning star. She came silently though, without the sounds of fury and frustration one would normally expect with such an attack, and this muted approach only added to the terror of it.

Anika stood her ground, her back against the metal side of the bottom container, her eyes like steel on Tanja as she approached, measuring every twitch of the old woman's face, the angle of her limbs.

Tanja was coming fast, her robe flapping in the wind, and she seemed to show no intention of slowing despite her proximity, which was now only a few feet from Anika.

Anika waited until the last moment possible, and then moved a half-step to her left. Tanja whooshed by her missing her by an inch, maybe two, and Anika watched as the woman smashed into the side of the container, her face bearing the brunt of the collision. She reeled backwards, stumbling, dazed, and as she fought to regain her bearings, Anika gripped her robe and wrapped it tightly around the old witch's neck.

Anika jabbed her mouth up to Tanja's ear, touching it lightly with her lips. "You're going to pay the price for what your daughter did to me. Did to us. For all the pain she inflicted on my family. And I want to thank you for being alive, and for being as awful and vindictive and evil as she was. It will make it so much easier for me when I tear out your heart."

Anika released the robe and pushed Tanja away into the open corridor between two stacks of containers.

The old woman stumbled and then grabbed for her face, which was now bloody and bruised from the impact with the container. She moved her hands to her neck, massaging the place where the robe had constricted her, regaining her senses now and grunting in a show of frustration.

"I'm going to kill you," she growled. "That is how it was meant to be. I know the secret that Marlene discovered, and I plan to follow through with it this time. You're going to taste delicious in my next batch. And Gretel even tastier in the one after that."

Anika froze, Tanja's last sentence resonating at a place so deep in her gut that she felt nauseous with rage. "What did you say?"

"I know the secret. Your story has spread to even here." Tanja smiled again, satisfactorily, as if realizing she had once again regained control of the moment. "And I know why Marlene wanted you. And Gretel. You're kin to us. To me. You and your children. And I long to taste you all. I long to have your blood and bile flow through my veins like—"

Anika waited patiently for the final words to emerge, the final sentence to finish before she leapt upon the woman and sliced her throat. But the words never came. Instead, Tanja's eyes grew wide, and the smug look of her unfounded feeling of victory morphed into one of surprise and hurt.

And then the blood began to flow.

Anika stood in shock, staring at the woman, confused at what had taken place. It was as if some creature inside her body, lying dormant for centuries perhaps, had suddenly awoken to destroy her.

And then the woman staggered forward toward Anika, the alarm still ringing in her eyes, and Anika stepped aside and watched her cling to the cold wall of one of the hundreds of containers on the deck, a large knife sticking out of her back.

Anika turned back in the direction of where Tanja had just come, and there stood Petr.

"Petr."

"I didn't come all this way for nothing," he said.

Anika grinned and shook her head. "You've done far more than nothing."

"I know you would have killed her, but those things she was saying, about you and Gretel, I..." Petr cut himself off and his face became a map of distress as he pointed behind Anika. "Watch out!"

Anika felt the attack an instant after Petr's warning, and instead of turning, she leaned her body to the right, her legs remaining planted, and Tanja stumbled across her hip, her violent, jagged nails swinging forward and connecting with the air.

Anika grabbed Tanja by the top of her forehead, and with the ferocity and casualness of an eagle, she clutched all five fingers of her other hand on Tanja's chest, digging her nails in until she could feel the beating of the organ in her hands. With a second motion, she pulled her arm forward, and ripped out Tanja's heart.

Anika released Tanja from her hold and watched in satisfaction as she collapsed to the wooden deck of the ship, clutching her torso in agony and vain.

The woman sputtered on the ground, trying to catch the oxygen all around her, but her breathing capacity was gone. Anika looked at Petr, who wore a look of resolve. Whatever fear he may have had for Anika was now a memory. She was a hero.

"IT'S TIME TO GO, PETR. Go find the captain. If he's alive, tell him I'm ready to honor my end of the deal. After that, go. Stay away from the harbor for a few days before you come back, and when you do, take a cruise liner." Anika gave a weary smile. "I don't know how you'll pay for it, but—"

"Anika," Petr interrupted. "I'll be fine. Maybe I'll stay in the Eastern Lands for a bit. Earn a little money to get home." He stopped and lowered his eyes for a moment before looking up again. "I don't want to tell the captain anything. I don't want you to die."

Anika smiled. "What I said to Tanja is true, Petr, I'm already dead. There's nothing more for me to do. Go now, Petr. Find the captain. It's time."

Chapter 34

PETR STOOD AT THE TOP of the hill, looking down on the crashing waves of the bay. The gallows had been erected quickly beside the waters, in two or three days, and Anika's trial had been even shorter. The captain had testified as promised, mentioning only Anika's role in the murders. Petr's name never came up.

Anika walked the steps and stood alone on the platform, staring out at the crowd of hundreds who had come to watch the rare punishment play out. The executioner followed, his head bare, unmasked, unlike the custom of hiding the killer's identity when such hangings took place in the New Country years ago.

The crowd was quiet, solemn, seemingly empathetic of the death that was about to occur. Petr didn't know if it was a respect for life generally that caused the forlornness, or for Anika specifically, but he took solace in the mood.

Petr had made his pleas to the captain of the cargo ship, described to him the events that led to the killings, but to no avail. Anika was to be tried for the murders of his crew, he told Petr, and if the punishment was to be death, which it almost certainly was to be, then that is what would stand.

But the captain did offer Petr safe passage back to the New Country. It wouldn't be as a passenger on the *ESC Mongkut*, which was to be grounded for several weeks, but rather on a passenger liner, using the captain's credentials to sail for no charge. It was a generous offer but also fair, since it was Petr who had ended the hostage situation inside the wharf master's cabin. Petr had simply opened the door and walked to the desk, and then had taken the gun from the teenager's hand. The captain had looked at Petr with awe during the ten seconds or so during which the rescue unfolded, and ultimately offered him the free sail home as a reward. But there was to be no relenting on his promise to testify against Anika.

The executioner placed the noose around Anika's neck and tightened it with a jerk, and Petr, even from his distance upon the hill, could see her flinch in pain. But her body seemed relaxed, resigned to its fate.

The executioner uttered something in Anika's direction, which Petr was too far away to hear; but the ensuing shaking of her head suggested it was to do with last words. She had none. To whom would she be speaking?

The stillness in the air seemed to last for minutes, as if the world had stopped spinning and the moment was frozen in time.

And then the floor opened.

Anika dropped like a brick beneath the base, and then bounced back, the rope above her tightening its death hold around her neck. Petr looked away, not wanting to watch the struggle or aftermath, not wanting the last vision of Anika's life to be one of helplessness and ignominy.

When the murmur of the crowd subsided, Petr looked back to see Anika hanging limp. It looked as if gravity were putting forth an extra effort to pull the body to the terrain, tugging at the arms and head, not understanding why the dead above hadn't yet reached the ground below where it belonged.

Petr stared at her for hours, waiting until the last of the crowd had left and night fell, shrouding the corpse in its grasp. She would hang for a full day, per the custom; at the exact time of her death tomorrow, she would be removed and buried at sea. The captain of the *ESC Mongkut* had seen to this final arrangement also, bearing the costs himself, sparing Anika the shame of an unmarked grave.

"I'm sorry, Anika. And I'll keep your secrets from Gretel and Hansel. From everyone. I promise."

Petr finally looked away from the gallows, seeing nothing in that direction but the reflection of the moonlight off the waves of the bay. And then he walked toward the direction of the docks and his ship that, come first light, would be sailing for home.

Chapter 35

DARKNESS. AGAIN. THIS time tightening around her like a cocoon, encasing her in a cape of black. It was as if she'd been taken to the emptiness of space and released, where no air or sound could reach her.

But there was sound. Some. The muffled crashing of waves behind her. And earlier, the sound of voices.

Anika opened her eyes and saw her feet below, dangling, the moon illuminating the tops of her shoes. She felt the rope around her neck and she tightened her muscles there, and then lifted her head straight. Her arms followed.

She spread the fingers of her right hand wide and then released her razor-sharp nails from the scabbard of her fingers, and with one swipe, cut the rope above her.

She walked down the gallows stairs and turned back to see the flaccid rope, shredded. Who would care? she thought. She was unknown here, and it would be assumed the body was robbed.

Anika turned toward the dark hills in front of her and walked, knowing the Eastern Lands would be her home for a while. But not forever. She was alive again. For a reason. And all she could do now was wait for the voice to direct her again.

DEAR READER,

I hope you enjoyed reading Anika Rising.

But the story does not end here. It continues with The Crippling (Gretel Book Five).

In The Crippling, new evils, more terrifying than their predecessors, are rising and threatening the land. Order your copy of The Crippling today.

And please leave a review for Anika Rising. It doesn't have to be long. A simple, "I liked it!" is enough. That is, if you enjoyed Anika Rising, which I hope you did!

OTHER BOOKS BY CHRISTOPHER COLEMAN
THE THEY CAME WITH THE SNOW SERIES
They Came with the Snow (They Came with the Snow Book One)
The Melting (They Came with the Snow Book Two)
THE SIGHTING SERIES
The Sighting (The Sighting Book One)
The Origin (The Sighting Book Two)

Made in the USA
Middletown, DE
03 September 2023